MISSING, PRESUMED DEAD

MISSING, PRESUMED DEAD

KIRAN MANRAL

AMARYLLIS

AMARYLLIS

An imprint of Manjul Publishing House Pvt. Ltd.
• 7/32, Ansari Road, Daryaganj, New Delhi 110 002
Website: www.manjulindia.com
Registered Office:
10, Nishat Colony, Bhopal 462 003 – India

ISBN 978-93-87383-68-5

First published in 2018

Printed and bound in India by Replika Press Pvt. Ltd.

To Kirit
For never reading my books.
And leaving me to write them in peace.
May there never be a no man's land on our mattress.

...how anxiously I yearned for those I had forsaken.

—Fyodor Dostoyevsky
The Dream of a Ridiculous Man

Book 1

1

Aisha

It was a strange time for the doorbell to ring. Not quite time for the kids to be home. Not quite time for the husband to be home either. In fact, she was never sure when the husband would be home. The scraping of the key in the front door would announce his arrival, followed by the dull thump on the sofa, where he would throw his laptop. If it was still a while before their bedtime, the kids would squeal, as they ran to him so he could lift them up in his arms, his strong, real man arms, making a mockery of the fact that now, at ten and thirteen, they were both too heavy to carry. If they were awake, that is. And, if he seemed to be in a good mood. If he wasn't, they stayed in their room, ensuring their steps were soft, and their voices hushed. And that their bedroom door was locked from within. Their father seemed to lose his temper very easily these days.

But there it was again. The very definite insistent ring. Again. And then after a moment's trembling uncertainty, yet again. Without opening the door, she knew it was an unfamiliar person. There was no authority to the ring, no confidence that the door would be flung open unquestioningly.

Who could it be, at this hour? Located on the remote outskirts of a mountain town, this house was part of a retirement home complex that never really took off, and was eventually converted into vacation homes. It was a good couple of hours of an undulating drive from the main town. Folks from the city came here to get away from it all. They returned, lulled into somnambulism by the easy hill life, only to be startled back into the relentlessness of the city.

The sky was sullen and overcast. The rain came down like fine mist; at first tentative and uncertain, and then became droplets that made the gravelled little path from the gate to the porch of the house treacherously slippery.

The children would be home soon from school. 'Hungry, Mamma, hungry,' her son would yell as he stepped through the door, his growing frame needing constant replenishment. Her daughter, now conscious of the need to conserve her waistline at an acceptable circumference, would pick at her food. Sometimes she took her plate into her room and at precisely the count to ten, Aisha would hear the toilet flush, and swirling with the water would be the food on her daughter's plate. Maya's cheeks were getting hollow, her eyes sunken. She wore long sleeves to hide the cuts she inflicted on her arms. There was a descent into chaos that began at adolescence, and Maya was at the threshold of that treacherous stairway. The only way out of this personal hell was right through it, Aisha knew. She had travelled through it, as Maya would have to.

But now, at this moment, who could it be, she wondered? They rarely got any visitors, which was exactly how Prithvi wanted it. Prithvi was not a sociable person, never had been. Over the years, Aisha had slowly withdrawn into herself too. She had her reasons. It was just better that way. Staying in the hurly burly of a city, with neighbours peeking into one's every day was terrifying. She liked it here, as alone as she wanted to be. There was the internet that kept her company through the long, lonely days, when it was just her and the house.

She got up and moved towards the door, catching a swift, automatic glance at her reflection, as she passed the mirror in the hallway. She was presentable, as always. Being presentable, she had learnt early, was the one thing that kept her sane. And as inscrutable too.

She looked through one of the translucent glass panes on either side of the door. A woman stood outside holding onto a duffel bag. She was young, probably in her mid-twenties, around the same height as she was. The woman was looking around, taking in the small patch of garden, the wrought iron chairs and the round table on the veranda. Her face was familiar, with the disturbing unfamiliarity of a stranger one has passed a million times before but with whom one never exchanged a smile or a salutation. Her familiarity was like a whisper of a memory, and for a tremulous moment, slick with the promise of revelation.

She opened the door a smidgeon, after slipping on the safety chain, 'Yes?'

'Aisha appa? I'm Heer,' said the woman, a statement spoken with the certainty that the name would be recognised.

For a moment, the world went black before Aisha's eyes. She gripped the small table at the side of the door, with an uncontrollably shaking hand. Her knuckles turned white from the grip on the wood.

'Why are you here?' she asked, feeling an indeterminate dizziness that could only mean her blood pressure had skyrocketed. It was like looking at herself through a time machine, seeing herself as she had been over a decade ago. She had seen those eyes before. She saw them every day in the mirror—wide, light brown, fringed with thick lashes that curled upwards. She had not been the only one to inherit her father's eyes. She felt the bile rise up in her throat. The ghost of her father's indiscretions had just caught up with her, and was now standing at her doorstep, waiting to be invited in to tea and sandwiches.

'I just wanted to meet you.'

'Why have you come here? There's nothing here for you, what do you want from me?' Aisha asked, trying hard to keep her voice firm, and her sentences coherent.

The face, abbreviated in the gap that the safety chain allowed, crumpled into an expression of visceral pain. A tear formed uncertainly in the corner of one eye, and slowly trickled down a cheek, before it was wiped away with a hasty palm.

'I don't want anything from you. I just wanted to meet you. My mother died last month, and I have no family I can call my own. I just thought, perhaps we could connect, put the bad blood behind us and at least stay connected, as sisters.' There was a moment's pause, a pause so loaded that it weighed the listener down to the ground.

'You are my sister whether you like it or not,' Heer continued resolutely. The resistance sagged out of Aisha. There were many battles she needed to fight and this was not one of them.

She sighed deeply, before opening the safety chain and allowing the girl inside the house. Her father was long dead, and her mother had died a couple of years ago. Her maternal aunts were scattered all over the country. The children that had been born of her mother's womb after her had died in their infancy. She had put the existence of this love child back in the recesses of her mind, where unpleasant things were hidden, to fester until they turned putrid and decayed. Family skeletons locked in cupboards rattle insistently, and always find their way out, their fingernails broken and bleeding from the clawing.

'You're not officially my half sister,' she said, her words spitting themselves out with the acidity of denial. 'My father did not marry your mother.'

'He didn't. But he was my father. No one looking at me can deny that.'

That was true. The stranger at the door looked like a female version of their father when he was young. The sepia-tinted monochrome images that were within cumbersome photo albums, tucked into the unpolished silver photo frames, dotted the kothi. Any casual onlooker would peg them down as sisters, so undeniable was the force of the Y chromosome.

Aisha stood there, at the door, breathing heavily, wondering what to do. The rain continued to pelt down mercilessly. The water trailed down into the earth, which sucked it up greedily. It would emerge as tremulous unannounced rivulets merging into the swollen, tumultuous river streams that would go down into the plain.

'You had better come in,' Aisha gestured, opening the door. Heer had with her a small duffel bag, one of those cheap convenient ones picked up at a discount online, the logo similar yet dissimilar to the original brand of which it was an imitation. Her clothes were travel-worn and wet, as was her hair, plastered to her scalp, her face glistening with streaks of what could be either water or tears. The house was inaccessible if one didn't have a car or a mode of transportation. Had she hopped off the state transport bus at the junction and asked for directions from the local lads who stood around passing the time of day smoking beedis and drinking never-ending cups of tea? Had she dropped out of the sky, like most unexpected things did, including disaster?

Things did drop out of the sky sometimes, like the time a goat kid had been lifted by an errant gust of wind and dropped right into their garden when she was a child. Her mother had insisted that a jinn had brought the goat into their premises, and ordered it to be taken away and sold off. The proceeds were distributed to the line of beggars seated outside the mosque the coming Friday.

Aisha stepped aside from the door and gestured that the duffel bag be placed at the side of the entrance lobby. Heer entered, looking around her with an unrestrained curiosity, taking in the double-heighted ceiling, and the sunken living room, made possible by the natural slope of the land the house was built on, the silver frames holding the smiling photographs of the family polished to perfection, happiness glowing off every inch of the house. An illusion that wavered occasionally, like a projected hologram, when Aisha blinked and lost her focus.

Aisha took great pride in keeping a clean house. She could be found occasionally at 3 a.m. in summer nights, scrubbing windows and beating out carpets in the backyard in the dim lights of the garden posts. It kept her sane. In the winter she confined her efforts to indoor cleaning. It calmed her down, the rigour of cleaning. It kept her from wanting to put her head into a bucket of water, feel the water force itself into her windpipe, and choke off the oxygen to her brain, taking her to a warm, welcoming blackness. Only that blackness would silence the haranguing voices within her head that seemed to keep up a constant diatribe. For now, they were silent. They had been silent for a while now. But there was no telling when they would uncoil themselves and slither out.

'Please sit,' she gestured at the sofas, vacuumed to brilliantness just the previous day. She had washed her hands with scalding hot water after she had taken out the dirt bag, and disposed the dirt from the sofa into the dustbin. Aisha looked at Heer as she sat, noting absently, the evidence of a woman's ripeness in her late twenties. The wet t-shirt displayed the firmness not yet ravaged by pregnancy, or the midnight visits to the refrigerator to fill the growing void within. Heer had a hand-span waist blooming out into full and firm breasts that seemed disproportionate to the slenderness of her hips. Aisha felt the shame of having sunk into the morass of neglect, her face dragged down by gravity and discontent, of the silver lattice of stretch marks over her apologetically sagging belly.

'I'm soaking wet,' said Heer.

'Would you like to change out of those wet clothes?' Heer nodded. Aisha gestured towards the bathroom on the landing. Heer rummaged through her duffel bag, extricated some clothes and went in, emerging in a t-shirt and tracks. Aisha took the wet clothes she held undecidedly and put them onto the line in the washing room. She sank into one of the two rough-hewn wooden chairs set by a little round table by the window. This was where she drank coffee most mornings, and ran over the minutiae of what needed to be done through the day. A gas cylinder to be carted off to the gas depot for a refill, or the plumber to be called in to sort out the leaking pipe attached to the washing machine. The laundry list of day-to-day living that washed, rinsed and spun itself in a never-ending cycle. When they had just bought the house, Prithvi would sit in the chair opposite hers, drinking coffee, reading the newspaper. Now they were a travesty, never in the same room together, except at night, except the bedroom. They slept, backs turned to each other, nerves on edge in the event that a stray arm reaching out might be considered an olive branch of a truce. It was a relationship that was poised at a knife's edge—she had him weighed up, measured and he'd come out lacking. He'd realised that this was not the Aisha he'd fallen in love with. The Aisha with her easy, warm laugh had shed her skin, and what emerged from within the discarded carapace was a brittle, menacing woman, her fangs dripping venom.

The women settled in the chairs with a faint adversarial air, sizing each other up, imprinting features upon the memory to be taken as evidence of a tenuous, shared genetic inheritance.

'I'm sorry to hear about your mother,' Aisha said, always unfailingly polite, aware of the awkwardness at expressing condolences for a woman she'd grown up hearing her mother curse a million times a day.

'That whore, couldn't keep her hands off a married man. A wife who is thrown aside by her husband has no respect in this society, Aisha, remember that. If it ever comes to that stage in your marriage, kill yourself. Or kill him. Or kill both.'

Her mother had completely unravelled after her father had left home. Had she begun to unravel even before he did? There was that one night where the badibegum had been spotted walking through the kothi stark naked. Muniyaa, the old retainer who had come to this home with her mother when she was a new bride, had been compelled to take off her dupatta from her hitherto never-bared head and wrap it around her mother, before leading her back into her room, before the entire household would wake up. Aisha had been nine then, and remembered the shock of seeing her mother's naked body, alabaster white in the moonlight. And then the whispers, followed by the grim-faced doctor her father had brought, the rush of flurried footsteps, of not being allowed to see her mother for days, her questions going unanswered.

A few weeks later, her mother was in her room at daybreak, hugging her, the familiar fragrance of musk and roses flooding her dreams, bringing her to wakefulness and the mother she knew. It had never happened again for years. And then, it began again when she was fourteen, a slow insidious descent into a madness that her father could not conceal from the world. Aisha was sent off to boarding school to keep her away from the ugliness. When she returned for the holidays, her mother was glassy-eyed and thick of speech. By the time Aisha graduated, her mother was a stranger, someone who barely recognised her, and wasn't functional. Death, when it came, was a release too long in coming.

Her father died years before her mother did, in another town. The funeral was held in Aisha's hometown, only because her father's cousins stepped in and brought the corpse home. It was the first corpse she had ever seen. Her father, handsomely imperious in death, his skin stained a mottled blue from where the blood had congealed beneath the skin into patches, a map that had no countries. The chest did not rise and fall as it did when he was sleeping. His face had crumpled into that of a stranger she did not recognise, the smile in his eyes, covered by closed lids weighed down by coins. Her mother had been brought out of her room to pay her respects, her maid holding her gently, coaxing her to step forward, which she did, each step dragging her forward through a swamp of disbelief. The wails, when they burst forth, were animal in their rage, echoing through the high-ceilinged room where they had kept the body.

What kind of a person had Heer's mother been? Had she been the calm, comforting refuge her father had needed, to escape from the chaos of Aisha's mother's insanity? Had Heer grown with her mother mollycoddling her? Would she understand how it felt to spend her days locked in her room, terrified that her mother, who had embraced her a couple of minutes ago, was completely capable of flinging something sharp at her, convinced she was spying on behalf of her father.

Aisha brought her mind back to the present, to the woman sitting opposite. 'She had uterine cancer; we detected it at the fourth stage, unfortunately. She barely lived for three months post surgery,' Heer stated, her voice expressionless. 'It was for the best. She had nothing to live for now after Pappa died.'

Aisha registered a sharp flicker of chilly resentment pierce her at the casual use of the word 'Pappa.' She called her father Abbu. Her Abbu was someone else's Pappa. She set her face carefully to reveal no emotion; it was getting easier to do so now, after all these years of training her face to betray no response when provoked, of forcing it to be neutral.

'I have no one to call my own family now.' Heer looked down at her hands and studied them intently, seeing more than the clear skin and the nails painted a particularly virulent shade of blue. 'Except you. If we can call ourselves family that is...' She looked expectantly at Aisha. It was a gaze that Aisha couldn't meet, a question she dared not answer.

Aisha, too, had no one in the world bound to her by blood, except her children. Her mother had passed away a couple of years ago. She had been found lying in her bed by their faithful family retainer, a block of frozen flesh, her limbs already stupefied into rigor mortis, a small wry smile playing on her beautifully faded face. She was calm in her death, and even gentle.

A silent attack, the doctor had said. They had had a quiet funeral. Her three aunts had arrived from the various parts of the country where they were now settled, to attend it. Their children accompanied them. A distant male cousin on her father's side had contested her mother's will. Nothing had come of it. Her lawyer had seen to it that the kothi and the adjacent lands were hers. And her children's. Her aunts consoled her, told her to not consider herself orphaned, that she always had them to turn to, and returned to their homes, their families, their grandchildren.

Prithvi had accompanied her to the funeral, said all the right things, done all that he was expected to, made sure she was kept somnambulant with medication for the duration of the funeral, for fear that she would go hysterical.

The huge, sprawling mansion, a remnant of her father's ancestral inheritance, was now crumbling into a heap of cold, broken stones. The life force that held it together, fiercer than cement and mortar ever could, was buried six feet under the ground. Aisha had no desire to go live there, or even to let it out on rent, or sell it. If she let the house go, she would have nothing left of her childhood. Not even memories, already crumbling into dust every time she pulled them out to pore over them, minute pores that blew away with the faintest sigh that escaped from her.

'Where are you staying here?'

'Nowhere yet. My main purpose was to meet you, I haven't really thought of what I would do after that. I'd thought I'd go into the town, stay for a couple of days, do some sightseeing.' Heer looked out of the window at the downpour as it slapped itself against the glass pane.

Getting back into town would be difficult. The only available public transport was the local state buses or the tourist taxis that ran up and down from the railway junction down at the foothills. It was rare to find some mode of transport midway. Aisha lived in a different direction from the main tourist town. It was a turn away from the snaking mountain road, linking the hill station to the road going to the train junction. She would now have to drop this girl into town, or at the very least, to the taxi stand.

It wasn't where she would have chosen to live, preferring the buzz of the main town, but it was a long drive from the Agricultural Research Centre her husband was part of. Prithvi had wanted them to be slightly isolated. 'Should we just put an electric fence around the house?' she had asked when they'd moved in, 'And guard posts, with search lights?'

The house had been presented to her as a fait accompli; he had already gone ahead, seen the house and put down a deposit for it. It was a beautiful house. Built recently, it was designed in the old style of stone and wood, to make it reminiscent of a heritage property, with imposing wrought iron gates. The exposed stone, and the green painted woodwork, made it look quaintly welcoming. It was away from the main entrance to the vacation cottage complex, ensuring a level of privacy that kept them away from the enforced bonhomie of good mornings they didn't mean. The deep rumble of the trucks on the main road sometimes echoed back, hesitant murmurings of protest from the road, grumbling about a burden they did not choose to carry.

'I never did get to see the kothi,' Heer said, wistfulness tingeing her voice.

'Feel free to drop by and visit it whenever you are there next,' Aisha replied, a vacant offer. Her mother, who might have objected to Heer's presence on the premises, was dead. For a moment, there was an inexplicable yearning for the certainty of knowing Ammi was home, and that Ammi loved her, as much as she could, whenever she could.

'I will,' Heer replied.

She had a pleasing voice with an odd hypnotic quality to it, which was measured, cultivated and soft. It rose and fell in cadences that smoothened out the crumpled creases in Aisha's mind. Despite Aisha's initial reluctance to give her more than the initial few minutes of courtesy that the effort of tracking her down merited, she found herself in deep discussion with her—listening to her life, her memories of their father. This was another father Heer knew, not the one Aisha was familiar with. The memories did not match completely, but the broader details did. Perhaps her father had changed as a person while being a father to Heer. Perhaps his capacity for patience and infinite tenderness had given way to a rough functionality. Perhaps, Aisha consoled herself, Heer was a child he had not wanted to share his love with.

The rain had lessened in its intensity, and a watery sunset had begun dappling the walls of the house with a mosaic of moving patches of grey and yellow. Aisha looked at the clock on the living room wall. It was almost a quarter to five.

The doorbell rang at that exact moment, the insistent rings of children who have been drenched in the hard, unseasonal rain. They would come into the house dripping wet and stand on the hallway rug, get scolded, and then scamper into their rooms, to emerge changed and hungry. She hadn't noticed the school bus stopping at the end of the road, the bright yellow announcing itself aggressively against the dull grey of the day. She had been so engrossed in the conversation that she hadn't heard the honking of the bus, as it turned delicately on the narrow side road to get back towards the main road. Hours had passed, and she was still talking with a woman who she had hoped to pack off on her way, after a cup of tea.

'Oh damn, they're here already,' Aisha said, panicking, her heart thudding angrily against her sternum.

She opened the door to squeals of 'Mom, Mom… look we found a puppy on the road. Can we bring it in?' Aryan was holding a drenched puppy, which was squirming violently at being so confined. Her son's face was flushed with a happiness she hadn't seen in a long while. She wanted to grab him and smother him with kisses, but held herself back, not sure how he would react to any demonstrations of affection, when a stranger was around.

The puppy, clearly of indeterminate local breed, was taken to the little washroom off the entrance lobby and doused down with the faucet to much squealing protest. It was only after they had cleared the pup of the gunk accumulated from the muck and squelch of the path outside, that they noticed there was a visitor in the house.

'This is Heer, a friend from back home.'

'Friend?' Maya was quick to pick up the small details that would otherwise go unnoticed, despite her distracted air. 'You've never mentioned her ever.'

'She is a friend's sister from when I was in college. I can't be mentioning every single person I ever knew before the two of you were born now, could I?'

She knew she was being bristly and defensive, but it was a tried and tested reaction that stopped the uncomfortable questions. They wouldn't dig any deeper, the answer sufficed for now.

'Is she here to stay?' Aryan had noted the bag and arrived at a conclusion that was not his to come to.

'No, she isn't,' Aisha hastened to reassure Maya and herself, 'She was just passing through town and dropped by to say hello. She will be leaving now.'

Aryan was the more compassionate of her two children, getting from her, an inside that turned to mush at the slightest provocation. All knees and awkward angles, he had her hazel eyes fringed with long lashes, and his father's square jaw and determined lip. Completely different from Maya, who had taken her mother's delicately strong beauty and turned it into something lacerating and savage, tempered with the promise of youth.

'How will she get back into town? It's raining. She'll catch cold and get kneemonia and die.' Having grimly pronounced this death sentence, he turned his attentions back to his newly acquired puppy, rubbing it down with a fresh kitchen towel. It would be gently retired from kitchen duty once its tryst with this fur ball was done.

The puppy wriggled, determined to escape, and whimpered for his freedom. It was white, furry, much like an overgrown rabbit, the offspring of some interbreed escapade that seemed to have wandered away from its home. These were not the breeds that wandered around on dangerous roads ending up as road kill. These were collared and vaccinated, and then neutered.

Maya, the more effective of the two, poured out milk into a saucer and placed it on the kitchen floor. Aryan took the puppy to the saucer and watched with an oddly proprietorial expression, as it slurped the milk up so eagerly, it made Aisha want to sternly tell it to stop making sounds, and to remember its manners.

'She could wait until the rain lessens, couldn't she?' Maya asked, 'Or Pappa could drop her to the bus stand when he returns. Or you could drive her to the bus stand. If you are feeling okay today. Are you feeling alright today, Mamma?' She looked at Aisha warily, uncertain of how Aisha would react. The unpredictability had reached a stage where she sometimes reached out to hug her children, and found them flinching and moving away from her.

Aisha drove the car when she felt 'okay'. Okay was a word that was used variably in the household. Some days, she was okay if she could get up to go bathe. Other days, she was okay if she could manage to rustle up a meal. Still other days, if she was not talking a thousand words a minute, she was okay. And on yet other days, if she didn't feel like throwing herself off a mountain road, into the welcoming abyss of mist and fog deep below, she was okay. When she wasn't feeling okay, she didn't touch the wheel of the car.

'I'm not very comfortable driving on these roads when it is rainy,' she replied.

'Don't worry,' Heer replied, jarringly chirpy, 'I'll find my way back, it's a short walk to the main road and I can always hitch a ride.'

Sunsets were always sudden and abrupt in these parts. Aisha moved lightly through the house, switching the lights on, and they cast a hesitant glow on walls and round corners, where unseen things lurked. The rain began to patter again at the roof, first hesitant, then more insistent.

The children looked uncertainly at Heer, who was now gathering up her bag and bending to put her wet sneakers back on. 'I can always stop a bus. There will be plenty of those going up and down on the main road.' As she said that, a great flash of lightning tore the darkened sky into bits of jagged blue flame, followed immediately by a terrifying clap of thunder that shook the sides of the hill the house was perched on. With the screeching wail of a banshee, the huge spreading tree with its benevolent canopy shading the front porch of their home, tilted slowly onto its side, and paused for a long contemplative second, before toppling right across the path leading to the house. The ground beneath them shuddered from the impact. The air was thick with the smell of something burning and the sizzle of raindrops falling on it. The tree broke the lamps on the gate posts as it fell, and the glass shards tinkled gently, as they rained onto the path, deceptively musical in their destruction. The gate gave an anguished groan and separated from the post.

The children, fearlessly curious, had already opened the door to look at the destruction outside the main porch. For a brief moment, Aisha felt the familiar sense of oncoming dread churn her stomach. This is the sign, the monsters in her head said. This is when it begins. She scrunched her eyes shut, and tried to calm the waves of panic rising in her stomach with bile.

The puppy bolted straight out of the front door into the rain and the darkness, whimpering as he escaped his new-found captors.

'Oh damn,' Aryan yelled. 'Maya, this is your fault, you left the door open…' And he rushed out in the rain behind the puppy which was soon a fading white speck beyond the fallen tree.

'Aryan,' Aisha yelled, 'Come back in right now…'

But he was gone too far ahead to hear her voice in the slamming rain. 'I'll get him,' Maya said, her determined thirteen-year-old big sister act in full throttle, grabbing an umbrella from the little basket placed at the entrance.

Aisha ran behind the two of them, unmindful of the fact that she was leaving behind a virtual stranger in momentary charge of her home. The rain was falling thick and fast, the icy droplets stinging her face. The path was dark, strewn with broken glass that could pierce through a sneaker and draw blood. Maya and Aryan had scrambled over the fallen tree. She could not see them clearly now. Her heart began slamming against her sternum. What if Aryan ran all the way down to the main road? What if oncoming traffic didn't spot him at the sudden turn? What if he was a heap of broken bones by the time she ran after them, what if…?

'Aryan, Maya…' she yelled, aware that the wind and raindrops were hurling her voice in a different direction. But she continued to call out. They were her children, and she needed them back in the house, safe.

'I'll go get them, you get back in the house,' Heer said, coming up at her elbow, and swung herself easily over the splayed branches, negotiating the snapped twigs and glass shards on the slippery path, with the ease of one who has been negotiating difficult terrain on a regular basis.

Aisha took herself back to the safe confines of the porch, still worried out of her head. Within a few minutes, she could see three shivering figures making their way back to the house, drenched to the bone.

'I lost the umbrella,' Maya said apologetically, 'it just blew away.'

'That's okay,' Aisha replied, 'Just come in and get dry quickly.'

Getting drenched in these unseasonal chill rains always led to a cold, then fever, and worse, bouts of pneumonia, from which it took weeks to recover.

The phone rang inside the house. She ran in to answer. 'Yes,' she replied on the third ring. She knew it would be Prithvi. Even the ring of the instrument sounded like him, impatient, insistent and disinterested. She told him about the fallen tree blocking the gate.

'I'll inform the fire brigade about the tree. I don't think they'll be there soon though; there've been a few landslides further up. I'll be back when I can. The roads aren't open now.'

'Okay,' she replied, and put the phone down without further discussion. Prithvi was an absentee husband most of the time. She was accustomed to him entering the home when the rest of them were asleep, crawling into bed, and sleeping with his back towards her all night. The marital bed was now a no man's land, a minefield of rejection, and distances that couldn't be measured. There were times she craved to be held, and held onto her extra pillow, searching in it, the humanity of touch across the arid desert of a marriage that was without even the mirage of normality.

Voices alerted her to the fact that Heer had managed to drag the kids back in. Aryan was sobbing at the top of his voice, 'He's gone… he's gone…' His eyes were red and his nose, redder, if that were possible. Aisha soothed him and simultaneously rubbed him down briskly with a towel, drying his hair, and ordering him to change out of his wet clothes. Heer stood by silently, looking on, an undecipherable expression in her eyes. They looked like stones set in wax, Aisha noted with a shiver running up her spine, the eyes of a basilisk.

Maya removed her wet jacket with an expression of great suffering. 'Stop bawling like a baby, it wasn't like you really had that puppy as a pet—you just picked him up when we got off the bus,' she scolded Aryan.

'Mom, Maya is being mean to me again,' he gasped through his sobs, her sensitive, loving boy, a complete contrast to her matter of fact, practical daughter.

'How will you go now?' Maya asked Heer. 'Shall I call for a taxi?'

'Yes,' Aisha butted in, 'Call for a taxi, will you, Maya, before it gets too dark? I'll just go upstairs and get this boy out of his wet clothes and wipe his head dry. Thanks for getting them back in, Heer.'

The local travel node a few kilometres away had itinerant tourist taxi drivers, stopping for a bit after drops, smoking a beedi or two, sipping from glasses of the strong, sugared tea. One of them might just be convinced to drive over to pick up a passenger for the bus depot or the rail head down, a few hours away on the winding mountain road.

Aisha was getting a change of clothes out of Aryan's wardrobe when Maya yelled from the living room. 'No taxis available, Mom. The roads are closed. There's been some problem with the bridge. They will start once the bridge is repaired.' And of course, there was no telling when that would be. The one thing she knew about living in the foothills of the Himalayas was that roads were their lifeline, and there was often no option but to wait it out until things cleared. Outside, a brisk wind churned the wind chimes on the porch into a forbidding cacophony of discontent.

'Okay,' Aisha yelled back, wondering what was to be done about the unwelcome guest in her house.

She dragged a pullover down Aryan's tousle-dried head and went to the living room. Outside the tinted, reinforced glass panes, the rain fell hard, smacking the earth with salacious delight.

'Stay here for the night,' she heard Maya offering Heer generously, 'You can sleep in the guest room. We rarely have any guests anyway.'

As she said that, the lights went out and the world went black.

2

The night was a ferocious litany of pounding rain, of lightning that split the sky, followed by the petulant growling thunder. No moon was visible through the blackness that obliterated both the stars and the universe beyond.

It would be morning soon, she told herself. The modicum of brazen familiarity would resume. The routine of a school day, making it to the bus on time, getting the washing put out to dry, getting a meal made without succumbing to the whispering urge to slit her wrists, while she wielded the knife.

Right now, all she knew was that there was no electricity, she had an unwanted visitor staying in her house for the night, and that her husband hadn't come home, and wasn't likely to do so.

Aisha's maternal aunt called. It was her mandatory once-a-week check on her niece, and her functionality. 'Are you alright, Aisha?' she asked her, her voice reedy with age and cheroots. It was tinged with the defiance of a generation of women who were so well bred, that in spite of reaching a point of smouldering rebellion of all the norms that kept them cloistered, they never broke out beyond the doorway of the zenana. 'Are the children okay?'

Aisha assured her aunt that they were.

'Is Prithvi home?' her aunt asked, after a moment's pause, knowing what the answer would be.

'No, he's stuck at work,' Aisha answered, by now used to making excuses for Prithvi. 'There's been a landslide and the roads are blocked.'

She did not mention that they had a visitor, about whom her aunt had whispered conferences with her mother, back when her mother could still have a conversation without meandering into wild-eyed diatribes against whoever she thought was trying to kill her.

'How do I even begin to compete with her? She's so much younger than I am,' her mother had sobbed. That was the only time she'd allowed herself to break down before the teenaged Aisha, who was finding it difficult to wrap her head around the fact that the father she hero-worshipped had feet of clay.

She'd heard the rumour about her father's other family. 'She looks exactly like Aisha did when she was a baby,' Natty khaalaah had told her mother, shaking her head gravely. She'd been dismissed from the conversation.

'I tell you, Jammy, that child made me believe it was Aisha back as a baby.'

'All babies look the same, don't talk to me about that haraami, Natty,' her mother had replied, spitting into her spittoon in disgust, quite not in the elegant manner her upbringing would have mandated, before fixing herself another paan.

And here she was, Heer. Aisha's half sister. The bastard child. The one she had hated throughout her life, imagining that all her little deprivations were caused by the expedient fact of her existence. It was startling how similar they were. Heer could have been Aisha, when she was a decade and a half younger. The same open face, the same skin that was poised delicately between tawny and olive, the same eyes that could go from melting caramel to piercing copper shards in a split second. It was disturbing, looking at her, realising that she was staring at someone who could have been her doppelganger had they been the same age.

Aisha was older now, the tautness of her shoulders was now a defeated curve, her body was apologetic. Her face was shuttered, her eyes dulled with unseeing, her voice heavy with trapped sighs that crowded up within her chest, rattling hollowly with each breath.

She remembered she hadn't taken her medication that morning. Had she taken it the previous day? She couldn't remember. If she skipped it for too many days, the red curtain of rage dropped over her eyes, making her lash out at whatever came before her. She had tried to do without it earlier. Sometimes, it worked well, and at others it didn't. She found herself falling swiftly into the trapeze of mood swings, without warning. Sometimes, the children bore the brunt of her unannounced rage. She could see herself reflected in their eyes, a feral creature, when they began backing away from her, fear flooding their hearts. If she could find the strength, she would hold herself back, walk towards the kitchen and start cleaning up. It soothed her. She would clean and scrub and scour until her fingers bled. It kept her calm. Sometimes, she wasn't quick enough and the rage would take over, and she would fling and break things. The kids would flee to their rooms and lock themselves in, trembling at the monster unleashed from within their normally placid mother. It happened rarely, now that she had the medication to keep her brain chemicals on a leash.

Prithvi was the only person who could manage her when this happened. Managing her sometimes meant that she woke up to a bruise on her face and no idea how it had come about. They circled each other like gladiators in a ring, terrified to give an inch or lose their lives. Their weapons were words that slashed, stabbed and eviscerated the soul.

Prithvi was careworn now, like Aisha was. She kept away from him, and he from her. The mattress of their bed sagged at the sides. They slept, backs turned towards each other, at the edge. That succinctly defined their life together, a careful negotiation of treacherously demarcated territory that neither dared cross. A no man's permafrost of land in their bed, between their bodies, the bone-numbing chill taking up the space, where love had disappeared.

Sometime in the night, she realised Prithvi hadn't come home. She had checked the children in their beds twice, thrice, four times. It was what she did, every night. Unfailingly. Drop off to sleep and wake with a sudden sinking sensation that something had happened to the kids, that she had killed them in a fugue state. The psychiatrist Prithvi had taken her to, had talked her through her fears, but it didn't abate, her obsessive checking up on the kids when they were asleep.

The first sign that something was truly amiss was when Haria didn't cycle up with the milk that morning. The occasional sounds of vehicles passing on the road up ahead, with the musical cacophony the drivers played when approaching the bend, were few and far between. The world was on hold today.

School was closed until further notice, due to damage to the road leading to it, said an SMS she had received from the school early in the morning. The tree outside lying askew on the path was still to be cleared. There was no way she could drive out. She let the kids sleep in, peeping into their room early in the morning. Aryan splayed on his bed, snoring gently, his high forehead and sloping brow taking after his father, he of the sculpted profile and stern brow. Maya, curled up in a foetal position, as she always did, protecting herself against night terrors, her back to the window that was alongside her bed. She took after Aisha, a thinner, younger version. 'Save her from the monsters in my head,' was all Aisha could think, as she kissed her forehead softly, a whisper of a kiss, infused with all the maternal love she could summon, before the brain chemicals went awry again. 'Let her mind be clear and strong.' It was a benediction she muttered to herself like a litany, a million times a day.

Heer emerged from the guest bedroom at around eight in the morning, stretching and yawning with the litheness of limber limbs, her face glowing with youth and a good night's sleep. Aisha had eggs whisked and ready to be poured into the saucepans for cheese omelettes. The hiss of the beaten eggs, as they hit the butter in the pan, was strangely reassuring. Routine was reassuring. It gently turned one back to the brink of normalcy, from the precipice of chaos.

'Good morning, hope you slept well?' she asked Heer, from mandatory politeness, rather than genuine concern. She hadn't slept well herself, but then she was terrified to let herself fall into a deeply medicated sleep if she could help it. She was afraid she would never wake up again.

Heer was fresh-faced and rested. Perhaps a splash of cold water on her face was all it had taken to sting the roses into her cheeks, which had been pale and drawn the previous evening.

'I slept very well, thank you so much.'

The sky was now a washed out shade of indeterminate fog, and the sun was still in absentia. Yesterday's wrath of thunder and lightning had dulled into a dispirited trickle, dripping down steadily from the drainpipes from the roof, falling with an afterthought of a splat onto the earth.

The two half sisters, strangers to each other, sat at the breakfast counter looking out at the unhindered view of the hills. A distant grey fog blurred the edges of the scene, rather like life itself was with Aisha, a pristine perfect focal point, which slowly merged into a terrifying indistinctness as she moved further away from the centre.

'Didn't your husband come home last night?'

'No, he didn't. The roads are in a mess. He's probably not taking the chance of stepping out until things clear up a bit. And anyway, they have a wonderful bunk facility and a very efficient canteen, so he's well taken care of.'

She didn't mention that Prithvi had a spare set of clothes in his locker, and in a duffel bag in his car. As well as a set of the copies of all his important papers, his passport, his certificates, his bank details. She'd come across them when changing a tyre, on the rare occasion she'd taken his car down to the market herself, to get the weekly provisions. It was the bag of a man prepared to flee at a moment's notice, she knew. It also had a shaving kit, and a pair of sunglasses and a cap. Plus a change of clothes and shoes. And a spare mobile. She hadn't asked him about it. He'd never mentioned it.

'The kids have a holiday from school today. I'm letting them sleep in. Please help yourself.' Aisha gestured expansively at the spread on the counter. 'If you would like some fried eggs or omelettes…'

Heer declined it all with an apologetic smile and gesture, 'Actually, I'm not a very heavy eater the first thing in the morning. I'll just have some juice, if you have some that is, or else coffee would be good. Then I need to get myself ready to leave—I need to figure out how to get back into town.'

The tree was still sprawled ominously outside the gate, blocking all access and exit. They both looked out at it. 'I can climb over it,' Heer stated impassively.

'You could,' Aisha agreed, eager to get her out of the house, before Prithvi returned and began asking too many questions. Heer went back to the guest room and emerged, in approximately ten minutes, dressed in a pair of jeans and a t-shirt, similar to what she had worn when she arrived the previous evening. Her sneakers, which she had removed at the doorway, were still sodden and she shook her head with a vague expression of disgust, as she slipped her sock-clad feet into them. The electricity was still out. In the light of the yawning day, Aisha realised that the fallen tree had taken down some electric poles with it.

Maya sauntered down the stairs, yawning widely, the last vestiges of sleep still clouding her face. 'Mom, what's for breakfast?' Aisha got up, automatically, and began heating sausages in the skillet, pouring the beaten eggs into the frying pan. Maya settled herself down at the table. 'Aryan's got a bad cough. He was hacking away all night yesterday. Why can't I have my own room now, Mom?'

'We'll discuss that later,' Aisha said, 'We are basically housebound until they clear that tree, and you have no school until the road gets repaired, so I suggest you sit down with your books.'

'Can I go to Rhea's house later… please, please, please? I swear we'll do some studying together. I'll walk it down and I'll be careful, you don't need to drop me there.' Rhea was her friend, who lived a good half an hour's walk away at the very least, if she took the curving paths that led off the main road. But, the paths were too deserted to have a mother's mind at peace, if she went through them on her own.

'Oh, are you leaving, Heer?' Maya saw that Heer was dressed and ready, hovering uncertainly at the door. 'Stay for a few days, it was such fun having you here.' Maya and Heer had spent an interesting evening discussing fashion trends, which included stuff Aisha couldn't fathom or relate to. Aisha had given up on fashion a long time ago; her wardrobe was now purely functional. Track pants and t-shirts in the house and fitted shirts and jeans to step out. Saris were too much of an effort. She had given away most of what she had owned, largesse that had benefited the local women who had come to help in the house occasionally, when she called them for an additional pair of hands for the annual cleaning up. Sometimes, she would, as a concession to dressing up, apply a coral pink lipstick. She preferred it bright, but she was slowly giving up on that too.

Vanity seemed meaningless, in this outpost in the back of the beyond, when the only person looking back at her was the reflection in the mirror.

'Heer has to get back home, Maya,' Aisha said, setting a plate of sausages in front of Maya, who did not begin attacking them instantly, as she used to. Instead, she took a slice of toasted bread, and carefully scraped a smidgeon of orange marmalade onto it, so slight it could be nonexistent, and held it in her hand for the longest time, while seemingly holding a debate in her head, as to whether she should bite into it or not. Maya hadn't been eating, Aisha knew. She determinedly ladled out some sausages and a cheese omelette into her plate. 'Eat,' she commanded, putting the steel into her tone, steel that was instantly deflected by an adolescent's insouciant defiance of parental authority.

'Stay for just one more day.' The expression in her eyes was pleading. 'Mom, she can stay for one more day, can't she? The roads won't be cleared anyway.' Heer stood undecided at the door, picking up her bag and putting it down again, looking out of the window. The landline buzzed insistently. Maya got up indolently and answered it. 'Yes, yes, okay, Dad. We're okay... I'll tell her... no, the tree is still there... we have a holiday today, that's why... no, you know Mom won't let us bunk even if it is raining cats and dogs... yup. Mom's friend is here, she came yesterday... Heer. She's leaving now. No, she's not from here...'

Aisha stepped in, 'Give me the phone.'

'Are you coming home today?' She could feel the terseness in her heart spilling out into her words. He hadn't bothered to call them all through the previous night to find out if they were safe, nor had she returned the favour.

'I have no clue when I will be able to get home. There has been some damage to the bridge and they've warned of falling rocks.'

'Okay.'

The sound of a disconnected line blocked out other voices in the background. She placed the receiver down, very slowly, realising that there was a conversation going on which was independent of her contribution, and that Aryan had emerged from the land of nod, and was singlehandedly demolishing the by now cold sausages on Maya's plate, without waiting for an invitation.

'Maya's on a diet,' he told his mother by way of explanation when she pulled him up, 'Because she's getting too fat and has a paunch. She threw up her dinner last night by sticking her fingers into her throat. She throws up her dinner every night.' He supplemented his statement with grotesque upchucking noises. Aisha looked at Maya with horror. She had been suspecting an eating disorder for a while, but when confronted with it, she was at a complete loss as to how to handle it.

'Shut up, frog-face liar! He's been watching too many serials he shouldn't be. Mom, I do nothing of the sort,' Maya replied, swatting him with the comic book she had been browsing through half-heartedly.

'You did, you did. I hear you every day after dinner.' Aryan came to Aisha and hugged her unexpectedly. 'I'm not lying, Mom.' She hugged him back and kissed him on the forehead.

'You are not eating well, I did notice, Maya, and you've lost too much weight.'

Maya scowled and went back to her phone. Snapchat. WhatsApp. She had lost her daughter to an alien world, the blinking white-blue light behind a screen.

'Never mind that, Mom, ask Heer to stay for a few days, please.'

Aisha looked at Heer at the same time that she looked at her. There was a pleading in her eyes that Aisha couldn't ignore. She couldn't be so heartless as to send her out in this chaos. The roads were probably not safe for a woman travelling alone at the best of times, and now, there was every possibility that things could get ugly.

'If anything happens to her, it will tap dance on my conscience even when I'm in the grave,' Aisha thought to herself.

'Why don't you wait back for a day or two until things get a little normal around these parts? You probably won't even be able to find transport into town, to the bus stand. I would have driven you there, but I can't take the car out with this tree blocking the road. And it is a very long walk down to the main road where you could stop a bus. And it isn't exactly very safe to be walking alone on these roads. Sometimes, we hear unpleasant stories of people going missing…'

Heer looked out of the window from where the soft rays of the morning sun fighting through the intermittent, straggly clouds filtered in, lighting up her face, and bestowing a delicate nimbus upon her head. Aisha caught her breath. For a moment, she was looking at herself from almost fifteen years ago. The same half apologetic, half defensive stance, the same hair falling straight to her waist, the jawline before it had slackened into the beginning of belligerent jowls, topped by soft, full, pliable lips, ready to break into a smile.

'Are you sure I won't be inconveniencing you?' Heer asked, her black hair swinging like a curtain begging to be parted, as she turned to face Aisha.

'Stay,' Maya squealed in excitement, 'Teach me how to make smoky eyes. Mom is clueless about makeup.'

Heer laughed, a deep, unguarded laugh that rolled over hills, and mountains and skimmed through valleys, as Aisha's once had. A laugh she had long since forgotten she ever had. 'I'd love to stay.'

Aryan, in an uncharacteristic burst of helpfulness, hopped down from his chair and promptly lugged Heer's duffel bag back up to the guest room. They liked Heer, they did, Aisha realised. Her children were generally prickly and mistrusting of strangers. They did not take kindly to people visiting and opened themselves up layer by layer to folks they didn't know. How had it come to this, Aisha wondered. How had they become a family of strangers to each other? They finished breakfast, and Heer helped with the clearing up. There was still no electricity, and the landline went on the blink too, after a sudden startled squeak of protest. They were cut off from the world, and it felt womb-like, cocooned.

It was then that Aryan asked Aisha the question she knew that they would eventually ask, and didn't have a ready answer to give. 'Why does Heer look so much like you, Mom?' Aisha looked desperately at Heer, feeling her heart sink to her toes. A cold clamminess begin to claw itself out from the pit of her stomach, and reach into her chest, squeezing her heart with fingers that were icicles.

Heer smiled at him, took his hand in hers unhurriedly, bending down to look him in the eye. Her voice, when she spoke, was soft, so soft you had to strain to hear it. 'That's because I'm her sister. Say hello to your new aunt.'

3

Aisha froze, expecting the world to crumple up and fall to pieces, with this revelation That it did not, shocked her. The kids took in the information with surprising equanimity. She stood, a statue of salt, waiting for their questions about why their mother had kept the existence of this aunt a secret. 'Cool,' said Maya, 'I thought you looked too much like Mom anyway to be just a friend's sister.'

'Do you also get very angry or very sad at times like Mom does?' Aryan asked. Heer laughed again, wave upon wave of laughter that hit the eardrums and broke into a scatter of happiness around the room. Aisha missed laughing like that, unhindered by the weight of resentment. At times, she missed the woman she used to be.

The children had no moral compass to judge their grandfather for his transgressions. They accepted this new-found aunt with an imperturbability innate to childhood, when everything is black and white and the grey has yet to fall into their lives. And in any case, to them, their grandfather was a shadowy figure, whom they met for a few days in their summer vacations. Over each year, the pauses in his sentences had elongated themselves to become silences. The silences eventually stopped punctuating conversations, and the conversations became silences punctuated with words.

They would never understand how the presence of this half sibling in Aisha's adolescence had made her question everything: love, her existence, her parents, god, and all that came in between. Her half sister, or her existence, had followed her like a dark, malevolent shadow through her teens and early twenties, making her feel stained, miasmal, the offspring of a morally decrepit man. Would she be the same, she had wondered. After all, she carried his genes. Would she be faithful to her husband, or would she, like her father, betray him the first chance she had?

It disgusted her, brought up as she had been with a strict moral code by her almost puritanical mother, who would even drape her soft muslin dupatta in a manner that no part of her neck would be visible beneath it. This was of course, before her sudden desire to bare all of herself to the moonlight.

The world had coagulated into binaries for Aisha. They blinded her to the distances that had percolated day by day into the relationship between her parents. She knew now, when she was older, that marriages came with no guarantees. That the person you loved fiercer than life itself, when you were twenty-three, could morph into a person from whom you wouldn't think twice, before walking away, when you were forty.

The municipal truck came in the afternoon to clear the fallen tree. Aisha called the local odd-job boy, Gopal, to clear the pathway of the remnants of the shattered glass and twigs. He sauntered up an hour later, his sole pair of jeans mottled with dirt patches, wearing the sweater that never left his body. He was, what the residents politely called, a little 'touched', but he managed to eke out a living doing odd jobs. He also did odd jobs for her and didn't ask too many questions. That suited her.

'Aagey rastaa band hai,' he informed her. The road too had collapsed in pockets ahead. A bridge had debris on it. No one could go further up into the mountains unless they decided to walk it out. It was going to be one of those times when they just had to wait for things to come back to normal.

The electricity had still not been restored and the house was an ice box. The damp from the earth outside seeped in through the stone and brick walls, and the stone floor. The chill infiltrated every corner of the house. The sun refused to show itself through the day, a day so cold, so damp, so miserable that it kept them all quiet and huddled. Evening fell, as it had the previous day, dark and sudden. They lit candles in every room with organised precision. Maya put the candles in the candle stands with plastic mats beneath to catch the drippings. Aryan following her around with a cigarette lighter in his hand, delighted to wield his momentary power over its flickering blue-white flame. For a brief moment, everyone gets a chance to play God in their life. This was his.

The kids were in their rooms hunkered down for the night, when the key scraped in the front door. It swung open with a squeak that oiling would fix, but which neither she nor Prithvi had gotten down to doing. One of those détentes that marriages negotiate. Her stomach knotted itself into a tight fist that hammered at her diaphragm, taking the breath out of her lungs in panicked bursts of breaths. There was a time when his entering the home made her heart leap with joy. Now, it only brought fear and an edgy panic.

She hadn't heard the car pull up into the lane; she hadn't heard the squeal of the tyres as he turned to enter the small bit of driveway where he parked. She looked outside the window. There was no car, and the yawning gap where the gates once stayed closed at night seemed disconcerting.

She moved down the stairs, her feet moving automatically in the darkness, her hands on the railing, a route she had taken in the darkness a million times through the night, when she was in one of her manic stages and couldn't sleep, or switch on the lights.

He was visible by the light of the cold moonlight trickling in through the glass panes.

'Do you want dinner? There is no dinner,' she spoke in the general direction of him, without looking at him, knowing that she wouldn't be able to handle the indifference in his eyes. When had he last looked at her with any longing, she wondered. When had she last given him reason to look at her with love?

'No, I've eaten,' he said, his eyes not meeting hers, flinging his laptop case on the sofa, throwing his socks in the general direction of the laundry basket, knowing the disarray would incense her. The last time she'd pleaded with him to keep things in their place, he'd yelled at her. 'You're stifling to live with. Can't you be normal about things?' It was a purely rhetorical question. He knew that she couldn't be normal about things, she had moved away from normal a long while ago. The spectrum she inhabited had normal at one end, and at the extreme end was the stage where he would call the folks to take her to the institution for a few days. The last time was a couple of months ago. His sister had come down to take care of the kids. But she'd been fine since, Aisha told herself. Really fine. Functional. No rages. No blackouts. No days of gibberish, which she had never believed of herself, until he set up CCTV cameras all around the home, so he could monitor her behaviour even when he was at work.

Mood charts meant nothing. Her moods were a weathervane, fickle, turning with the wind, kept on an even keel by medication he tried hard to ensure she took.

The more he tried to force-fit her into his definition of normal, the further she retreated into her kitchen, to arrange her jars with the colour-coded lids, or into the bathrooms scouring the tiling for grout, scrubbing till her hands were raw and blistered, the skin peeling off in patches. This was her normal, to be stoic in the face of the world collapsing around her, to hold herself together with will and a prayer, because she couldn't dare allow herself the luxury of collapsing. Until it happened, the tipping point was reached and the chemicals in her brain went awry, and she would be the person she had no idea she was being.

He walked up to the children's bedroom and opened the door, peeping in with a hesitancy that was endearing. Aryan was asleep; Maya was sitting by the window, looking out into the velvet blackness of sky dotted with stars.

'Beta,' he spoke, softly, so as not to wake Aryan up.

'Pappa,' she turned with a start at his voice, then came to him to hug him. Aisha looked on from the landing where she'd been standing.

'What did you kids do all day? I'm sure no studies got done. Has your mother been taking her medication, Maya?'

Maya turned around, with the grace of early adolescence. 'Yes, Pappa, we studied, Mom took her pills,' she replied smoothly. Her mother had probably thrown the pills away in case her husband counted them.

When he was home, he would insist she took them in his presence, and then open her mouth wide to show him she had swallowed them. Otherwise it was spit, not swallowed. Such a metaphor about the state of their marriage too. But she was fairly placid now, she told herself. She could risk tapering down her medication. When she would feel the high or the low coming on, she would begin taking it again. It was a delicate rope she walked on every day, judging whether she could be trusted to keep her sanity through the day. It wasn't easy on the kids to have their mother zoned out from medication for days, unresponsive, catatonic. Some days were walking through rivers of sludge to function. She felt her brain slow down to a point where to even lift her hand was an effort. And she would keep a watch on herself before she escalated into one of her unbearable highs, which made her feel invincible, indestructible and omnipotent, and completely unfocused.

It had been eight months since the last time. After three sleepless nights of just doing stuff around the house, and yet feeling a recklessness that would not be stemmed, she had just taken off from home one fine morning while the kids were at school. She left a note for the kids on the kitchen table, and the door key under the door mat. She hitched a ride to a popular tourist hamlet higher in the mountains, spent a week at a commune of foreigners, blissing out on the cheap and readily available marijuana, and the even more readily available sex. It all ended when Prithvi tracked her down via the locals and the taxi driver network, and brought her back home. She'd left a trail of course, and deliberately so. She'd called home from where she was, to tell the children to survive on the packets of two-minute noodles she'd stocked in the pantry, and she'd told them where she was. She was hiding in full sight, waiting to be found.

When she had seen Prithvi drive up, the flood of relief rushed straight to her ganja-addled brain. The first thing that had alerted her to his arrival was the tyres screeching, as the car turned in through the steep turn up to the cottage where she was currently shacked up. A slow-voiced, languid-limbed Israeli student had offered her a bed and a room for a ridiculous amount of money. Prithvi had come up and stood at the door without saying a word, his face carved from stone, his jaw clenched, the nerve at the base twitching like it always did, when he was too angry to trust himself to say anything. She packed her things back into her duffel bag and walked out without saying a word either. It was understood that he would come to get her back and she would go back with him. They were tied to each other by tenuous bonds that perhaps only death would break.

When they got back, he'd spoken to her gently about how she needed to stay on her medication, about how he would need to put her into an institution if she didn't, and send the kids to a hostel, if she went off the edge again. She nodded her head meekly. She was over the high of invincibility and was slowly sinking into the blackness of the catatonia that would inevitably follow.

Maya looked at her father as he stood at the door to their room. 'Pappa…' she began and stopped, just as Heer emerged from the guest room. Prithvi turned, following Maya's gaze and took her in. In the flickering light of the shaky torch she held, Heer looked other-worldly. The expression on his face was familiar. Aisha had seen it before, many years ago, before Maya was born, an expression she had assumed was love but she now recognised as unfettered lust. She absently noticed him straighten his shoulders and suck in the slight softness of his belly. A nervous hand ran through his hair in an unconscious gesture of grooming himself. He had been terrifyingly handsome once, a face that was made to be magnified by cinemascope, had he chosen to. There was still that consciousness of a fading attractiveness, albeit a little crumpled. He was a little dishevelled right now, with the stubble of a couple of days that hid the beginnings of the jowls, around what had once been a granite slab of a square jaw. She could almost see the hormones leap up and begin skittering through his bloodstream.

'Pappa, meet Heer, mom's sister, actually her half sister,' Maya continued, having accepted this new addition to the family as a given, and assuming that her father would do so as well. 'She's staying with us till the roads clear up.'

Prithvi looked at Aisha, a single eyebrow lifting itself in unspoken query. 'Now that is interesting, Aisha's half sister?' he said, each word slow and deliberate. She could almost see the synapses within his brain, grey pink, soggy with tiredness, flash instantly, making the connections. She had vaguely hinted about her father's other family to him many years ago when they were dating, and had never ever it mentioned again.

Every family has their skeleton in the closet, and this was hers. She had not expected to have to bring it out and tango with it at this stage in her life.

Her husband, the father of her two children, once the love of her life. Director of a privately funded research institute that had lured him away from his position in the backwaters of a government organisation. This position offered him complete autonomy from the principal funding conglomerate based in the US, and set him apart from the rest of his peers who worked in government-funded institutions. He was in his mid-forties, surprisingly fit for a man who barely got any physical workout on a daily basis. He still carried the restrained menace of his days as a prize-winning pugilist for his university. It made people think twice before disagreeing with him, even if they didn't know that he once was known for his upper-cut. In fact, that was their first meeting. She had accompanied a friend to a bout, and went up to congratulate him, still bloodied and woozy, for a bout well fought. He held out a gloved hand to her, as his coach mopped up the blood oozing from a cut on his forehead. She shook the glove, still sticky from the blood that had flown from his opponent's nose. He asked her out to dinner that night. Touching that bloodied glove had felt like a covenant she had entered into. That night, she gave up her virginity to him. And notably, for all his small town upbringing, he hadn't thought of her as easy and available after she had done so, but instead proceeded to fall completely and irrevocably in love with her.

They were married, five years later, a civil wedding conducted in the impersonal environs of a court office, piled with the musty files slowly gathering dust on the tables by the sides of the room. The jaded marriage officer announcing them married with a studied disinterest that came from years of officiating at civil ceremonies, where the back stories of the couples could make a Bollywood blockbuster pale.

Maya was born a couple of years later. Aryan three years later. Then came the demons in her head, and Aisha was never quite the same again.

'Hello,' he said to Heer, pleasantly enough, shaking her proffered hand with the charming politeness he effortlessly donned in the presence of company.

He put on his man-about-town voice with its deep bass and rolling cadences that lingered and caressed the ears of his listeners. It had Aisha totally hanging onto his every word when they first met. 'Most good-looking men have voices that grate on your nerves,' she had told her then best friend, Ramya, when they'd discussed him the morning after she spent the night losing her virginity in Prithvi's PG digs. She had not realised it at that time, but when she had stated she would follow this man to the ends of the earth, he'd made her follow through on the statement.

Now that same man was looking at her half sister with an expression that teetered uncertainly between politeness and a full-blooded man's longing for a beautiful woman. 'Lovely to meet you, I'm sure Aisha was delighted to re-connect with you.' Aisha, listening in without comment, wondered when it had ceased to matter to him what delighted her and what didn't. Heer replied that she was delighted to meet Aisha after all these years.

Prithvi continued politely, a deceptively mundane conversation tinged with strong undercurrents that wafted back to Aisha, who stood looking on at both of them. She had a sudden unbidden sense of being an intruder.

'The roads are quite a mess, there have been landslides. I think staying back would be a good idea. At least until it clears up. You won't find transport until they fix the roads. I got a ride half way home and then walked it back for around five kilometres.' That explained not hearing the car drive into the road, and the squelchy shoes and raincoat that was now dripping puddles onto the floor from the dining table where it had been flung.

'Wow, Heer can stay for a couple of more days with us, then?' Maya asked.

'Let's see what the situation is tomorrow,' Aisha interjected.

Prithvi went into the bedroom, washed up in the dark, changed and went into his den. He closed the door behind him and she saw the thin blue light of the laptop glowing from beneath the closed door.

There was still no electricity. Aisha took out the long-handled mop and wiped the wet mud from the road off her flooring, and took a cloth to the carpet to get the mud out. After she was convinced she could do nothing further to repair the damage to the carpet, she went to the kitchen and began cleaning the counters again. The emergency light she had placed on the breakfast counter flickered blue and forbidding, casting strange misshapen shadows in the room. Heer joined her, sitting at the stool on the counter, pouring herself a glass of water. 'This is a lovely home you have, such a lovely family. I envy you.'

She couldn't help but notice Heer's hands—smooth-skinned, unspotted with the little bits of pigmentation that had already begun creeping up on the backs of her own hands. Heer's nails were square-shaped perfection, topped with an indeterminate shade of blue-grey that was more trendy than girly. These were not the hands of someone who did her own work around the house. Aisha looked down at her own hands with a fierce mixture of shame in their unkemptness, and pride in the conglomeration of calluses, the blisters, the sensibly cropped nails, untouched by varnish or file. These were hardworking hands, that had earned their years, their wrinkles, their crepey, textured senility.

'Thank you, my children are darlings,' Aisha replied. And they were. Maya, the adolescence bloom filling her face with the sharp promise of an unbearable beauty to come, like her mother and her maternal grandmother before her. Aryan's mischief dripping through from every pore, inevitably leading to scrapes and cuts and bruises, all of which speckled his body. The narratives he created for each featuring him in heroic deeds that almost saved the world, or if not the world, at least a couple of his friends.

'Did you ever want to meet me?' Heer asked. The answer she wanted to hear hung indistinctly in the chilly air between them.

Aisha took a long sip from her cup, weighing her words carefully before she let them escape. Then she replied, words she meant to cause hurt. 'I did for a while, but then I got caught up in my own life and forgot about your existence.'

She saw the hurt flare up for a moment in Heer's eyes, flicker into something vaguely hostile before dying down into embers. The eyes they had both inherited from their father, copper when annoyed, bronze when emotional, honey when overflowing with happiness that would not be contained.

'Will you go back to your mother's home now?' Aisha asked.

'No. I'm all alone now. My grandparents died when I was a child. And anyway, they had disowned my mother after she had me. And my only maternal uncle lives in Canada and hasn't been in touch with us. I don't have any contact with him anymore.' She shrugged her shoulders and put her glass back on the breakfast counter with a sudden abruptness.

'Anyway, I'd already moved out of home a few years ago. I lived in Delhi in a rented apartment, and I used to work at a digital agency. I left my job when my mom fell ill and needed me around. I need to get back and find myself a job and a house again. Start from scratch.' She sighed.

'Would you like something stronger than water to drink?' Aisha asked. 'Feel free to help yourself.' She gestured towards the well-stocked bar that was Prithvi's pride and joy.

Heer rose and moved towards the bar, inspected the contents in the dim blue light, pulled out a bottle of Absolut and poured out a heady measure into a highball glass she located in the cabinet. 'Do you have some orange juice?'

Aisha padded across to the refrigerator, now like any other cupboard, having been switched off for over a day, took out a tetra pack of orange juice and handed it across to Heer.

'What about you, would you like me to pour you some?'

'Nothing for me, thanks,' Aisha replied, half apologetically.

'Oh, why is that? Are you a teetotaller?'

It would have been easier to say yes, to say that she didn't drink alcohol because she didn't want to, but something made her state the truth, albeit veiled with understatement.

'I have some medical issues, for which I am on medication, and alcohol is not permitted.'

Heer looked at her curiously, the blue from the emergency light casting an eerie glow on her face. She began to say something and then stopped herself. 'Have some juice with me then? We'll pretend it's a Screwdriver.' She poured out some orange juice in another glass and handed it across to Aisha.

Aisha laughed. It had been a while since she had laughed. She felt the unnaturalness of the laughter from her ricochet off the walls and return to drill her ears with a prescient warning. They clinked the glasses together in a mock toast. The mood was the kind of mellow that Aisha had not experienced in a while. She could feel the prickly barriers she had hastily set up against this woman slowly dissolving into the ease of an enforced familiarity. She was thankful that Heer didn't ask her to elaborate further on what medication she was on. It would be difficult to explain how her mind sometimes twisted in on itself, like Kekule's snake and sometimes swallowed its tail.

Heer sipped her drink carefully, staring at it intently when it was on the counter, as they spoke.

'I have no option and nowhere else to go. All the little money we had, I spent on my mother's treatment. I am broke now. The house is mortgaged, and the bank will claim it, because I can't pay the instalments. I thought of going back to Delhi but it frightened me this time. Earlier, I knew I could go back to Mom, in case things went wrong. Now, I have nowhere to go back to, no one to come back to. No safety net, nothing to fall back on.'

Aisha knew how overwhelming that bereftness felt. When the call came informing her about her mother's death, it seized her—a realisation that she had nowhere to go to, that she was no longer someone's child anymore. In her last days, Jamila's mind had been elsewhere, in a distant dank place, from where she emerged only to howl and claw at whatever or whoever came within her reach. It terrified her to think that she might end up just like her mother. She *knew* she would end up like her mother. It was an inescapable destiny that awaited her, no matter how she tried to delay it with the pills and the denials.

Heer could stay here, Aisha thought, for a wild, irrational moment. She could live with them, they could be sisters, as sisters were meant to be. Together, walls of support for each other. They could build on the years of not knowing each other, and create a relationship that was all the more unique for the absence of a shared childhood, a void they would fill with the pristineness of a brand new history, build it moment by moment, as siblings who had first met as adults. The moment passed, and the prickly barriers, made of hurt and pain, and uncertainty went up again. She swatted the errant idea down as untenable. One didn't open one's house to a stranger on a permanent basis just because they claimed to share blood with you. One needed to first open one's heart to them and she wasn't sure she could find hers anymore, much less open it to anyone.

'No boyfriend?' Aisha asked, with none of the reticence that came into play regarding personal questions, considering this was someone she had met for the first time the previous day. Surely the rules could be discarded when it came to half sisters.

'No boyfriend,' Heer repeated, without elaborating, her face getting shuttered down. 'At least, nothing permanent.'

That was a nice place to be at, Aisha thought. Nothing permanent. She would have liked to be in that space as well, nothing permanent. What determined one would spend out an entire life with one person? Perhaps merely the simple expedient of that person's pheromones being in consonance with yours, when you were at a phase when pheromones mattered.

The pheromones had dissipated now, leaving behind the miasmal stench of discontent. It lurked behind doors, paused between moments of calm, and blackened the edges of memories with their acrid corrosiveness. Neither she nor Prithvi had been willing to negotiate the landmines of indifference that now dotted the charred landscape of their marriage.

'I think I'll call it a day,' she said, stretching and moving towards the stairs, peeking into the kid's room to check if they were asleep.

'Me too,' replied Heer, moving into the guest bedroom and shutting the door behind her with a soft goodnight.

Aryan was sprawled on his bed in a starfish pose in the dark, while Maya was looking out of the window, as still as a thing carved of stone. She started guiltily, as Aisha stepped into the room, and began picking up the scattered detritus of the children's day at home. 'Mom,' she yelled, 'Stop sneaking up on us.' Aisha planted a soft kiss on Aryan's forehead, and hugged Maya, despite the adolescent prickliness that exuded from her.

'Goodnight, Maya, go to sleep,' she said, as she turned away from the children's room, passed the study with its door firmly shut and moved towards the stairs to go up to their bedroom. From behind the closed door of the den, sounds of a conversation emerged, broken and muffled, cloaked with the impenetrability of the door.

Suddenly, Aryan tumbled out of his room and hurtled himself up the stairs towards his mother, grumbling loudly, rubbing at his eyes, 'She's not sleeping, troubling me and tickling me and disturbing me...'

'Maya,' Aisha thundered, as Aryan wrapped himself around her, his arms around her waist, in an instinctive seeking of security and protection that had often made her feel braver than she really was.

Aryan had more of her heart than Maya did; it was something she no longer allowed herself to feel any guilt about. Maya had been a difficult baby, stuck in the birth canal, so Aisha had to be cut open to allow her to emerge. A colicky, sickly baby, who drained her of all the energy. Aryan, on the other hand, was her golden boy, emerging laughing from the womb, suckling without fuss, sleeping for the better part of the day, drawing energy from the sun's feeble wintry rays she placed him in, to strengthen his bones. He was her darling child, but he had leeched out all the life energy from her, leaving her drawn and weary, turning her into this wretched creature, who couldn't be sure whether she was in her right mind or out of it.

Maya knew that Aryan was her mother's preferred child and resented him for it. And now there was the unspoken burgeoning of adolescent self-awareness, and the added resentment of having to compete with her own mother in the looks department. The boys in her class craned their necks collectively, when her mother stepped into the room on Parent-Teacher Meeting day. Her best friend told her it was a pity she would never be as delicate as her mother, because she'd got some of her father's features too. A boy she had a crush on blushed and got all goggle-eyed when her mother spoke to him. She would never be as beautiful as her mother, she told herself, and she threw up all she ate in protest.

Prithvi emerged from his study, and watched the two children complaining in tones too loud for his presence in the house, especially when he was working. They didn't realise he was standing there, silent, menacing. The flickering darkness hid him well. It was Maya who first saw him and stopped mid-sentence. Aisha turned around to see him slowly descending the stairs, every step reverberating in the quietude, each time his foot hit the uncarpeted wood. Aisha felt fear begin to crawl up her spine, her insides went cold and her palms went sweaty. Prithvi called Aryan to him in the voice he used when he was not to be messed with. Aryan walked with leaden steps to his father, his shoulders drooping with the burden of the weight of terrified anticipation of what undoubtedly would follow.

'What have I told you about making a noise when I'm on a work call?' Prithvi began in that deceptively soft voice that always led to a screaming rage, which would leave him shaking and the rest of them backing away into corners, behind locked doors where he wouldn't be able to reach them. Perhaps, she thought, it was Prithvi who needed to be on medication to control his rages. But he didn't see it that way. To him, she instigated it, she gave him cause, made him so annoyed that he was compelled to lash out.

'He didn't know you were on a call, he was trying to go to sleep,' Aisha said, moving swiftly up the stairs, putting her hands on Aryan's shaking shoulders and firmly steering the child into his room, handing him to Maya who quickly took him into the room, and closed the door behind her. They knew the drill. They would emerge now only the next morning after the storm had abated.

He focused his anger on Aisha, as she stood between him and the door of the children's room, her back straight and her gaze as steady as it could be. 'Aisha, have you been going through my things?' His voice had gone soft, deceptively soft. 'You think I wouldn't notice when my things have been messed with? How many times have I told you to stop going through my things?'

She shrugged indifferently, a non-committal gesture that hovered on the precipice of acceptance and denial.

'What are you hoping to find? Why are you so suspicious?'

Aisha went through his drawers to check out his correspondence. There was stuff that concerned her too, things that he kept hidden from her, things she had a right to know. She did so regularly, but he had not figured it out so far. She must have pushed things back in a hurry, or opened something and not kept it back in the way it had been kept originally. She hadn't checked his things in a couple of days, or more. And she had always been meticulous about placing everything as it was, down to the level of random disarray that she knew he created, as a trap to get her OCD into action.

There was a brief moment of silence, then he spoke again. 'Have you stopped taking your medicines?'

She didn't bother to respond. He moved a step towards her and grabbed her hand. She stepped back instinctively, trying to free her hand and tripped over a small step. She fell with a thud against the door she had just closed, her hands clawing at air to steady herself and finding nothing to break her fall. She felt a sharp sting in her lips where her tooth bit on it sharply and the metallic taste of fresh blood swirled up in her mouth.

'I am fed up of you,' he shouted. 'I've had enough of you and your madness and suspicions.'

'Stop it,' a voice shouted from the top of the stairs, and swift footsteps came clattering down. Heer. She bent down over Aisha in a strangely protective gesture, interjecting herself between Prithvi and Aisha, blocking him from reaching Aisha.

He stood over both of them, looking at them with a wary, perplexed expression for a long, heavy moment, then turned away, climbing up the stairs, going into the bedroom and slamming the door shut.

Aisha's eyes did not fill up with tears. Those would come later, she knew. And with them would come the howls she would stuff the hand towel in her mouth to muffle, after locking herself in the bathroom. She went, her knees shaking, into the spare bathroom by the landing and washed her face with a calmness that knew the procedure to be followed after such an incident.

'Are you okay?' Heer asked, 'Are you hurt?' Aisha stayed silent. Words seemed incapable of conveying all that she needed to say.

Heer looked around, handed Aisha a hand towel after dipping it in the chilled water that came out through the taps, indicating she should hold it against her lip. Aisha did so, and looked at her reflection, dark and shadowy in the flickering light, where she couldn't make out the dribble of blood from the cut lip. But, the sting and the swelling told her it was split and she hoped that it wouldn't need suturing.

A Rorschach blot bloomed on the towel, red and furious, spreading its tentacles wildly across the fabric as the blood continued to gush. She wrung the hand towel out under the running water and saw the blood swirl away into the basin, mingled with the tears that had now begun falling briskly, efficiently. There seemed to be a deliberate waiting, a silence, an explanation needed, but Aisha kept silent, unwilling to let her humiliation seep out from where she kept it locked, in the deep recesses of her mind.

She smiled quickly, a smile of gratitude, seeking to reassure herself more than the guest that this wasn't something that merited being alarmed about.

'Nothing to worry, just a silly argument. I'm fine. I really am.'

'You aren't fine. You're bleeding,' Heer replied, opening the bathroom cabinet and finding a small bottle of Dettol and some Betadine.

'I'm okay, just a small cut. Nothing serious. It was my fault, I tripped and fell. I'm always so clumsy. I should have made sure the kids were quiet when he was working. It just gets him angry.'

She made Aisha sit at the breakfast counter stool and daubed away gently with some cotton soaked with antiseptic liquid. It didn't sting. What stung were the tears that dripped unbidden into the ruptured skin. They were salty, a familiar taste of distilled sorrow. When they mixed with blood, they created a potion for grief, that when swallowed, could drown her in a morass of darkness from which it would take her days to emerge.

'As you can see,' she said, through thickened split lips, tasting the familiar metallic acridity of the fresh red blood on her tongue, 'This isn't such a lovely life after all.'

4

Aisha slept on the sofa in the living room that night. Sleep evaded her. Her mind churned with things to be done, one thought chasing the other, until she had to wake up and write them down, before they escaped her. She caught a bit of sleep just before daybreak, and woke up as the rays of the morning sun reached out tentatively, from the east, into the house. The electricity had been restored, but in fits and bursts. The house though was almost an icebox, the feeble rays of the hushed morning sun doing nothing to dispel the early chill.

There was a blue-black bruise spread over the left cheek from where she'd hit the ground. Her split lip was swollen. She looked into the tiny mirror above the sink in the utilities room. A stranger stared back at her. She did not look pretty anymore. But then, she hadn't for some years now. A woman who has grown up aware of her beauty is the most acutely aware of its gradual fading. Every woman handles it differently. Some clutch onto fading youth by resorting to surgical intervention, others step up the makeup, choosing colours that go brighter, applied by a hand that is heavy. Aisha belonged to a different kind. The ones who let the wrinkles creep up unrestrained, moving on matter of factly into middle age, where appearance was incidental to existence.

age. She'd lost her husband when she was
children, one from her late husband, and
over she had given up, were in their teens.
aid now, as she deftly offloaded radishes,
leafy bundles of vegetables into the basket
, 'I think your parcel has come in.'
, acknowledging the bit of information. She
into town today, to pick up what was waiting
cal store, while picking up the butter, the cake
ecessities of running a home. Gauri kept her
parcels. Phone calls didn't work as well, Gauri's
n law partner was the delivery man. He did the
veen the big city and their small one-horse hill
week. And every few weeks, he carried with him,
pped, a parcel for Aisha, something that she dared
vered in the house, in the event that it arrived when
t home. Gauri could have carried it with her, but
trust her to deliver it safely.
n't really need the groceries. Aisha had always ensured
ntry was stocked to the brim. When one lived in the
ng up for a month was a natural way of living, given
and the cold sometimes made it impossible to venture
of course, she had the added issue of her mood swings.
en months since her last relapse, but one never knew.
ways a good thing to stock up. She could be sure that
would be fed even if she was slowly disintegrating and
regular functionality. There would be days when even
out of bed was impossible, and all she could do was pull
nkets over her head and lie down, whimpering helplessly
n agony she could not put into words.
er visit to the post office had been long pending. She
ed to send off some papers. The back and forth on legal
ments wearied her. Sometimes, she wished she hadn't fallen

Aisha did her cleaning, sipped her coffee, tidied the rooms, organised breakfast and laid it out on the table. She scribbled in her diary, trying to put down the thoughts racing at 140kmph through her mind. Writing everything down kept her sane. She locked away her journals, taking them down when she was calmer and reading a stranger's hand, stories she would never know.

Her husband emerged from the bedroom, bathed and dressed. The fragrance of his familiar aftershave and cologne stabbed the indifferent morning with a sense of purpose, wafting into the kitchen ahead of his swift steps down the stairs. She knew, without looking at him, that his hair would still be damp and tousled from the shower, finger combed as was his norm. His face would be placid, unruffled. The unprovoked rage of the previous evening would be nowhere in evidence.

He sat heavily at the breakfast counter, poured himself some coffee from the carafe which had been plugged in, mixed his muesli with cold milk, buttered a couple of slices of bread, and ate them silently.

Aisha turned away as she saw him approaching and kept her back turned to him. Part of it was to deny him the pleasure of seeing her cut and swollen lip, and the purple bruise on her face. Part of it was the apprehension that it might lead to yet another confrontation. She hadn't taken her medication yet, or been into the bedroom yet. She couldn't risk conversation of any sort with him. She found her hand reaching tentatively towards the knife drawer where she kept the meat cleaver, and pulled it back with great difficulty. She could easily cut a limb off with that meat cleaver, she knew. She resisted that temptation on a daily basis. She didn't hate him that much, not yet though. But there was no telling. Wasn't hate merely love flipped over onto its back, kicking and squealing for attention, the angst of unrequited emotion that would not be denied?

She heard him put his cup down, walk to the den and pick up his bag. 'I might not be back home tonight,' he said to no one in particular, without turning his head to look at her, and slammed the door shut behind him. If he had looked at her then, he would have a memory of her with her shoulders squared and jaw determined, rather than that of the woman, who had tripped over a half step and fallen awkwardly against the door, her lip a sudden spurt of angry bleeding. But he didn't.

She watched him walk down the paved path to the gate, looking every bit the academician he was, with the black V-necked sweater he'd pulled over the blue-collared shirt. She recognised it as the one she had bought him as a wedding anniversary gift many years ago. It could be his effort at brandishing the olive branch. She was imagining it. It probably meant nothing, she told herself. It had perhaps been on the top of the pile, ironed and at easy reach.

He walked down the path and through the broken gate, swinging half unhinged, his step laden with the cold certitude of finality. She knew he wouldn't turn around. Just like she hadn't turned around to face him earlier in the morning. The distances between them were the ones that were only bridged by anger. The tenderness of a look or a gentle touch had long dissipated from their lexicon.

The children emerged, yawning and stretching from their bedroom, having blanked out the unpleasantness of the previous night, choosing not to comment on it, nor on their mother's slightly swollen lip. The cut was not as gruesome as it seemed in the light of the torch in the night. Daylight always had that ability to make things less fearful, whether it was cuts and bruises or the monsters in the dark corners of the mind.

Heer joined them at the breakfast table, smoothly taking over serving the kids, clearing the table, and washing up the dishes after they were done, while Aisha kept her face turned away as much as she could.

to the responsibility of so much property, that she was not the custodian of ancestral wealth to be passed down to her children. And she now had to collect her parcel.

'I have to get into town for some work. Hopefully, the roads have cleared up now. Would you like to come with me? Perhaps you could find some transport back to Delhi?' she asked Heer. Strangely, she wasn't quite as keen as she thought she would be for her to leave. The unease of an illegitimate sibling had all but dissipated, and Heer was now a comfort to have around the house.

'I'll stay for a day or two, I think, if you don't mind that is. I really don't want to get into town and not find transport back to the railway station nor a place to stay. That's if you don't mind me staying on?' The gentle question in her eyes demanded an answer, one that Aisha was not quite ready to give yet. An answer that would mutate into either acceptance or denial.

'Of course, I wouldn't mind,' Aisha replied. 'Do feel free to stay on for as long as you please. And yes, it might not be a good idea to travel in these times. Let things settle a bit and the roads get back to normal. But I do need to get to the post office today, there has been something I've been putting off for a while, and I just have to get it done.'

'Go ahead,' Heer told her, 'I'll stay back and watch the kids.' The kids didn't need watching anymore, she knew, they were old enough to take care of themselves. But it was a gracious offer, meant well, and she accepted it.

'Thanks, I should be back within a few hours,' Aisha replied, taking the keys of her tiny car off the key rack and riffling through her hand bag to check if she had all she needed.

It was a risk going into town on such a day, she knew. The roads would be uncertain, and there was no guarantee she would make it into town before the post office shut down for the day. She had no clue of whether the roads were navigable, or whether the danger of landslides had passed, or whether the clear-up crew had worked on the debris that had fallen from eroding mountains, denuded of their tree cover in patches, by illegal logging.

The rain began trickling down again in uncertain dribs and drabs as Aisha carefully negotiated the slippery curves of the roads, already slick with mud and debris. She drove carefully, wary of the headlight-flashing, horn-tooting city slickers, trying to overtake her on treacherous mountain roads, with the insouciance of those who have not yet known the finality of a fall, off the edge of the mountains. There was damage from the rains, she noted, roads piled with mounds of boulders and mud, sudden treacherous gaps where the edges of the road had given way. It was greater as she climbed higher.

The road dipped a bit, going down to where a sturdy bridge crossed over an angry chaos of rocks and gushing waters. She drove over the bridge without stopping, without stepping out of the car, without walking to the edge and peering over, swaying undecidedly for that short second that the swirling, dark waters lured her.

There was no oncoming traffic from the other side—it was a sudden warning bell. There might be trouble up ahead. And then she saw a bright red jeep which had overtaken her car, a short while ago, going back in the same direction it had come from.

Around fifteen kilometres from the market, and five kilometres after the turn-off to Research Centre, where Prithvi would be, a pile of boulders sat prettily in the middle of the road. There was only space enough to navigate a two-wheeler around it. Beyond it a patch of the road had caved in with the impact of falling rocks, with only a sliver of a ledge enough for a single person to walk on. Some police personnel stood guard, turning the cars back from either side.

'Landslide, madam,' said one, when she rolled the window

down to ask what the matter was. 'The road is closed, turn around and go back.'

'Damn,' she swore, getting out of the car and peering over the mound of debris to the other side of the road. There seemed to be a few cars backing up, probably returning to where they came from or perhaps looking for an alternative route to get to their destination.

She reversed the car, drove back a bit until she found a narrow little path that led upwards to a few homes perched on the edge of the mountain. She parked it there, after requesting a young woman carrying a baby on her hip, at the gate of the house, to keep an eye on it for a couple of hours. It would remain untouched until she returned. People in this part of the country did not tamper with things that didn't belong to them. She rechecked if she had locked the car, a couple of times, then moved swiftly back to the spot of the landslide.

A man got off from a vehicle behind her, walked swiftly up to the part where the road had caved in and looked across. He waved to a man standing outside a white SUV.

'Want to cross?' he asked her as he stood next to her.

She was trying to work up her nerve and not look down at the edge, beyond which the drop was suddenly dizzying.

'Come,' he said, holding out his hand, lithely making his way across the narrow strip of road, so narrow that he had to place his feet in single file on it or risk slipping into the abyss. She placed her hands in his, without a second thought, and followed him across to the other side.

The policemen didn't notice them trying to make their way to the other side; they had wandered further down the line of cars to tell folks to turn around. Aisha was surprised to find she could balance herself surely on the slippery path with a grace that came from years of training her body in dance.

The man walked up to the SUV, and a driver in uniform

opened the door for him. She followed him, with the curious camaraderie that comes from having done something death-defying together. He stopped at the door, and turned around, squinting his eyes against the faint rays of the sun breaking through the dappled cloud cover. The dark film of the window of the car reflected her as she approached, long and lean, in her sweater and jeans, her mirrored aviators camouflaging her expression, her hair falling straight down her back, pitch black woven with the fleeting strands of grey that she hadn't bothered getting coloured into uniformity. He sat in the driver's seat, while the liveried driver stood aside, waiting.

'I guess you could do with a ride into town?' he asked. His voice was deep, his tone surprisingly familiar. She felt like she should know him but she was certain they had never met before. She noticed, on an aside, that he was also very attractive. He smiled, his eyes warm, the skin around them crinkled into a fan from a combination of laughter and squinting against the fierce sun at high altitudes. His skin was toasted to a warm bronze, the V of the skin exposed at the neck of his collar, a startling contrast of almost pale white.

'I need to get to the main market road. Could you please drop me to the closest point convenient for you? I can walk the rest of the way.' She could actually walk the entire way, but the roads were slick with pebbles and squelchy mud that had poured down the slopes, and she wanted to return home as quickly as possible.

'Definitely, my pleasure, do step in,' the man at the wheel replied, a respectful politeness to his tone that almost made her weep. Politeness made her weep these days. She saw little of it from her own. And she expected less from strangers. She scrambled over to the passenger side of the vehicle and swung herself in, as the driver held the door open for her, before settling himself in the seat behind, his expression inscrutable.

The man at the wheel was looking her over in an appraising manner that wasn't offensive, and she instinctively squared her shoulders and pulled her stomach in, a reflex from a time of having been tremendously beautiful. Perhaps she should have applied a brighter lipstick before stepping out in the morning, she thought, in some flabby cranial fold where her vanity had retreated. Her lips no longer curved and laughed unbidden as they used to, flashing a moment of dazzlingly white, immaculate teeth. No amount of lipstick could redeem the pinched thin-lipped petulance her lips were now reduced to. And now, when they were slowly recovering from being split and swollen, they were far from beautiful to begin with. It had been a long, long while since a man, any man, had looked at her in that way. She felt strange, unsure of how she was to respond to that appraising glance. Would it be seemly to acknowledge it and smile back, or would it be better to look away and ignore it, to pretend that it hadn't existed, that momentary fierce flare of desire she had glimpsed in a complete stranger's eyes?

She wondered how she appeared to him. In her deep blue denims, functional sneakers and comfortable old sweater in a dreary sludge brown, she knew she was far from glamorous. Nor was she beautiful anymore. What she didn't realise was that there was a residual attractiveness that was even more compelling in its raw, gritty fragility. Her hair was shiny and slightly messy. She had not blow-dried it or pampered it with hair serum and protein packs. Her skin, untouched by makeup, save a quick application of a light moisturiser, was still clear and unblemished, if a little lined and weary, reflecting the lack of professional ministrations to her skin. There were faint semi-circular, blue smudges beneath her eyes, making her look haunted, vulnerable. A light blue bruise sat on the side of her left check, and her lower lip had the swell of a slight cut. She was acutely aware of how her face looked. She had slapped on some extra compact powder on her bruise but it only seemed to accentuate it. It was a rare moment when she gave in to vanity, and today was one of those.

The sweater camouflaged the spread of her waist, the slight overhang of her belly, the slight droop of her breasts. She was glad she wore the fitted jeans Maya had insisted she pick up for herself the last time they went shopping together. 'You are so out of style, Mom, you're practically back in the cave age,' she'd said, in that scathing manner teens adopt when their parents don't live up to their definitions of cool. 'Skin-fits are in now, not these granny jeans.' Much against her inner censorious gaze about what was appropriate for her age and what was not, she had bought herself a skin-fit, and then realised she found them very comfortable. It was the stretch and give of the lycra. And the deep blue, invitingly deep, the deep blue of sleep she longed for, blank and intense, and dissolving everything that would make her toss and turn endlessly through the night. They also emphasised the still toned pair of limbs she had, legs that once had been so jaw-dropping gorgeous that the boys in her college were known to line up the corridors the day she wore a dress or a skirt. They detracted attention from the current lack of perfection along the waistline and the chest, but wasn't that what life was all about—skilfully shifting the onlooker's gaze from what one wanted to hide, to what one wanted to display?

The man at the wheel reversed the vehicle deftly. The driver had hopped into the backseat and remained silent through the journey, unless spoken to about something routine. The route was lined with cars stuck in a jam, tooting the occasional perplexed, enquiring horn.

They drove on for a short while in complete silence. She took a surreptitious glance at his profile, noted the strong hawk-like nose, the eyes intent on the road, the hair, which had grown out to lengths beyond acceptable and was lazily brushing his shoulders now.

'I'm Daljeet,' he said, without her asking him for his name, perhaps feeling her eyes on him. 'I needed to come to meet my nephew, he's at Pinewood.' Her children's school. 'I wasn't going to drive back, having driven all this way, so just asked for a car to be sent down for me.'

'Good to meet you, Daljeet. I'm Mrs Thakur. Aisha,' she replied, stating her married name through force of habit than choice, it just sprung automatically to her lips. 'My children go to Pinewood too, but they have a holiday today.' A common ground was established. His nephew was in a grade between Aryan and Maya, and they might just know each other. He seemed to know a lot about the school, the teachers and the school-related events. It was puzzling.

'I am my nephew's guardian,' he said, in response to the question in her eyes. 'His parents, my sister and her husband are dead.'

'Oh, I'm so sorry to hear that,' she replied, suddenly aware that the conversation had turned from the politely superficial to the intrusive and the personal within a moment. She was at a loss as to how to steer it back into the territory of grey neutralities. But did strangers, bound together by the few kilometres they would travel together, need to have a conversation? They would inevitably be separated by the flotsam and jetsam of their individual existences.

'Do you have a place to stay?' Aisha asked him, and then instantly regretted her lapse into premature familiarity with a stranger.

'Actually, we have a summer home here,' he replied.

She did not ask any further questions. He asked her nothing, neither where she was going, nor why she was out alone, how she planned to get back, nor whether she planned to get back. The silence was not uncomfortable, and that made her uncomfortable. Outside, the familiar landscape flashed past in a daze… the terrace farms, the houses built precariously on the edge of the roads, the undulations of the hills making way to the grey outlines of the Himalayan peaks at the distance.

He drove expertly, negotiating the curves on the road with a comfort that denoted an old familiarity with the mountain stretches. He knew the protocol for mountain driving. The slowing down at a curve, the sharp enquiring blast of the horn, the gentle pip if one wished to overtake another vehicle, a polite request, a communion with the slopes and the steep hairpin bends. They were drawing closer to town. She noticed bristling queues at the taxi stand, while the main mall road was hushed and quiet. Most of the stores had their shutters down. No red-cheeked, blazer-clad children scampered down the sloping, winding streets, on their way home from school. It was a town that was on hold.

They were at the crossroads that led into the market. 'Thank you for the ride,' Aisha said, as she stepped out of the vehicle when he stopped at the point beyond which cars were not permitted.

'My pleasure,' he replied.

As she moved down the road, something compelled her to look back. He was still waiting there, having got out of the vehicle, standing at the side of the road, almost as if he knew she would stop, turn back and look for him. He raised a hand and waved at her. A simple enough gesture, but it unnerved her. She looked away, suddenly uncomfortable with the unsought, tremulous intimacy the gesture implied.

When she looked back again, the SUV and man contained within had both gone away, driving off in the opposite direction, towards the other end of town. Here, the homes began to clamber up the sides of the mountains, moving further up into the grander residences built back in the days when the rich and the royal looking to escape the lunacy and heat of the summer in the plains, built their summer homes.

Thankfully, the home supplies store she frequented was open.

The post office was a short walk away from there, and beyond that was the bank. She would get through her tasks one at a time, in the order in which they presented themselves. It was the way she had always done it and it had never occurred to her to deviate from the format. Mr Negi, who had been manning the store for as long as it had existed, which was over forty years, and who knew all his regular customers by their names, smiled a gentle welcome at her as he spotted her, his round face with its latticed wrinkles and white ringed irises, exuding a Buddha-like calm that never failed to soothe her.

'How are you, Mrs Thakur, how are the children?'

'I'm well, thank you. The children are fine too,' she replied, a sudden panic beginning to seize her. 'I'm here for my parcel,' she said, her voice low.

He shook his head in an edited movement of regret. 'Nothing has come in this week, Mrs Thakur, I'm sorry. But then transport has been disrupted. Maybe it will come in when things settle down.'

She felt the sudden panic begin to claw at her chest. 'I was told it had arrived,' she said, her voice suddenly higher.

He shook his head. 'It hasn't reached me yet then, maybe it will tomorrow. No vehicles have come through since last night.'

She took a deep breath, she would manage without them, for a while, and perhaps her parcel would come in soon. She wasn't at the precipice yet, she was still tightrope walking the delicate edge of sanity and invincibility. She would be fine, she told herself, trying to still the fluttering panic that began welling up in her chest.

She should have realised that the roads were peppered with landslides and parts of them slipping away along with entire surfaces of the mountain. The consignment, a tiny wrapped package, the lifeline to her sanity, one among the many secrets she kept from Prithvi, wouldn't have made it across the last leg of the journey from Gauri's hovel to town.

'The children haven't accompanied you today? Hope they're alright?' he asked, with distant familiarity.

'They're well, thank you, just enjoying the unscheduled holidays they've got from school,' she replied.

A hassled-looking woman, evidently a tourist, raised her voice in irritation at not being attended to immediately, the urban pace of needing immediate attention making tempers begin to fray. 'I asked for that first,' she said, snatching a packet of sliced bread away from a man who had picked up the last one in stock. He made to snatch it back, and voices were raised. Mr Negi tried ineffectively to control the tempers, but he was too soft, too gentle to be heard above the din.

A whistle pierced through the voices and everyone fell silent. Aisha turned around, as did the rest of the people at the counter to see what had caused that authoritative whistle. Daljeet was standing at the door, his face impassive. 'Let's get into a queue, people,' he said.

Such was the authority in his voice that the warring factions immediately had the fight deflated out of them, and fell into a reluctant order. Aisha smiled at him. 'That was impressive. Are you sure you haven't been commanding armed forces on the sly?'

He laughed, a rolling laugh that drew annoyed glances from those who had now resigned themselves to waiting their turn. 'I don't think you should pick up any groceries right now,' he said, inclining himself towards her, creating a sense of isolation between the two of them despite the crowded store. 'You might not be able to get back home at all today.'

She looked at him in alarm. 'Why ever not? I'll hitch a ride back, the same way I got here.'

'I actually came back to find you and warn you. I just found out that they're cordoning off the road completely, they suspect more landslides. Until they build a makeshift bridge or an alternate path, nobody can cross. And definitely not any vehicles. You could be stuck here for a couple of days.'

'My car!' she exclaimed.

'It should be safe, unless some rocks fall on it.'

The fist in her stomach clenched again, anxiety spilled over into her gullet with the acrid taste of bile. Fear. She looked around, outside, at the distant end of the road where the bus depot was. It was crowded and none of the buses were moving. The tourist taxi drivers, instead of calling out for fares, had taken themselves to the tea stalls, and were calmly sipping on their tea, the fronds of smoke drifting upwards, wreathing their countenances with unaccustomed otherworldliness. Her hands began quivering involuntarily, she had to get back. What was that story she'd read in a school textbook about the milk woman who had climbed down the walls of a fort and the steep sides of the mountain cliff to get back home to her infant boy, when she found the gates of the fort closed for the evening, making it impossible for her to go home via the conventional path? She had no courage to scramble down the mountain, she told herself, and her children were old enough to not need her to supply them with breast milk. But yet, the disquiet persisted.

'What am I going to do?'

He shrugged his shoulders. 'I have a very comfortable bungalow, and plenty of vacant rooms available.'

'I can't impose on you.'

'You wouldn't be imposing at all, I would quite welcome the company. It is rather tedious with only the staff for conversation. I'm going to be the first one out of here once they manage to set up some variant of a motorable road, and I could drop you at the spot where you left your car.'

She looked around and noticed the signs of things steadily descending into the tumult of chaos. Raised voices, gathered around ticket windows asking for information that was not forthcoming. And the sense of resignation to the inevitable that hung morosely over it all. The usual throng of tourists pacing the mall road was scattered, waiting in groups. A police van stood at the entrance to the mall road, a few men in uniform were manning the barricades erected, diverting the traffic, letting the cycle rickshaws through. She looked at Daljeet and walked purposefully out of the store towards them.

'Have you closed the road completely?' she asked the man in uniform. 'Is is there no way back now? Not even midway?'

The police inspector, his eyes impenetrable behind a pair of dark Ray Ban aviators, nodded. 'The bridge has gone completely. Forget traffic, even humans cannot pass now until they manage to rebuild. It could take days.'

She should have jumped off the other bridge when she had the chance, she thought to herself, then chiding herself mentally for the selfish thought. She groaned, the despair shredding her voice into rough raggedness.

'Where are you from?' the police inspector asked, looking at her, perhaps realising that she was not quite a resident of the town, but not a tourist either. She named the four-road junction outpost her home was a little away from. He shrugged. 'Not today for sure. The road will not open today. You could check tomorrow.'

She turned around despite herself and looked back. Daljeet was standing behind her, a few steps away. He came up to her and took the single bag she was carrying with a few provisions in them. 'Let's go home,' he said, in a manner so definite she didn't seem to have much option but to do so. But where was home for her? Was it where she chose to be? Was it the home where her father had left her mother alone, to slowly spiral into ever-increasing insanity, or the home where she spiralled in and out of highs and lows herself? Or the home he was taking her to, a home that was not hers, yet at the moment, her only option?

They walked silently down the road, which was simultaneously crowded, yet isolated in its spilling crowds. 'I need to call home,' she said, fishing out her cell phone from her bag, sliding her finger across the screen to unlock it, pressing the digits that made up the home landline number, listening to the interminability of the unanswered ring that made her mind run riot. What could have happened in her absence? Her heart slammed around in her rib cage with the mercilessness of a cage match fighter in a WWE bout.

Aryan lifted the home line. 'Where are you, Mom?' he asked. His voice wasn't worried, his was the reassurance that children have that their parents will come home eventually.

'I'm stuck here in town, Aryan, but I'll be home as soon as I can. I promise. Where's Maya?'

He handed the phone across to Maya who squealed into the receiver, prescient with an adolescent's worst-case scenario intuition. 'Mom, what happened, is there something wrong? You don't normally call up when you go into town.'

'I know, darling. There was a landslide blocking the road while I was coming here. I should have just turned around, but I parked the car a little distance away and decided to hitch a ride into town, and…' She felt Daljeet's eyes on her. She paused. 'And now, the bridge has collapsed along with a bit of the mountain and I'm stuck here. I'll be back as soon as it opens up but tonight I'll have to wait here.'

'Where will you stay?'

'I don't know. I'll find some place. A room at a hotel or something.'

She did not know why she had lied and what it was about her accepting an offer of hospitality from a stranger, this stranger, that made her feel guilty. She closed her eyes.

There was a brief pause in the conversation. 'Is Heer there?'

'Yes, she is.' Maya handed the phone across to Heer. Aisha explained the situation the best she could.

'I'm sorry but I seem to be stuck here for a while. Can I trouble you to watch the kids till I return?'

'Of course I will, don't be ridiculous. And stay safe. Have you told Prithvi?'

Prithvi. And not your husband. For the briefest of seconds, the use of the first name by someone who had barely met him once, rankled of an uneasy familiarity. And then the moment passed. 'I will. Thanks.'

They had almost reached the car. She called Prithvi. His mobile rang on, until the call was disconnected, with the impersonal, metallic female voice telling her that the customer she had dialled was not reachable, did not want to speak to her at this moment, was busy, had better things to do with his time than answer a call from his wife in the middle of a busy work day. She should have known better than to expect he would take her call. He never did. They communicated through the impersonality of messages, which could abbreviate words into single letters and emoticons into afterthoughts.

She typed out a message to him. 'In town. Road collapse. Landslides. Bridge broken. Stuck here. Will be back when road re-opens.' She did not expect an answer. She had informed him of her whereabouts. She would face him when she got home.

They had reached the parked SUV. Daljeet opened the passenger door for her. She climbed in and closed the door. He looked at her through the tinted glass of the window for the longest time, their gazes locked. She could feel her heartbeat race in a manner it hadn't for a while yet. Within her, the deepest part of her, long-forgotten warmth slowly coursed its way through. When their gaze finally broke and he climbed into the driver's seat, he did not speak, nor did she. Somehow, between the two of them, all that was needed to be said had been said.

5

They turned off the road, and went higher into a small path enough only for a single vehicle to pass. She realised they had left the main town far behind. They were so high above the town that the lake which was the mainstay of the town seemed like an inconsequential puddle below, at the edge of the drop of the road. The path ended into a sudden looming pair of gates, set into stone gate posts attached to a wall that ran away from what the eye could see. He'd called it a 'small summer home,' but Aisha realised that it was an ancestral manor. He probably had a family crest adorning his personal stationery and grew up with faithful uniformed retainers, one of whom sprang to attention and swung open the huge gates as he honked; a single, impatient honk.

Her jaw dropped as they drove down a winding driveway that sloped gently upwards, shaded by spreading old trees. The house rose in front of them, revealing itself bit by bit, with imposing gables, grey stone cladding, with parts of the wall clad with a carpet of climbing ivy. The sun dappled it with a pale, late afternoon light as it gently began its descent to the opposite side of the earth.

'You have a beautiful home,' she said, her voice low with awe.

He smiled. 'Glad you like it.'

The vehicle came to a halt by a small porch. Another uniformed retainer sprung forth and opened the car door on her side. She stepped out and was immediately assailed by the heady fragrance of roses hanging heavy in the air. 'Please…' Daljeet gestured to her to enter the house. For a moment, it felt as if she was breaking a code she had imposed on herself by entering the house. She entered a lavishly furnished hallway which opened up into a formal drawing room. The walls had ornately framed prints of hunts, heads of kills mounted, the rifles that shot them displayed ostentatiously on the walls. Occasional tables were peppered with photo frames of sepia prints, with elaborately dressed people seated with the ease that the privilege of birth bestows.

Daljeet instructed one of the staff to have a particular bedroom opened up, aired and readied to be occupied. The Memsaab was going to stay the night. They seemed to accept that information with an equanimity suggesting that there had been Memsaabs who had stayed nights and it was not in their place to question why. And he enquired what was available for lunch. At this, there was some scurrying around. A wizened cook emerged from the recesses of the house, rattling off a menu of options he could present within the hour at the dinner table.

'I was supposed to have left today,' Daljeet explained, his tone apologetic for this perceived lack of expected hospitality. 'They only stock what is required for a day or two.'

Tea was served in fine bone china that had delicate pink roses on white, edged with scallops of gold. It was so delicate that she was terrified it would crumble into pieces if she gripped it too firmly. Vintage Wedgewood, she knew it would be, without turning it over to check. There had been a similar tea set at home, a different pattern though, which her grandfather had ordered all the way from London, packed safely in a crate and shipped via cargo ship. It had probably been in the family for generations. She was reminded of the Japanese art form where broken crockery was fused back together with gold making it even more beautiful than it had been in to begin with. *Kintsukuroi.* That's what she was, broken pottery, patched up with gold, the gold shimmering through the places where she had been cracked open, and left bleeding.

Daljeet took her on a tour of the property after the hurriedly put together lunch. 'It's been in the family for generations, and we're debating on whether we should convert it into a boutique hotel. I already have two heritage properties up and running as hotels, but this is a family home. Those were acquired properties, so I don't have that kind of sentimental attachment to them that I have with this home.'

The cottage, built of solid stone over a foot thick, was built in the late nineteenth century as a summer retreat. 'It wasn't built by my grandfather; he bought it from the family of the Englishman who had built it, when they chose to return to England. We've retained the original look, along with much of the original furnishings, maintained it pretty much the way it was. In fact, while we've tried to modernise it as much as possible, we've done so without changing the original character of the place. The most difficult of course was running water and plumbing. Thankfully, we have no outhouse now. Everything is in-house.'

She laughed, a laugh she had long forgotten she owned, but which surfaced occasionally, when the rays of an overpowering joy began cracking through the blackness of her everyday mind.

'This is lovely,' she said, words failing her. She was overwhelmed, not merely by the house. It was the freedom of the moment, where she was no longer playing her roles of a mother, a wife. Now, at this moment, in the middle of nowhere, she was just an ordinary woman. Albeit, tired, middle-aged, disintegrating wrinkle by wrinkle, failing to see the edgy vulnerability that made her enticing to a man who was surrounded by fiercely predatory women every day. Daljeet had no such parameters to judge her by, he saw her as she was. Her skin, untouched by a cosmetologist's ministrations, had fine wrinkles crumpling into diffused fans at the edges of her eyes. The vertical crease in her forehead furrowed itself when she listened intently, unsmoothened by glycolic peels or Botox shots that had frozen most of the women her age he knew into gargoyles with frigid faces, their voices as polished and cutting as their words.

Aisha, as he saw her, was fragile, edgy, unaware of the raw sensuality she exuded, in her functional jeans and sweater, the curve of her breasts unaltered by surgical intervention, their gentle sag unfettered by a push-up bra attempting to alter the natural contours of her body. She was wearing no perfume, the scent of her filling his nostrils every time he came close to her, flooding him with an inexplicable desire to bury his head into her hair. Her lips were swollen, one was split and healing. It was all he could do to keep his hands off her. He sensed that should he touch her before she was ready to be touched, she would crumple up and disintegrate. The rawness of unslaked desire that he could smell on her made him crazy. He wanted her from the moment she sat next to him in the car, fidgety, apologetic for having imposed herself on him, running her fingers surreptitiously against the fine-grained leather seats, a soft sigh escaping her involuntarily, before sitting back with the pleasure of someone who was once accustomed to the fine things in life.

He felt her presence next to him with a keenness that pierced him, that made him at once comfortable and anxious. She made him feel he was being evaluated and found lacking. It was unnerving, the realisation that this woman, unlike those who knew him and would consider him a prize catch after his divorce, had no clue of who he was, and wasn't intimidated by his lineage or his perceived wealth.

Daljeet went to the school to meet his nephew in the evening. She amused herself by going through the house and poring through the books in the rather well-stocked library.

Now, sitting in the den in the early evening, he poured out some red wine for her in a crystal wine goblet, and some scotch on the rocks for himself.

'How's your nephew?' she asked.

'He's alright, just a little rattled by not being pampered enough. He'll toughen up quickly in hostel.'

She nodded. Children toughened up in hostels, they learnt to depend on themselves, to rock themselves to sleep. She'd fought tooth and nail to keep her children out of hostel. She'd been in one ever since middle school, and longed for the regularity of home every single day she had been in it.

'In fact,' he said, 'This was a totally unscheduled trip, and the roads aren't in the best of conditions after all the rains that have happened recently. But I welcomed the opportunity to come here for a couple of days. It is my detox. I spend the days walking around the mountain trails, and the evenings, I sit by the fireplace, switch off from the rush of city life. There's nothing that draws me back to Delhi. And no one. What about you?'

'Only my children. Only they draw me back. Nothing else.'

'I'm sure your husband…' the words he didn't say hung in the air between the two of them.

She made a dismissive hand gesture, the expression on her face changing. He noted the still not healed cut on her lip, and the bruise to the side of her cheek facing him, and narrowed his eyes.

'My marriage is as good as over,' she said. When the words came out, she examined them closely, realising this was the first time she had said this aloud, and accepted it as a fact.

'And my marriage is over,' he replied. 'My divorce came through last month. Strangely, it doesn't hurt anymore.'

That she would be sharing these confidences with a complete stranger was something she could not reconcile herself with. But right now, with the world shuttered outside, it seemed completely natural. She would never see him again, she thought. The next morning, the roads would open up and she would leave. And he would go his way, there would be no more tomorrows. They would never stay in touch.

'Staying in some marriages could be more painful than a divorce could ever be,' she said, and felt a tear trickle down from one eye. It went down the side of her cheek where the grooves were settling in, where the dimple she had merged with lines of disappointment. She turned her face away and looked out into the distance, where a wall of deodar trees blocked her view of the sky, unwilling to raise her hand and wipe away the telltale tear. It spilled secrets it shouldn't be telling the world. Secrets that no one should have been privy to, except she and her mirror.

Daljeet reached out and took her hand in both of his. It was an oddly intimate gesture. 'You are beautiful. And hurting.' He stroked her hand with the other, like one would stroke a pet. She felt her hand begin to quiver under the touch.

She made no move to remove her hand from his. She just looked at his hands like it was something unique she was seeing for the first time ever. A human hand touching hers, feeling every point of contact between skin, ablaze with the awareness of the unacknowledged attraction between the two of them. Firm solid hands, with a slight fuzz of hair on it, pale at the knuckles, long-fingered, nails trimmed. This man with his hawk eyes and wavy hair that got mussed up every time he pushed his hands through it, was the first human who had touched her in years, apart from her children. All she had craved for, she realised, was to be touched, the inexplicable real rush of being touched. At that touch, something had seeped through his skin and into hers, an inexplicable sense of yearning for something she could not and did not want to define. She drew her hand back, and pushed an errant lock of hair off her face for something to do with her hand, now that she had freed it from his grasp. She felt awkward, adolescent.

She looked at him closely, her eyes questioning yet guarded, this man who had met her this morning and who was now touching her with the intimacy of someone who had known her for years, accentuated by the fact that they were alone in this huge home. Perhaps she had no inclination to get back home. Perhaps they had already come too far away down the road to go back, she thought, staring now at the hand that had pressed hers, and was now holding a glass of single malt, molten fire, reflecting the yellow light from the old chandeliers that were now lit above them. She imagined his hand caressing her body, kneading her flesh, exploring the folds and crevices untouched by hands other than her own for so long. She closed her eyes for a brief moment, feeling the anticipation of his fingers probe within her. When she opened them, his eyes were on her, looking at her intently, an expression that was simultaneously gentle and hungry. He reached across the small round table where they sat, and took her hand back, cradling it within both of his, stroking it gently, and lingering over the calluses and the roughness, with a longing that was palpable.

'Are you feeling alright? You're looking a little pale.'

She pulled her hand back again, feeling the buzz of a tangible electrical current run through it, pulling the soft fine hair on her arms to attention.

'I'm fine, just tired perhaps,' she replied, feeling every nerve in her body tingling with the awareness and anticipation of what she knew, without doubt, would inevitably follow.

He stood up, took the glass of wine she was holding with her other hand, and placed it on the table, without releasing the hand he had been stroking. His movements were sure, practised.

He'd done this before. He lifted her to her feet, and then gently drew her into him, one hand burying its fingers in her hair, and the other, pulling her body into his, pressing into the small of her back. His lips explored hers with a deep, searching kiss that blacked out everything in her mind but a blaze of uncontrollable desire that welled up within her. She winced from the pressure of his lips on her split lip and he withdrew, for a moment, and then came right back, pressing his lips gently on hers. The sudden wetness surging between her thighs embarrassed and scared her. She felt her knees sag as she put her arms around him, holding onto him for support. She pushed him away, with not much conviction, when they broke for air.

'This is not right. I barely know you.'

'How does that even matter?' he whispered, and pulled her right back to him, running his hands over her entire body, feeling the folds which had once contained burgeoning embryos and the apologetic breasts, no longer firm with the arrogance of youth. They were soft, pliable and yielding against his chest, the nipples hard and aroused under the scratchiness of the rough, knitted sweater. He reached up and pressed them roughly. She moaned. It was madness, and she was unable to stop herself from pressing herself against him.

He pulled away, tilting her face up to him. 'Do you want me to stop?'

She shook her head. 'No. Don't stop.' And pulled his face down to hers, exploring his mouth with ferocity that she had forgotten she ever possessed. She could feel his body respond to her, as he put his palms against her buttocks and ground himself into her, his breathing becoming ragged.

She allowed herself to be led to an adjoining bedroom, where after carefully locking the door and drawing the curtains across, he peeled off her sweater and jeans and made love to her in a gentle, unhurried manner that brought tears to her eyes. Over and over again, until they were so wrung out with exorcising the ghosts within each of them that they lay limp, drained, curled into one another. Then, with a tenderness that made her weep even more, he kissed the faded bruises on her body one by one, barely visible in the dim glow of the solitary bedside lamp he lit, creating a map on her body. He caressed her hair, soft and thick and dark, and settled her body against his. And she thanked him, over and over again, for what she did not know, in a soft tremulous voice as the tears continued to flow down her cheeks. She lay, her head on his chest, her eyes damp, feeling his heart beat under her ear, loud, insistent. For a moment she felt she had been searching all her life to rest her head here.

6

The next morning dawned hurtfully clear and bright. She felt the gentle sunlight caress her closed eyelids, and opened them to find herself sprawled on a strange bed. She realised she was nude, and chilled to the bone under the blankets, and watching her silently was the man she had made love to through the night. She could feel her brain popping and buzzing. This was one of those days, the start of the climb up. Her medication. She should have stuck to it.

'Good morning,' he said softly, unsure as to what her reaction would be.

'Good morning,' she replied, amused at the formality of the conversation. She gathered the sheets around her, aware of her morning dishevelled avatar, complete with dragon breath, realising with horror that she needed to attend to her bodily functions. There was the sinking scare that they had used no contraception the previous night, the dried stickiness between her thighs testament to yet another episode of unfaithfulness that she dare not justify as a momentary lapse again. Prithvi need not know ever; the last time she had run away and been found, had been a mistake. She had not realised she would ever be found or need to get back.

'Irresponsible woman, irresponsible mother,' he had spat at her. The words were branded into her forehead and she struggled every single day to prove him wrong. And now she had done it again, been unfaithful and abandoned the children. This time she would return on her own and not need to be found, she told herself. She sat up, panic making her movements jerky.

'What is it?' he asked, sitting up too, the blankets falling away, revealing a bare-chested and well-toned torso, with a scattering of chest hair, contrary to the current fashion amongst well-groomed men. 'Is there a problem?'

As his hand reached out for her, she twisted her body away, trying to find her clothes. 'I should be getting home,' she said, 'My children would be waiting for me.'

'What's wrong?' he asked, noting the sudden flare of panic on her face, the rejection implicit in the way she turned herself away, and prepared to get off the bed.

'Nothing's wrong, nothing,' she kissed him, more to reassure herself than him that nothing was, feeling the desire flare up again, fierce, unrestrained, feral. Nothing was wrong, she told herself. There was nothing wrong in giving herself some pleasure. She had almost forgotten the feel of skin on skin, to dig her nails into the back of the man over her, while he drew himself in and out of her until she spasmed into shuddering waves that crashed through her, spreading from her pelvis right to her head and her toes.

'But I'm hungry and I need to go to the bathroom,' she laughed, after a short while.

He rose, unselfconscious of his nudity and the chill morning air in the unheated room, pulled on his trousers and pullover, hastily discarded on the floor the previous night. 'Stay here in this room,' he said, softening the imperious tone of his command with a soft kiss on her lips, 'I'll be back in a few minutes.' She pulled a bed sheet around herself and went into the bathroom adjoining the bedroom.

The woman looking back at her from the mirror looked a little different from the woman she was used to looking at in the mirror back at home. This one seemed younger, happier, the frown lines between her brows miraculously erased, a flush tingeing her light skin into a delicate pink on the cheeks. Her skin felt tauter, firmer. Her breasts felt fuller, swollen. It felt like something had switched on, reversing the accelerated ageing that had taken hold of her, or perhaps just halted it in its relentless march across her cells. She splashed water on her face, the iciness making her cheeks flush even more. Broken capillaries, she told herself, nothing to do with reverse ageing. She found a tube of toothpaste and used her finger to brush her teeth. The shelves by the basin were lined with face wash, moisturiser, body lotion, body shampoo and all that could possibly be required for a woman's morning routine. She had discarded a beauty routine years ago. Now, she was purely functional in her upkeep of herself.

'You're beautiful.' His words echoed in her ears. Aisha had let go of vanity years ago. Now all that was left was a faint consciousness that once upon a time, she had been considered very beautiful. That a man would still find her beautiful was incomprehensible to her.

She emerged, after a quick bucket bath with tepid water, wrapped in a towel she had found within the bathroom, and dressed in her clothes which she now found carefully folded and placed on the back of the chair opposite the bed. She wondered who had entered and folded the discarded clothes. All she could remember from the previous night was that her clothes had been taken off her body and thrown onto the floor. When had hushed footsteps entered and put things back into a semblance of order, she wondered. Had it been Daljeet, because she had heard no other footsteps enter, nor the door open except for when he yelled through the bathroom door that he was going out of the room.

She straightened the bed through force of habit, of mornings spent in a fixed routine of tidying the house, which numbed and palliated. And then she drew the curtains back, letting the sharp morning light filter in, and watched the dust motes floating in the rays dancing to music audible only to them, a cosmic dance, unfettered by gravity or convention.

There was a gentle knock at the door. 'Come in,' she said, concerned about the lapse in her own morality that she would eventually have to confront in the mirror.

A uniformed man entered bearing a tray with a tea pot and two cups that he placed gently on the table by the window. 'Chotey Saab has asked me to inform you that there are clothes for you in the cupboard should you wish to change.'

He bowed slightly and moved out of the room, his feet not making a sound, a deference born from years of being trained to make one unobtrusive. Curious, she moved towards the cupboard, a deep polished mahogany, which swung open without effort, revealing shelves of shirts, cardigans and trousers within. Some of them still had their price tags on, jackets, woollens, all tinged with the nostalgic fragrance of a perfume once used, intermingled with the ruthless dismissal of mothballs. Most were practically unused, the sheen of newness still crisp on them.

'My sister's clothes,' Daljeet said cryptically, having walked into the room while her back was to the door. 'She loved coming here. She was approximately the same size as you are. This is her room. I thought you might like to change into something fresh. I've been meaning to have them disposed for some time, but somehow never got down to it.'

For a moment, the information disconcerted her. Why had a dead person's clothes still been kept and not given away, as one normally did? And had she felt a cold, unearthly touch gently brush her fingertips in what could be only a warning as she had run her fingers over the wools, silks and denims that lined the shelves?

She was glad of the opportunity to change into fresh clothes. She was fanatical about bathing a couple of times a day, except when the greyness of winter came upon them. She pulled out a pair of denims, straight fit, and a pullover knitted in warm, red wool meant to keep the bite of the wind at bay and made to go into the bathroom to change. There were undergarments too, in the drawer, but she couldn't bring herself to use them.

'Change here,' he said, his eyes deepening in hue from tawny to copper as he looked at her, closing the door behind him and locking it. She stood uncertain. She couldn't remember the last time she had done something as simple as changing her clothes in front of another human being. After she had given birth, she'd taken to going into the bathroom and locking the door before daring to take her clothes off. The body in the mirror mocked her, with its folds and flab and the silvery lines across the abdomen, glinting unevenly, the beauty in the imperfection invisible to her. She closed her eyes and took off what she was wearing before stepping in hurriedly into the clothes she had selected from the cupboard, averting her body from his direct gaze. When she opened her eyes, he was sitting in the armchair, his eyes fixed on her.

'You're beautiful. Do you know that? Why are you so embarrassed of your body?'

She shook her head. 'It is no longer a body to be proud of.'

He got up and gathered her into his arms. She realised he had to bend his head down to her, and she had always considered herself taller than the average woman at almost five foot eight inches in her bare feet. Her husband was a couple of inches taller than her.

He kissed the top of her head, a gentleness from a stranger that brought stinging tears to her eyes. 'Let's go have some breakfast, I'm starving.'

Breakfast was leisurely. 'I have to get home,' she said again, the regret suffusing her voice with a layer of dullness, noting the missed calls from home on her mobile that she had left behind in her handbag, when she'd allowed herself to be led into the bedroom the previous night. 'My children will be worried about me.'

'I've sent someone down to enquire whether the roads are functional now. We'll know soon enough. Till then, why not just call home and tell your children you're fine and you'll be home as soon as you can?'

She did just that. Maya answered the call on the first ring. 'Mom?' Her voice was worried, there were undercurrents she couldn't quite put her fingers on that layered her enquiries. 'Where are you? We called and called and called and you didn't answer, we were so tense, and no one knew where you were…'

'I'm sorry,' she replied, trying hard to sound repentant for having been as irresponsible as she was, in more ways than one. 'I was so tired I just went off to sleep and didn't hear the phone ringing.'

'When are you coming home?' Maya's tone was imperious, certain that her mother would return home. 'Are you okay? You're sounding…'

'I don't know,' Aisha said, replying to both questions, looking at the man sitting opposite her at the dining table, sipping slowly from his coffee mug, staring back at her intensely, which no longer made her nervous, but which now wrapped itself around her and made her feel caressed and wanted, without his hands physically touching her. 'Perhaps today, perhaps tomorrow. It depends on whether the road has been fixed, you know how long that could take. We're finding out, I will call you and let you know if I'm coming home today.'

She was okay, but slowly sliding into one of those days which kept segueing into each other because sleep would not come unless she medicated herself. And days when all her body wanted was another body and didn't care about the person that came with the body. 'Immoral,' her husband had called her. But then, when the haze descended over her, there was only hunger and energy and restlessness. Nothing else mattered. It was why he kept her isolated, she knew, away from the world. She could not be trusted on days when her brain was a hallucinogenic chiaroscuro of speckles. Then would come the days when even getting out of bed was like traversing through miles of swampland that suctioned her into it.

'What's Aryan doing?'

Aryan grabbed the phone from Maya and screamed into it, 'Mom, Maya is not letting me play video games.'

She laughed. 'Don't trouble your sister, and don't trouble Heer. Go play in the garden.'

'I can't, it is raining.'

She looked out of the window. The blazing sunlight the day had begun with had gone away and the clouds had begun rolling in.

'Is your father home?' she asked, realising there had been no missed call from him. Nor had he replied to her message. Maya came back on the line. The phone was obviously on speaker, she could hear Aryan mumbling to himself as he'd probably been shoved aside by Maya to answer.

'He came home late last night, he's left already for work. They have some project they need to complete and something he said which I didn't understand.'

'Okay. If he calls, tell him I'll be home when I can and that I'm safe and sound.'

'Cool, Mom. Bye.' The definite click of a disconnected line ended the conversation.

The children were managing okay without her. Her husband was least concerned about her whereabouts. 'I don't need to get back today,' she said, looking directly into Daljeet's eyes. 'Can I stay here a day longer?'

'Of course, for as long as you please.'

'If I didn't have the kids to worry about, I probably would have,' she answered, 'But I do. I need to get back to them. This…' she moved her hand vaguely, 'has been so…' Words failed her but her smile left him in no doubt as to what she was trying to convey. She smiled at him, across the table, lifting facial muscles that had forgotten to move, little realising that her face had lit up like a child's upon receiving an unexpected gift.

'It will come to an end. You will go back to your life, and I will go back to mine,' she continued, her voice high. 'But we will have had this. Yesterday and today. And perhaps tomorrow, if this continues.'

'Do you want tomorrow too?' he asked, his voice going soft, so soft she had to strain her ears to make the words out.

'Yes,' she said, tremulously, feeling an unbecoming quivering begin in her body that coagulated and rushed into her pelvis, making it throb and quiver. Could he see it, she wondered, on her face, the lust within her, her nipples standing to attention beneath the thick knit of her sweater and a gush of liquid warmth coursing through her and wetting her undergarments.

'It doesn't look like any road repairs will be possible today either,' he said, looking out of the window, patting his lips with the napkin, waiting politely for her to finish her breakfast and rise from the table. It was basic social courtesy, but something she had long forgotten existed in this world, after years of eating alone most days, or of eating after the children.

'It does seem like we're stuck here today. And unless things clear up, tomorrow looks unlikely too. Is your husband home to watch the children?'

'He isn't, but my sister is with them,' she replied, tasting the sound of the word 'sister' turn on her palate, examining its unfamiliarity, testing it for taste, flavour, and digestibility. 'She will watch them.' He knew that, but he didn't tell her so. He held his silence. She would know soon enough, the kids would be watched and so would her husband. And she would be watched too, but all in good time.

She had also called the grocery store owner at the crossroads a little away from their lane to deliver bread and eggs, and knew that the house would be stocked with adequate food for them to get by for a couple of days. Schools were still shut, and would continue to be shut until further notice, until the situation returned to normal. They were used to contingencies like this when they lived in mountain terrain, but it was rare that she was not around to watch the kids.

She rose from the table and moved towards him, wondering if it would be seemly to lead him back to the bedroom from which they had emerged down the passageway, or would that seem too forward. Then, she decided that it was well past any chance of her appearing too forward after all that had transpired between the two of them since the previous night. She smiled at him, a smile that held all the secrets of the body she had revealed to him. He made the decision for her, and led her back to the room they had spent the night in.

It was strange, this feral creature, the body. It would stay denied for months, for years, and then, at one touch, a moment's trembling indiscretion, it would raise itself and reach out without a moment's hesitation for what it wanted, in complete contravention of all previously held notions of honour, propriety and morality.

The room had been tidied in their absence, she noted, the bed made, the pillows discarded on the floor settled back into position, and all the seminal evidence of their indiscretions peeled off and replaced by another sheet, pristine, smooth and waiting for the spill of semen, the drip of vaginal fluid. He pulled her to him and kissed her again, deeply. She felt the world drown itself out beyond the roar in her ears, as her mouth responded to his.

Her handbag and her phone were in the other room. It didn't

seem to matter that perhaps the children would try to reach her if there was an emergency. For the moment, she was here and now, detached from everything that had comprised her everyday life. After they were spent and lay back on the bed, the world around them still a languid blur of post-orgasmic bliss, she realised she hadn't asked him something that had been niggling at her.

'How did your sister die?' She gestured at the clothes she had discarded.

'I'd rather not talk about it.' His face shuttered over, with secrets he did not wish to tell.

'Why not?' Perhaps it was unwise of her to ask, people were entitled to what they wished to share. Every heart needed to contain stories that were too overwhelming to reveal to another human being, for fear that sharing them would diminish their enormity.

'It wasn't very pleasant, what happened to her.' He turned his face away. Perhaps there was something in his expression that he couldn't conceal, which he didn't wish she caught. 'She was unwell, we had to institutionalise her. It was perhaps the most difficult thing I had ever done, sending her to that place.'

There was a silence in the room while she assimilated his words. She wondered how far and how many dosage changes away she herself was from institutionalisation. She had meant to but forgotten to take her pills that morning, she always had them in her handbag, just in case. But she had been experimenting with phasing herself off them, promising herself that if she felt it coming on again, the blackness, she would. If she didn't, the descent would be swift and rapid. She pushed her luck. It was strange to know a person's body intimately, and know nothing about him except his name, and the fact that he drove carefully on mountain roads.

She pulled on the clothes she had been wearing, clothes that belonged to a dead woman. It didn't creep her out anymore, the hair on her arms didn't stand on edge, the chill finger of a dead entity didn't caress her back. Perhaps, she thought, death wasn't so far from where she was, given how often she had flirted with it. A knife in hand and yearning wrists that throbbed for the stinging release of a sharp cut, made precisely to slice through a vein. A mountain path that led to nowhere, a vertical drop off the side of a narrow road that it would be so easy to drive off, a handful of the pills she took, instead of the one pill she was prescribed to have when sleep eluded her. A skipping of the monthly blood test to measure dosages of the chemicals in her blood, letting them settle into the realm of the toxic. She had toyed with the fantasy of death in all its fascinating forms every so often, but so far, life had always won.

'Tell me about her,' she said, sitting down on the leather upholstered sofa, positioned opposite the fireplace in the room. He had got dressed too, and went to the shelves lining the wall from where he pulled out a photo album bound in brocade fabric, the photographs within mounted with gilded corners. The pages were filled with ceremonial family portraits.

'That's me,' he said, pointing out to a frowning-faced little boy standing reluctantly in the corner of the frame, looking angrily into the camera, the molten brown of his eyes still blazing through the print. Holding his hand, standing next to him, was a young girl, almost twice his height and evidently some years older, with the flawless features of an angel. Aisha caught her breath. 'She's beautiful.'

'She is. She was. The most beautiful creature God could have ever created. Her beauty was the stuff of legend. When she was a child, she was indulged by everyone around and got away with all the mischief possible because she was so beautiful. Sometimes the mischief got warped. She would have episodes, violent episodes. We got her the best treatment, she would be fine for months, years and then…'

Aisha had that same edgy fragility. That disintegration of self hovering around Aisha had reeled him in, when he first saw her clambering over the rocks. The same build, the same jumpiness, the jerkiness, the unravelling beauty that was slowly blowing out into the ethers of discarded molecules and shortening telomeres. With it, the disconnect from it all, spacing her out into being present and absent simultaneously, a mind that travelled down pathways it shouldn't, taking the crossroads into dank, deserted places populated only by screaming ghouls of insanity.

He shut the album and placed it back where it had been, between hardbound books, putting away the rest of the photographs that she presumed chronicled his childhood and his family. She was suddenly greedy to see them, to assimilate everything there was to know about this man, a stranger to her yesterday. She noted the haunted expression in his eyes, the constant running of his hand through his hair, the straightening of it into a measure of certitude that defied the natural curly unruliness that made it spill over his face. He was wearing a pair of baggy denims, a shirt under a pullover knitted in a cable knit and was evidently hand-knitted and well worn. His hair was rumpled and a day-old stubble had grown on his chin, adding to the interesting angular planes of his face.

'It was only when she was around thirteen that we realised that there was something endemically wrong with her, it was the first time we used the word evil. She would do the strangest of things, cut up pets, set things on fire, speak obscenities. My mother couldn't understand what was happening to her, but my father was convinced she was possessed. He tried everything, babas, tantriks, taking her to various dargahs to exorcise whatever it was that possessed her. It would go away, she would be normal and lovable for a year or two and then she would have a relapse, and go back to her episodes. It began getting scarier and scarier. By the time he agreed she needed medical help, it was too late. She was married, a new mother and a threat to herself and her son.'

He paused, drew in a deep breath and released it in a shuddering sigh. He looked at her, tilting her face up to his. 'I don't know how to explain her to you. But she was nothing I can explain. So beautiful and so dangerous.'

His face shuttered down again. 'Have you dealt with someone who is mentally ill?' he asked, his face vacantly brooding. He absently picked at a cuticle on his finger as he spoke, avoiding eye contact.

She became very, very still, scared that even the slightest movement would reveal what she really was. Someone who walked the thin line between normalcy and full-blown insanity every single moment, someone who stayed functional through carefully calibrated dosages of medication that her doctor adjusted and fine-tuned each time she came into town to consult him after getting her blood tests done.

'Not really,' she replied. Which wasn't technically a lie because she hadn't had to deal with herself, her family did. There were labels, diagnoses and combinations of labels that different doctors had applied to her. She had heard them all. She didn't like to use them. She only dreaded descending the way her mother had, into a place from where no one could pull her back.

And the highs, when she was invincible, didn't need food, water, sleep and could walk on the skies if she chose. Followed by the lows, crashing, terrible lows, that dragged her through the muck and stench of a dark, rancid place, where all that she could long for was the oblivion of not existing.

The pills would shut those voices down when they began, but the little they whispered through cracks and crannies in her cranium was enough to set her on edge. And she would pass it on to Maya, she feared, just as her mother had passed the brain demons down to her. It was an inheritance she could have done without.

She could pinpoint the day it began. She'd had episodes in her teens, when she'd starved herself into a skeletal frame that made her lose hair, her breath stink and her periods stop. She would still look into the mirror and see herself as humungous. Her aunt had taken her to a psychiatrist then. She learnt to begin eating again, morsel by morsel, bit by bit. She was back to a functional normal. For years, the demons lay dormant within her, and then suddenly, the hormonal tsunami of the postpartum, after Aryan, kicked them awake again.

It began the day her husband recoiled from her body when she reached out to him, barely a month after she'd borne Aryan. After they found her trying to smother Aryan with a pillow, they took her to the doctor. He diagnosed it as postpartum depression. All she knew at that moment was that he was what had made her ugly. And the rare times that she was not depressed, she was either too sedated to know differently, or as she was now, on an endorphin high that made everything brighter, like a grubby window being hosed clean, clearing it of the patina of soot and dust, that had clogged up everything. It got uglier from there. It was then that the voices in her head began. The pills got upped. Sometimes she was functional and lucid. At others she could go days in a drugged-out haze. Then there would be months she would go through completely even-keeled before the disintegration began again.

She had worn Prithvi down to a shell. There was no love left, not even a residual tolerance for her. She wasn't easy to live with anymore. But within the layers of the woman she had become was the woman she had been, struggling to break out, to be able to laugh again, a laugh that was not suffused by the precursor of the mania to come.

'Tell me more,' she said, knowing that perhaps what she would hear would be a version of herself, a version she would recognise in bits and pieces. The details were perhaps altered slightly to fit another person, another life, the intensity varying, but the basic premise the same, that of a woman who wasn't in her own head or too much in it.

'Some other time perhaps, not now.' He rubbed a hand wearily over his eyes. 'It is still painful to think about her and how her life ended.' He put his head into his hands and shuddered.

She kept silent, watching the glowing rods of the heater placed within the grate. 'You remind me of her. You have the same beauty, the same vulnerability, the same fragility.'

Because there was nothing to be said, Aisha put an arm around him and pulled his head down to her shoulder. There is a trembling eloquence to certain silences that words would only diminish, that can draw two people together the same way other silences tear two people apart. He settled his head into the nook of her shoulder, and kissed the exposed skin there, with lips that were cold but soft, kissing and biting the lobe of her ear, seeking out her lips, crushing them with his.

She wanted nothing from him, just the weight of his body and his need for her. And then they were kissing with a passion born of pain, exploring each other's bodies with a lack of hesitancy that belied the fact that they had only met the previous day. And she would stay there, for days and nights that would segue into each other, until she forgot that she had a home and children to return to, and he wished she didn't.

7

The battery in her mobile drained out. She did not bother charging it. She hadn't carried her charger with her, nor did she try to locate a substitute. It was a shackle that had been cut loose. The feeling of being disconnected from her every day was intoxicating. She revelled in it, trying not to think that this would eventually end. The thought brought her no joy. She kept it tucked away at the back of her mind where it banged frenetically, asking to be let out and mulled over. The 'what if there was an emergency with the children' kept nagging at the back of her mind. She ignored it as stoically as she could.

Nothing could go wrong. And there was the here and now and the things she wanted to say that knew no pause, no full stop. The words tumbled out of her, as she spoke to him, telling him everything about herself, and more, answering questions he asked as well as those he didn't. It was so rare that anyone wanted to know about her, that she had almost forgotten most of the answers. She dredged them out of her memory and laid them out to dry. He listened to her, laughed, barely interrupted, and wondered why she was absolutely in no need of any sleep. The brain chemicals were careening through her bloodstream now that she had stopped taking the little tablets that kept them at an even keel. She was controlling this demon. Or was she not?

When she looked at herself in any of the many mirrors that adorned the walls in passageways and on wardrobe doors, she barely recognised herself. Her cheeks were flushed almost unbecomingly so, her hair shone and swung as she moved even though she had done no additional pampering. The lines that weighed her face down, and dragged her expression to the floor, had righted themselves almost miraculously. There was a smile in her eyes and on her face. She looked and felt a decade younger. The dark fog that clouded her brain most times, needing a pill to clear itself and allow her to function normally, had lifted too. She felt clearheaded, strangely like she was observing herself from the outside.

It was someone else who had spent the previous night writhing under a stranger, naked, casting aside all her inhibitions about her body, and letting herself sink into the maelstrom of reciprocal desire. Was it the mere slaking of animal lust, or was it the elation of being desired, or the demons in her head slowly casting off their fetters?

She called home, ascertained that the children were fine, fighting furiously with each other, and that Heer was keeping them fed. 'But she's not cleaning the house,' Maya hissed in a whisper. Aisha could imagine her speaking with her face turned to the wall, her body almost into the little alcove where the telephone instrument was placed, so that no one could hear what she was saying, 'And all the laundry has piled up. When are you coming back, Mom, it's been four days now.' Had it? It was four days gone by too quickly.

'I'll be back tomorrow, hopefully, and I'll get the house in order, don't worry.' She breathed deep and then asked. 'Is your father at home now? Or has he left for work?'

There was a moment's silence at the other end of the line. 'He didn't come home last night. He called to ask if we were alright and said he might come home today. School is still closed till the end of the week, apparently the wall at the back of the building has been damaged by some rocks that rolled down, and they need to repair it. And of course, the bridge is still to be repaired.'

'Where's Aryan? Has he been eating properly?'

Maya's voice dropped to a whisper, 'Actually all we've been eating are sandwiches or Maggi. So he's really happy. But I'm missing your cooking, Mom, come home soon. You better come home because Heer...' She paused.

'What...?'

'Nothing. I'm missing your food, Mom.' Her daughter was not missing her. Her daughter was missing her cooking. Her daughter who didn't eat what she cooked, was now missing it. Or perhaps that was her daughter's way of telling her that she missed her.

'I will be back tomorrow if the road opens up. Tell Pappa to take the spare key of my car from the safe and bring it back home, it's just at the turn after the chowrasta leading up to the market.'

'You tell him. You know how annoyed he gets if we call him at work. Okay, Mom, bye, I gotta go,' she said, putting the phone down hurriedly, before Aisha could ask to speak with Heer.

She stared at the disconnected receiver in her hand with an alien sense of detachment. That was that. She wasn't really needed, but then had she ever been? What had Maya been trying to tell her about Heer? Did it matter right now?

Daljeet was pacing the patio speaking softly into his phone. She watched him through the glass windows, his movements, precise and controlled, lithe and restrained. He reminded her of a leopard she had once seen in a cage at the zoo, during a school visit. She smiled now, at that memory, as she watched Daljeet, the now familiar planes of his body moving and flexing under the denim jeans, his shoulders stretched under the black leather jacket. Her fingers ached to have them hovering above her again so she could dig her nails into them and moan.

Perhaps the roads would clear tomorrow and they would go their separate ways if the roads allowed them, till then she had him and he had her. This dalliance was one where she had allowed her body to get the better of her head and didn't regret it in the least. Perhaps she would later, when sitting by the window at her bedroom, watching the rain pour down over the small patch of garden. Perhaps it would have been better continuing the way she had been, without reawakening her body to its physicality. Getting back to a relationship where the only contact between her and her spouse was that of a tenuous tolerance would be her punishment, she decreed, for breaking the codes of morality she had imposed on herself. Perhaps she was her father's daughter after all. Hadn't he taught her that monogamy was a social construct that held no relevance with the reality of the human heart? That the heart could love, over and over again and unshackle itself from the bondage of loyalty it owed one person without a smidgeon of guilt.

Daljeet entered the room, having ended his conversation, and sat next to her on the sofa she had finally settled down on, pecking her neck with tiny affectionate kisses. She pulled away gently, it embarrassed her, the thought that they might be on public display.

'The doors are open, anyone could walk in.'

He laughed, making her wonder how often he had kissed a strange woman in these rooms without bothering about open doors. Or were the staff trained well enough to be non-intrusive at such moments? 'Let's go outside then.'

He led her out to the glass conservatory in the grounds, where they sat on a broad wrought iron and wooden bench in the midst of verdant foliage.

'This is much better,' he said, as he sat beside her. The soft mist-like rain fell on the surface of the glass with a slight musical tinkling. It felt isolated here, a world by itself, away from the house. It was chilly, despite the woollens she had pulled on, and she shivered. He pulled her closer into him, and she could feel the warmth flow from his body to hers. He worked his hand down the neck of the round-necked pullover she had on and caressed her erect nipple like a prayer bead. She laughed, 'This feels like college and going to the movies with a current fling.'

'But that's what I am, the fling of the moment,' he replied, a wry smile on his face.

They sat in silence, within the glass panes, cocooned by the green cover of the plants being grown within in pots, the smell of compost and peat rich in the air, made headier by the dampness outside.

'Tomorrow we go back to our lives as they were.'

'But that was always how it was going to be. You have your husband and kids, and I have a life back in Delhi.'

For a moment, resentment flared within her.

'We could stay like this, forever,' she said. 'I could get my children here, they could go to school from here. Unless…'

He looked at her, his face empty. Her mind filled in the words he did not say. No matter, this much was enough to keep her going. She traced the outline of his face with her fingers and kissed him.

'My husband doesn't need me, my kids do.'

'Do you need your husband?' he asked, his voice curious.

'I think I do. Somewhere, part of me still loves him, or loves the man I married. I often fantasise about getting out of this marriage, but something holds me back from running away and it isn't the children. It is him. I still love him, even though I hate him. Am I making sense?'

He shook his head in the negative.

She took a deep breath, knowing she was going to speak about what she had never spoken of before, not to her husband, not to her mother, not to her children, not to the few friends she had once had, and had now fallen out of touch with. It was difficult to open one's soul to one to whom one had opened one's body.

'I have not had sex with my husband ever since my son was born. Over ten years ago. Our relationship has completely broken down because of that. A month or so after I delivered my son, he looked at my postpartum body and lost his desire for me. Ever since, I've not been able to touch him or let him touch me. And when he did try later, it was no use, he didn't get aroused or stay aroused long enough to climax. My body repulses him, he said. He blamed me for it. Said I was unfuckable.'

He turned her face towards him and looked deep into her eyes. There were shadows behind the shadows that he could not decipher. 'You definitely aren't unfuckable,' he lied.

He drew her closer, sensing that this wasn't the end of what she had to say, there was more to be said and she would not be stopped now.

'He's been patient though, and takes as much care of me as he can. And I am not the easiest person to live with anyway, I have issues, mood issues, and I'm on medication for them They made me fatter and uglier and even more unfuckable. So I stopped taking them…'

She sighed. She dared not speak about the voices in her head, they had been quiet for a long while now. Speaking about them might tempt them to start screaming to be let out again.

He ran a finger along the barely healed cut on her lip that he knew had been inflicted fresh.

'What mood issues?'

'My husband took me to some psychiatrists. They put me on some pills. Sometimes I am better. Sometimes I go off the edge.'

'What does going off the edge comprise?' he asked.

She angled her head and looked up at him, the expression

in her eyes suddenly cold and eerie. 'This. Running away from home. Or running away from myself within my home.'

He kept quiet.

'Tomorrow,' she repeated, her voice now flat and dead, the incandescent spark that had lit her up from within for the past few days was slowly flickering, fading. 'Tomorrow, I must go back.'

He cradled her face in his hands, wondering at the sudden surge of tenderness that flooded him when it came to her. This wasn't love. He'd seen love, lived through its peaks and crevices, and emerged warped from its crucible. This was different, just a connection with another human being who was as broken as he was. Broken in different places, but hurting just the same.

In his circles, he had a reputation of being one of the modern-day rakes who had been through half of the unhappily married women, and the happily unmarried ones too. He made no promises and offered no emotional solace to any. He didn't seem to need to do much of chasing, he found. It worked that he had emerged from an unhappy marriage and had little to say about it. It was his silence that drew the women in like magnets. They had heard the whispers, no doubt, and the rumours of him having caught his wife being unfaithful. He had never ever confirmed nor denied it, it had just added to his allure. Then there was the pedigree and family he represented. He realised that while some might think he was notching up holes on his belt, he was probably a notch on their belts.

Aisha was different. He hadn't set out to seduce her, the sex was an unfortunate by-product of his plan. It just complicated things that little bit, but he would resolve it, he knew. It was always a stupid idea to mix business and sex.

He had been a faithful husband for five years, besotted with his wife. It all changed the day he found his wife and his best friend drunk and naked in the bathtub at his farmhouse. The image seared itself into his brain, an image that had wormed itself into his nightmares and woke him up sweating and disoriented.

He had stepped out of the bathroom, instructed the handwringing attendant who had stood respectfully outside, to inform his wife to meet him in their room when she was dressed. This was after calming himself down from his initial impulse to pluck one of the hunting rifles off the wall in the den and riddle both of them with bullets.

An imperious click-clacking of the heels she hadn't been upset enough not to slip on, informed him that Devyani was approaching their bedroom. Sure enough, she stood at the door, looking at him with the imperious assumption that he needed her more than she needed him.

'Don't tell me you're surprised and shocked. I thought you knew you don't satisfy me. I always needed more,' she said, petulant in her dismissal of his devotion. She had wrapped herself in a bathrobe, with nothing beneath it, uncaring of the domestic staff witnessing both, her indiscretions and her near nakedness. The arrogance of her hold over him making her confident that the overpowering obsession he had for her would allow her to worm her way out of this too, like she had so many others before.

Those were minor misdemeanours. Overdrawn credit cards, a cocaine habit that he had inadvertently funded to keep her stable, public incidents of flying off the handle at parties that had found their way into tabloid gossip. But this was different. This was betrayal. Betrayal of the body. Betrayal of the mind. Betrayal of the covenant of marriage that he had believed in.

'I want out of this marriage, I never wanted to get married to you in the first place. You bore me.' Her voice was shrill, echoing through the high ceilings of the rooms, bouncing off the crystal chandelier that hung indolently above their heads, disinterested in the misery of the lives unravelling below it. This was her ultimate threat, wanting out of the marriage. She had used it often, and to great effect. She was confident she would have him again reduced to a mass of trembling, distraught flesh, determined to plea bargain everything to have her stay with him, in the vain hope that someday, perhaps, she would find some affection for him. That someday she wouldn't stare blank and expressionless at the ceiling above, while he heaved and thrust into her, the boredom on her face reflected in the impassivity of her marble-like body beneath him.

She picked a Baccarat vase from a sideboard and threw it against the wall of the room in a swift, unexpected gesture. It hit the wall with a surprisingly muted thud and then the tinkling sound of it shattering into pieces echoed in the silent room, long after the fragments had been swept up and discarded. It had been in the family for generations, something they had cherished. At that moment, Daljeet had felt something crack within him. It was probably his heart.

She had rushed at him and clawed him when he told her that he was ending the marriage this time. Her face, twisted with rage, was still the most beautiful face he had ever seen and it was all he could do to stop himself from holding her down, ripping off the bathrobe she had carelessly put on her wet body and throwing her onto the bed.

'I gave you everything you ever wanted,' he told her. 'Was it too much to expect you to be faithful?'

She had looked back at him, her eyes black pools of contempt.

'You don't satisfy me. You knew that when you married me. You knew what you were in for, I need more than you could ever give me. Don't whine now like the mamma's boy you are.' He noticed, for the first time that night, how her face resplendent in its ivory beauty morphed into ugliness so unimaginable, it repelled him.

He stepped away from her, and walked out of the room, leaving her sitting on the bed, the bathrobe askew. Her breasts, the exquisitely formed marble globes tipped pink that used to drive him berserk with a mere hint of them through the décolletage of her blouse covered lightly by a chiffon sari, were on full display now. They evoked nothing in him.

He had Badri Singh, his major domo, escort her back to her maternal home that very night, a long trip made by road through dusty highways and narrow side roads.

When he had the maids clean out her wardrobes, and pack her things into suitcases and trunks to be sent to her later, they handed him her medical files, hidden beneath a pile of woollens in a trunk. What she had told him were miscarriages in the early years of their marriage were in fact abortions. He did not know whether to mourn the unborn children or to be relieved he didn't have to question their paternity every time he looked upon them.

It had taken him a year and a half and a hefty payout to get the divorce through, and he had thanked his stars that they hadn't gotten around to starting the family he had yearned for with all his soul. All that kept him going was a succession of bodies he had bedded, some paid for, some seduced, all attempts at restoring his sense of worth, which had been wounded beyond repair.

Infidelity, he now realised, had nothing to do with the lack of love, and everything to do with the lack of respect. The carefully calibrated balance that made a marriage, never applied in his marriage, where the weight of his need for her completely outbalanced the scorn she had for him and his pathetic obsession with her.

Devyani was eighteen when they first met, or rather, were introduced to each other at a social gathering under the benign approving gazes of the elders who were hoping they would take to each other. He was twenty-eight, the right age to get married and produce an heir to the family, an heir who would take the lineage further by another generation. The wild oats had been long sown, he was now practical about matters of the heart, or so he thought. His man-of-the-world carapace was shattered when he first saw Devyani. It was an early winter afternoon, he would remember, reliving the moment with a passion that was untinged with the burden of reciprocity. The air was crisp, sharp, the light was soft and warm, as it faded into the forgiving greyness of dusk. She was standing at a window, framed against the soft late afternoon light, her hair lit up like a nimbus, her skin pale, her eyes glowing, her features so precisely set in her alabaster perfect skin that she seemed carved out of a single block of marble. The flowing pale chiffon sari she was draped demurely in, clung to her firm flesh in a manner that concealed, and yet, paradoxically seduced.

She felt his eyes on her, turned to look at him full in the face, and gave him a slight nod, acknowledging that she had noticed him noticing her, but without a smile, and turned back to look outside the window. He stood transfixed, every rational thought in his head blanked out except for how to make her his forever. When she was brought to him to be introduced later, by her maternal grandmother and his mother, he found himself dumbstruck, unable to respond coherently. She was then part child, part woman, the two disparate halves of her clearly visible in the yet burgeoning body, which would fill out more in the years they would spend together. The knowing gaze in her eyes was one that belied the unsullied innocence on her face. It was a combination that drove him crazy just looking at her.

When they were finally engaged, he realised that the knowing in her eyes came from experience that he didn't ever stop wondering where she'd picked up from. He asked no questions, he had had his share of women and on the wedding night, he genially conspired with her as she pricked her finger with a pin used to hold up her heavy veil, blotting the blood that oozed onto the pristine whiteness of the new bed linen, which no doubt would be taken for examination by the women of the household to ascertain the new bride's virginity.

He looked at Aisha, her bruised body and her disturbed soul, the flickering of something quite not at peace with itself evident, much like a lake that glistens with the reflects of the sunlight falling on its gently lapping water. She had betrayed her husband too, with him. But with her, he wasn't sure who was the betrayed and who the betrayer.

His marriage to Devyani lasted five years. The divorce took up three. Getting her out of his head was taking longer. Much longer than he thought it would. When relationships end, however one-sided they might be, the one who loves the other more is the one who ends it. They reach a tipping point beyond which they give up trying to carry an unequal burden.

He wondered how Aisha's husband would react if he had seen her naked with him. In the few days she had been away from home, he had not called her once. Nor had she called her husband. There was a resignation to her, a miasma of being unwanted, and unloved, that hung over her like a mantle, cloaking her every move. Her husband wanted her out of his life, he knew. And it showed on her, the uncertainty with which she reached out to touch him, the uncertainty of someone who doesn't know how a simple reaching out will be received.

She began kissing him with the greed that someone who doesn't know how long this could last has. He'd had his fill of her though, it was time to call an end to it and move onto the next phase.

Aisha pulled away. 'What are you thinking about?'

'Nothing.'

She pulled his face down to hers again and looked into his eyes. It seemed impossible that a pair of eyes could contain so much human misery within them.

'Well, stop thinking about nothing then. We might only have today to think about us.'

'There is no us to think about, there will never be an us,' he replied, and drew her down to him wondering what dystopian forces in the universe had conspired to get the two of them, with their destroyed souls, together, in this dance of despair.

8

'I need to go home,' she told him as soon as he woke up the next morning. She had barely slept for two hours, spending most of the night marching around the room, rearranging the furniture and then waking him up to have more sex. The guilt at abandoning her children was clawing her. There was a sense of closure to this, their little escapade.

She could feel things changing within her. She needed to get back to the comfort of the space between the bed and the wall, where she could roll herself up in blankets, and lie undisturbed, until it passed. There was an uncontrollable urge to scream, welling up within her, the urge to smash something to pieces, to take a blade and pierce her skin and see the blood dribble gently to the floor, drop by drop until the life drained out of her. She got up from the bed, her limbs quivering, and moved naked to the sideboard her handbag was on.

Her hands were shaking, as she fumbled in her bag for the bottle of pills. They would keep these feelings at bay until she could get home and crawl into darkness, until she could face the world again, without cringing or attacking it. It was coming upon her, she could feel it, the swift sink into the morass of blackness that saw nothing but knives that could slit her wrists and let all the blood out of her body, or ropes that could tighten themselves around her neck and choke the breath out of her. She couldn't find them, the pills that would work their magic with her brain, allowing her to stay on this side of the razor's edge, the side which had her children not back away in fear when she reached out to hug them.

'Okay,' he replied, 'We leave today.' He bathed and changed into jeans that fit him well at the hips, a sweater that hung gently on his broad shoulders, and having shaved away the stubble that had scratched the most delicate hidden skin of her body raw the previous night when he had rubbed his face all over it. She was already dressed, and waiting by the window. She didn't bathe, it felt like too much effort.

They had a quick breakfast, or rather he did. She drank down mugs on mugs of pitch black coffee that would keep her coherent and functional, her hands quivering just that bit as she lifted the mug from table to lip. She needed cigarettes.

There was a sense of relief, though she wouldn't acknowledge it even to herself, that this, whatever she could call it, an affair, a romantic interlude, an adulterous encounter, was over, that she need not ever see him again. She could just erase him out of her memory and get back to the routine of her every day. She could slip back into the carapace of the woman who kept her mind occupied by being obsessed with the order of the jars in the kitchen cupboards, and who locked and unlocked the doors to make sure they were locked, who scrubbed every possible surface of the kitchen clean. Return to the sterile marital bed, where her body atrophied under the phantom touch of caresses that never reached her skin.

The drive back was in strained silence through the descending roads. When they reached beyond the main nodal exit point of town, they realised that the roads were still blocked. A little beyond the main market, police barricades greeted them. She felt the tremors begin in her hands and legs, a nervous churning in the pit of her stomach that needed a drag of nicotine to silence it for the moment. She pulled out her almost depleted pack of cigarettes and offered one cursorily to Daljeet, who declined politely. He didn't smoke.

'Curfew,' the constable manning the barricade informed Daljeet. 'Rioting, the workers have burned down the factories at the food processing cooperative and set the manager of the estate on fire. The poor man died. The road won't open until the situation comes under control.' With an imperious blow of the whistle around his neck, he directed the oncoming traffic to turn around and go back from where they had arrived.

The friction between the locals and the immigrant workers had been building to a boil for the past many months and it was the sudden devastation that had pushed things over the edge. There had been firing, and a couple of locals dead from the firing. The local authorities, already brought to their knees by the landslides were taking no chances.

Aisha looked at Daljeet, terrified. Her cigarette was almost down to the butt, she flicked it out of the window unstubbed, its tip still flickering ominously as it disappeared from sight. Her gesture was practised, imperious, a side he hadn't seen in her this far. She lit another one smoothly, drawing in deeply, almost like the nicotine was her oxygen. 'What now? Is there no alternative route?' she asked, knowing that there was no option but to turn back and return to the summer home she had just left with its thick stone walls that told no secrets.

'Sadly no, unless we try to walk through the forests off the road, and that too won't be safe. We have to go back,' he said, his expression not that of regret. 'I can't say I'm sad. I'm not really looking forward to going back home.'

She looked at him, her expression curiously blank, her eyes blank dark holes that revealed nothing. She blew the smoke courteously in the direction of the open window before speaking, keeping her demons under tenuous smoke ropes of control. 'Why is that? Won't your family be missing you?'

'There's no one to miss me. My sister, I told you, is dead. My parents died a few years ago, in quick succession, I think my father died of heartbreak after my mother passed away. My nephew is my only immediate family now. He's like a son to me.'

'What about your sister's husband?' she asked.

He changed the gear, putting the vehicle into reverse. His mouth was set in a thin, grim line.

'He's dead too.'

'I'm so sorry to hear that.'

'My sister killed him. Slit his throat while he slept. We pleaded insanity. She was put in an asylum. She killed herself when she was there.'

There was a moment's silence after this statement while she let it sink in. She thought back to all the uncountable moments over the past five years, when she had physically stopped herself from padding down to the kitchen and taking the meat knife to chop up her husband's body systematically into many parts, and then disposing the remains in the dry leaf incinerator. She had it all planned in her head, which of the older bed sheets she would use to mop up the blood that would spill, and the disinfectant she would use to wipe all the surfaces that came in contact with the spilt blood. An involuntary shudder ran through her body. Some nights, she found herself barefoot in the kitchen, opening the drawer where the knives were kept, and taking out the one she used for the meats, testing its sharpness by drawing a razor thin line of blood on her finger, and then licking the blood off, its tangy, metallic taste bringing her out of her reverie. Somewhere, within her, the residual love for her husband always won over the insanity, always held her back when the monsters tried to take control. Prithvi didn't know she had these thoughts. One day he would look into her eyes and know, it was more than a falling out of love that had happened between the two of them. She had fallen, irrevocably, into the turgid cesspool of hate.

What of the children, what would happen of them if Prithvi were dead, and she was behind bars? Her aunts were too old, half in the grave themselves, and their children had their own lives to live. Prithvi's sister would be only too pleased to have the children with her. She had been trying to convince Prithvi for years to have the children sent across to her.

'It is not good for the children to grow up in the midst of madness,' she'd told Prithvi, when she didn't realise Aisha was listening in from the extension in the bedroom.

The world was unforgiving to children without parents.

One morning, she had woken up after a dark, stygian, chemical-induced sleep, with the knife clenched in her hand, and deep gashes in the mattress in the side where he slept. She had sewn it up swiftly before he returned, hasty unequal stitches with shaking hands, from the crash that followed a medicated high. Luckily, he hadn't come home from work that night. Since then, she had taken to locking the knife drawer at night before sleeping.

Daljeet noticed the slight tremor in her hands as he changed gears. He also noticed her hands, as he hadn't noticed them in the past few days. These were rough hands, chapped with detergent and scouring, blistered with bleach. These were common hands. They didn't match the sharply delicate aristocracy of her features. He looked at her. She was suddenly a stranger again, not the divine creature who had fascinated him for the past few days. Just another tired, middle-aged woman, with nervous eyes that looked everywhere and nowhere at the same time, and hands that were trembling despite her efforts to hold them down in her lap to still them. And she had a way of suddenly pushing her hair off her face that was almost a gesture of defiance against the gentle softening of her profile that it brought, when it fell around the edges of her cheeks. But she was still stunningly beautiful. The vestiges of the mesmerising beauty she must have been still evident, in a way that ruins remind one of the overwhelming magnificence of the monument past. He had the feeling that if he touched her now, she would explode into pieces, she seemed so tightly strung. He knew that look before; he had seen it on his sister.

The drive back to the house was silent. Guilt wracked her, guilt for having abandoned her children to the care of a stranger, guilt for having been unfaithful to a husband who had stopped giving her reason to remain faithful. She was rapid cycling, she knew. It was her punishment for deciding to do away with dosages she thought she didn't need, for skipping therapy sessions and lying to Prithvi that she had been to them, even when her husband had got his office to set them up, and convinced the therapist to fit her in on the day he visited their small hill town, once in a couple of months. But it had been months since the last episode. She was allowed to slip, or wasn't she?

'When do you think I could get home?' she asked in a voice so small, he could barely hear her. She had gone from elated to despairing in a matter of minutes. Her eyes, as she looked at him, had the light switched off from within them, and something terrifying, even feral, awakening within them. He noticed she was chain smoking now, reaching for the last pack of cigarettes she had kept hidden in her handbag for moments like these, when her body craved the nicotine.

He drew a deep breath, before replying, acutely aware of her eyes on him, now raising a slight hackle of unease down his spine. 'I honestly don't know. But I have to get back to Delhi too, I will figure out a way. I have to.' She was not going to get home, he knew. Not if he had anything to do with it.

'I need to go home. My kids need me. I need more cigarettes. I need my medicines, I need a chemist. I don't have my prescription with me.' She said this in one breath, punching the words out with difficulty.

'We can try tomorrow. There's absolutely nothing we can do.'

She ran a shaking hand over her forehead.

He stopped at a hole-in-the-wall store by the side of the road and purchased a pack of cigarettes of a brand that wasn't the one she was smoking. He gave her the pack, which she accepted without comment, lit up one, exhaling the smoke with short, sharp gasps, the furrow in her brow deepened by squinting against the smoke that rose from her lips, and wreathed her face in another layer of fog, making her look otherworldly.

She called home as soon as they entered the house, dialling with shaking hands. Aryan answered.

'Aryan, it's Mom.'

'Mom, are you coming home today?'

'Not today my darling, now apparently, there have been riots, there's a curfew on the route near the food factories. Don't step out of the house, okay. And tell your father to come home. It isn't safe for you to be alone in the house. Don't open the door to anyone, okay?'

'Okay,' he replied, with the nonchalance that came from the belief of youth that nothing could go wrong, and whatever could already had.

She was terrified, though she did not say it. What if the rioting workers managed to get to her house, and what if they entered and found only a woman and two children within? It didn't bear thinking about. But there was a gun, and Maya knew where it was and how to use it, if required. That was what came of living in the middle of nowhere. You kept weapons to be used against wild animals, knowing within yourself that sometimes humans were worse than animals and that you would not hesitate to use it against them.

'Mom… Mom, come home, Mom, I'm missing you so much.

And I'm tired of eating sandwiches and Maggi noodles every time.'

There were sounds of a slight scuffle and Maya's voice came on the phone. 'Like hell he's missing you. He's enjoying that he can eat Maggi all day and he's doing absolutely no studying. The milkman told us there was trouble higher up and that some people had been killed. I guessed as much you would be stuck there again today.'

Her words came out in a rush, as though she was afraid to pause in the event that the phone would get disconnected, and she wouldn't be able to tell Aisha all that she needed to say.

'Did your father come home yesterday?'

'Yes, he did, he came with a driver from the institute, gave him the spare key of your car and told him to get it back home. He called an hour ago from work to tell us there had been trouble. He's told us to keep the doors locked and not to go out unless it is urgent and not to let anyone in. Haven't you spoken with him?'

There was a brief pause. Maya knew that Aisha and Prithvi barely spoke anymore except for the functional. 'I messaged him. He knows I'm stuck. Tell him to come back home. There's a curfew in these parts. You children can't be alone… what if there's trouble? But then he wouldn't be able to come back even if he wanted to if there's a curfew…'

There was a brief silence while mother and daughter digested this half truth. And that Prithvi and she hadn't spoken.

'Anyway, Heer's here and we're okay, you don't worry, Mom…'

There was a pause, too brief, too loaded with uncertainty, when the line went silent yet was not disconnected, and a sudden change followed.

'Hey, Aisha, where are you, are you alright?' Heer's voice was too cheerful to ring true. Demons with hammers began making their presence felt at the back of Aisha's eyeballs, a precursor to the beginning of yet another of the debilitating migraines she suffered on and off.

'You must do it today,' came the demon voice inside her head. 'Find a knife and end it now.'

She closed her eyes, trying to separate the voice within her head, from the voice coming from the telephone.

'Not today,' she thought to herself. 'Please. Not now.'

The only thing she could do when the voices began was to pop a pill and take herself into a quiet dark room until they stopped. It had been months since they last spoke, and she had almost kidded herself into believing she was over them. She spoke first, before the voices did and drowned out her voice.

'I'm so terribly sorry to put you into this situation of having to watch over the kids, I'm sure this wasn't your plan when you came on this holiday.'

'Tchchah,' Heer said, a sound that seemed proprietarily dismissive. 'In the first place, I didn't come on a holiday. I came in search of my family. They're my niece and nephew, I'm glad I got the chance to get to know them at leisure, rather than the few hours I'd originally thought I'd get with you, although I'm sure they're missing your cooking. My repertoire doesn't extend too much in the kitchen apart from packaged ready-to-cook.'

'Make Maya help you. She's good with cooking, I've taught her basic cooking and she is good with chopping things as well.'

'Now you tell me this…' Heer laughed throatily. Aisha could imagine her throwing her head back and letting the laugh rip out of her and echo off the silent walls, uncaring of a disapproving husband demanding quietude, while he hammered out his reports to headquarters. 'I'm going to get her to make lunch and dinner today.'

Aisha could hear Maya's voice protesting in the background. Maya snatched the phone.

'Is this the hotel's number you're calling from?' Maya asked. She froze, realising the number she had called from would show on the caller ID phone they had at home.

'No. This is the number of the home at which I'm putting up, a friend's home.'

'Which friend, Mom?' Maya asked, ever the inquisitive one, ever the one to dig deep to unearth what was not obvious. 'You never mentioned having a friend in town.'

'I didn't then,' she replied, clamming up with guilt and a smidgeon of fear of being tracked down by Prithvi. 'I do now, someone offered me a lift when I crossed over the path where the rocks had fallen. I'm staying with them.' Daljeet, who had just walked into the room as she said this, looked across at her and smiled. Something she could not quite decipher came into his expression that made her just that bit wary.

Maya spoke again, her voice hushed. Aisha knew she must have turned her back to the room and was now speaking hunched over the receiver so that she was almost inaudible. 'Mom, you better come home fast. There's something I need to tell you, it's about Heer...' and then she paused, 'Okay, she's back. I'll tell you later.' The click of the phone echoed in Aisha's head for a long moment, followed by the buzzing emptiness, as she held onto the receiver.

She hugged herself as she sat down in an armchair that wrapped itself around her. Daljeet pulled a footstool across and sat himself down in front of her.

'What is it? Why are you suddenly so jumpy? Are you okay?' She wasn't but he didn't need to know that. She nodded, not trusting herself to say too much.

'You don't seem okay?' he persisted.

'I'm not feeling too well. It's my head. I need to lie down for a bit, in a dark room and hopefully, it will go away.'

She also needed to get her hands on some medication which she didn't have with her, not having kept the bottles in her bag because she had assumed she would be home by the end of the day. Was it because she had slipped on her maintenance medication? The monsters within her were uncoiling themselves, slowly, surely, slithering within the flabby grey folds of her brain, biding their time till they would strike and overpower her. She needed to be alone, to draw on every reserve of her strength to bat them down, to send them back into the Hadean Styx where they dwelled. Surely a chemist would be open and give them to her without a prescription; there were only two big chemists in the small town market that she knew. She had never ordered her medications from them, preferring instead to have them sent in from a supplier in the city. It was bad enough that her children went to school here, without rumours of them having an insane mother dodging them into the classrooms, and getting them laughed at by the rest of the kids.

He looked at her curiously, but escorted her without comment to the room she had been occupying for the past three days, the room that used to be his sister's in the days when she visited this home, the cupboards still replete with her clothes, the walls still bearing her photographs. 'Here,' he handed her a pill. 'For your head.' He poured out a glass of water from the jug kept on the sideboard. She gulped it down without asking what it was, without thinking. She lay down on the bed fully clothed, the effort to move from one spot to another beginning to drain her. Her mind, which had only a day earlier been racing with thoughts, so wild, so disconnected that her tongue couldn't keep up with her stream of thoughts, was slowly becoming a sludge of thick mud she had to struggle to walk through.

He stood over her, watching the light in her eyes begin to dim, as the pill he had given her began to take hold of her. 'I'll see you when you're feeling better. Now rest.'

She smiled wanly, with the hint of physical pain in the effort, and closed the door. The mattress received her body like a benediction and she sank into it, a fall that did not stop until she hit pitch, psychedelic blackness.

When she opened her eyes, the room was dark and unfamiliar. The sound of rain pounding on the roof had woken her up. She could faintly discern the outline of a person sitting in the chair opposite the bed in the darkened room. She pulled the covers around herself in an ineffectual bid to protect herself from whoever it was in the chair. Her hand reached out to the bedside table and groped for the switch to the lamp. She flicked it on. Nothing. There must have been a power outage. The room was chilly, almost freezing, even though a rough blanket covered her. The light flickered on apologetically, another bulb in the centre of the room, a naked bulb. Daljeet was sitting in the chair, his eyes unblinking.

'Good evening, this is the right switch, not everything in this room works,' he said, in a voice so soft, she had to strain to hear it. 'Did you sleep well?'

She struggled to sit up. Her limbs refused to obey her, the blanket felt as though it had been nailed down to the sides of the bed and held her down. 'How long have you been sitting here?' she asked, noticing her voice was slurring in the strangest way, her tongue reluctant and heavy in her mouth, which was all at once dry and acrid.

'For as long as it took.'

The room seemed different from the one she had gone to sleep in, she realised. This was smaller, and no longer on the ground floor with the lights of the distant gate visible from where her head was on the pillow. This was higher, the window was under an eave, the armchair where he sat was not one she had seen before, the stuffing on this was coming out in patches and an acrid, disused smell reeked through the room. The walls closed in on the bed and the ceiling was low, so low that when he stood up from the chair he had to bend down in order not to hit his head.

'For as long as what took?' she asked, feeling the unease

growing within her, realising that what emerged from her mouth was undecipherable, but he understood her perfectly.

'For as long as it took you to come back to consciousness.'

'Why?' she asked, feeling the confusion swirl through in her brain, with the after-effects of the stupor induced by the medication he'd given her making coherent thought difficult.

'Why?'

'You needed help. I need something you have. Your property. It seemed like the perfect option.'

She shook her head. Nothing seemed to make sense, the room she was in, the man sitting opposite her, him shifting her to this room from the room she had fallen off to sleep in, nothing made sense. Her mind was filled with disoriented thoughts that she found impossible to wade through.

Daljeet. Daljeet. Why had the name seemed familiar, why had he seemed familiar when he had offered her the ride into town? She scrambled to find a foothold within the flabby folds of her mind, something she could identify him with, anything. The property, what did he know about her property, she hadn't spoken about it to him. She never spoke about it with anyone. Prithvi had never let her speak about it or handle it herself. 'Don't bother your head about it, I'll take care of it,' he would tell her. 'Don't tell anyone that you are the sole inheritor of all that property. You're not well enough to handle it, I'll handle everything for you,' he had said.

She knew then, as she knew now, that all he had been trying to handle was a way for him to sell it off and siphon off all the money before getting her committed into a mental asylum. She knew it, and she had made her own plans. But this man, this stranger, what did he know about her property, how did he know she needed help?

He smiled, a smile that had the effect of a knife lacerating her exposed skin. His expression terrified her. It was cool, deliberate, detached. This was another man, not the man she had spent days and nights being unfaithful with.

'You aren't in the main house anymore. This is the cottage at the end of the estate. No one is allowed here. You are here now, for as long as I want you to be. And after that, for as long as you want to be.'

She shook her head slowly, feeling the trailing images on her retina blur into a psychedelic fairground of moving lights. Every movement seemed amplified, every sensation heightened. Yet, she was unable to respond, unable to speak; her tongue felt like a stone in her mouth. Dried. Dead.

'Why?' she asked, 'Why, why, why…?' No other words emerged from her mouth.

'Because you need to be away. And I need to get your signatures on some papers. And believe it or not, I want to help you. I don't know why, I can't explain it, but I want to help you.'

'I don't need your help. I want to go home.' It was difficult getting the words out, she had to force them off her tongue.

He sat beside her and stroked her head gently. 'You know this is for the best, don't you? You don't need to go back to your husband ever, if you don't want to. And I can help you take your kids away with you too, but first, you need to give me what I want.'

The tears began flowing down her cheeks, a drop or two at first, and then a steady stream that went into her ears, worked their way through her hair and formed asymmetrical wet patches, dampening the lumpy pillow below her head. He put his arm around her head and wiped her tears with his fingers, cradling her as gently as one would an infant.

He then sat her up, gently fed her a meal from a plate that was already there on a side table, cold unappetising khichdi, congealed into lumps that stuck in her throat as she struggled to swallow them, and put her down to sleep after that. He handed her two pills after she ate. She was unresisting, compliant, the energy whooshed out of her by the blackness overtaking her mind. 'Go to sleep,' he had said, stroking her hair as she closed her eyes, suddenly fragile, uneven and unable to focus on anything around her or within her. 'We'll talk tomorrow.'

The world had slowly gone black after that. The only sound in the room was that of the howling wind banging at the window panes, crying to be let in.

9

When she woke up from a sleep so dark she had been unsure if it was death or oblivion, it was morning, a grim deathly morning. Outside the grimy window, the fog smothered everything with the blanket of grey. Her limbs were leaden with the chemicals swirling through her system. She gingerly stepped up to open the door. It was locked. She tested the windows. They were nailed down. The glass looking out, she realised, was covered by one of those one-way films, she could look out through but no one could see her. An iron grille boxed the window in. The outhouse was at the very edge of the property, he had shown it to her the first day he had taken her for a walk around the estate.

'This,' he had said, 'is where I keep my guilty secrets.' She had looked at it, going steadily to ruin, this decrepit little outhouse, down a sloping part to the back of the house. The mountain fell away to a chasm on the other side, with only an old, crumbling stone wall between them and certain death. The outhouse was uncared for, the masonry exposed, the vines creeping up the walls, and the solitary chimney climbing high out of the back with no smoke emanating from it. She'd felt a shudder go up her spine. At the time, she didn't realise why. Now she did.

This was his guilty secret. And now, she was his guilty secret.

'It is a miserable life you will go back to, Aisha,' he told her last night, 'your children won't need you, now that they're grown up. Your husband doesn't want you anymore. He's already fucking your new-found sister. Yes, I know about that.'

'How do you know about her?'

'That's a long, long story.'

'Why should I believe you?'

He leaned back in his chair and templed his fingers, resting his chin on them. His expression in the dim light of the single bulb that lit up the room, was a curious mixture of cold calculativeness and a tenderness that scared her more than the coldness did.

'Because you really have no choice if you want to ever get out from here.'

'What do you want?'

'Just your signature on some papers. The kothi, the grounds, the adjoining properties. I'll pay you for it, a fair price I promise you. And I'll even help you to disappear with your children, so far away your husband won't be able to find you. Isn't that what you want?'

She nodded slowly.

'What if I don't want to sell the house?' He hadn't answered her, just smiled slowly, very slowly.

'Then I will have to just kill you.'

She had absolutely no doubt that he would kill her if she didn't agree. Perhaps it would be better to give him what he wanted, to sign the papers. He might still kill her after he got what he wanted. She shivered. She would negotiate with him when he came next. Perhaps it would be for the best if he killed her, after all wasn't it what she had been tempted to do so very often, take a knife to her wrists and end it all.

The room was chilly, her flesh felt like that of a freshly plucked chicken. She went to the bathroom, realising that no matter how the mind stayed disturbed, the body had its need for functionality.

The room had a small bathroom attached, with a commode that was cracking dangerously, tiles which were chipped, a washbasin with a tap that dribbled a few stray drops like an old man's penis, incontinent. She opened the tap and splashed some cold water on her face, starting at the impact of the chilliness. The chill stung her skin. There was a wizened, dubious-looking water heater in the corner of the bathroom, but bathing felt like too much of an effort. Even washing her face and brushing her teeth was too much of an effort. She knew that, in two days she would be in bed, emerging only to use the bathroom, buried under the blankets, refusing to emerge until the darkness passed. She didn't have the luxury of losing her mind now, at this point, when she was in a strange place, being held captive by an almost stranger. But then, had she ever had the luxury of losing her mind, even when she'd become violent and had to be taken away by four sturdy attendants in an ambulance to a care centre? It was a luxury she had taken without it being hers to take. She had paid for it with children who loved her, and were terrified of her simultaneously, and a husband who had stopped loving her.

The bathroom was clean. There was a bottle of phenyl perched precariously on the window sill, a broom and a mop tucked away under the basin. It would have been kept ready for her incarceration. The medicine cabinet beside the mirror revealed shampoo, conditioner, a bar of soap still in its wrapper, toothpaste, toothbrush, floss, mouthwash, even a vaginal wash, Savlon, cotton, a pack of sanitary napkins, and in a thoughtful condescension to feminine vanity, body lotion and night cream. This room had been stocked in readiness for her arrival. Or had there been others before her locked up in this room, in this outhouse, waiting until they were let back out into the world? There were no razors. If there had been she knew she would have slit her wrists until all the blood drained out of her body in slow, excruciating drops. She could drink the phenyl, she told herself.

She emerged, and positioned herself at the window, waiting for something to cut through the unrelenting grey fog. Nothing did. It was a morass of uniform grey. She hammered at the glass with her fists, heaved a chair against it, and fidgeted with the iron rods, kicked at them hard. Nothing gave. It had been created for imprisonment, reinforced with the careful planning that goes into creating a space to keep a human being captive. She pushed at the metal reinforced door to the room, ran her fingers around the edges, looking for a spot where it would give. It wouldn't budge.

Through the windows, she could see the black hounds pacing the gardens, unleashed this time, black shadows in the mist. She couldn't hear them barking, but they moved, silent, prowling, ominous. Perhaps he had let them loose as a warning to her in the event she thought of escaping. He had told her of how they had once torn a thief to pieces. They would not hesitate to do the same to her, she knew, if she attempted to run away.

A whirring sound at the door made her turn towards it. A small metallic inset grate at the bottom of the door was raising itself. She saw a tray being pushed in by unseen hands, the grate whirring down with a sudden thump.

'Help me!' she yelled, aware that another person was present on the premises, watching over the closed door, 'Get me out of here.' She fell down to her knees, and tried to peer through the rapidly shutting metal sheet. All she could see were a pair of scruffy sandals on feet covered with hand-knitted rough wool socks shuffling quickly out of her line of sight. She banged the door with hands that were desperate, and then raw, on the unforgiving metal. The sound of the footsteps echoing on the timber floorboards, and clomping down the wooden stairs, died down. The slam of a door shutting downstairs reverberated through the room. The overwhelming silence that wreathed the house took over again, a silence so heavy that she could hear the sound of her heart thudding in the cavity of her chest.

She picked up the tray. Roti, sabji, daal, chawal. It would keep body and soul together.

She kept the tray on a small side table. She had no appetite for it at the moment, just an overwhelming sense of nausea that kept raising acrid bile to her throat.

Her handbag had been kept carefully on a dresser, next to an old cupboard. She opened it, and took out her mobile phone, hoping against hope that she could switch it on. Surely, she thought, they would trace her last location from the signals and track her down. Who would, she thought to herself. The kids couldn't and her husband wouldn't bother. Or would he? Her phone was dead. She opened the back of the instrument, her sim card had been removed and probably disposed of as well.

Time was elastic in the greyness of fog-filled days. This would be day four of her having gone away from home, perhaps, or was it day six. She had completely lost track of time and days.

Surely they would put out a missing notice for her. She hadn't called home for the past couple of days as she had been doing every morning for the first few days, nor had she reached home. What had happened while she had been passed out? Just how long had she been in the fugue state between awareness and chemically-induced unconsciousness? How many days had she lost? There was nothing in the room to determine time, date or even year.

She opened the rickety cupboard. It contained clothes. Most were from the cupboard in the room she had earlier been in. She went back into the bathroom, dampened a hand towel with some water and wiped the exposed surfaces of her body clean. She needed to force herself to be functional. The silence was cloying. It hung thick over the outhouse. Not even the wind whistled through the cracks in the window pane.

With nothing to do, she ate the food on the tray. She needed to keep up her strength, if she wanted to escape. Ten minutes later, she felt her head swim with giddiness. She lay down on the bed and fell fast asleep from whatever it was that had been mixed carefully into what she had eaten.

The dreams she wandered through were a purgatory of chill and fog that pierced through her skin. She woke to a room that was dark with the overhang of night and still with the presence of someone watching over her as she slept. There was a familiar shadow in the armchair.

She attempted to speak, feeling her tongue, heavy again, with an induced lethargy that made her sluggish. 'Daljeet,' she slurred. 'I'm thirsty, I want water.'

He rose from the chair, in a manner almost eager to be of service and poured out a glass of water, before coming to where she lay.

'Sit up,' he commanded. His voice was soft, even gentle. She obeyed. He opened her mouth and poured a dribble of water down it, with an assuredness that told her he had done this before. Played caretaker to someone who couldn't care for himself or herself. His sister, she realised suddenly, with complete clarity. That's how he knew with what to medicate her.

She gulped and swallowed, feeling the liquid go down her parched throat. He wiped the side of her mouth gently, where some water had spilt unwittingly, and then kissed her softly where he had wiped it dry.

'Are you cold?' His voice, honey smooth and polished, the clipped boarding school accent which had been so attractive when they first met now made her wary. She turned her face away.

'I need to go to the bathroom. I can't walk.'

It had descended on her, the blackness which had only one way out. Through it.

He lifted her up carefully to her feet. She felt disjointed, like a marionette. Her legs were shaky from lying down for the hours she had been knocked out. She walked with faltering steps to the bathroom. In the bathroom, she closed the door and sat down heavily on the commode, feeling her body respond to the Pavlovian stimulus of being on the commode, with the automatic release of urine. Her body was still functional, although her mind might have begun going to pieces. She tested the bathroom window again. She could work on the slats and figure out how to wriggle through it if she got an opportunity.

The bathroom couldn't be locked she knew, but it still came as a shock to her to realise that he had thrown the door open and was looking at her. 'Do you mind?' she asked, gesturing at him to close the door and go away.

'There's no point, the box grille outside is electrified.' Without waiting for a reply, he turned around and walked out of the narrow bathroom that had filled up with his entering it, closing the door behind him.

She could hear his heavy footsteps walking about in the room outside the bathroom, pacing the floor like a caged beast. Why? Why? Why? The question hammered within her brain with no answer. Why was he keeping her prisoner? What did he stand to gain by taking her hostage? Why had he created such an elaborate plan to confine her? Was this what prison felt like? The disquieting sense of being watched constantly, of having absolutely no privacy, of being kept in a confined space, against one's will. Undoubtedly he must have a way of keeping an eye on her. She looked up at the corners of the room. Nothing. Could she discern the circular aperture of a camera behind the mottled silver of the looking glass?

She splashed her face with water, and looked at herself. If

anything, she looked younger. The hollows in her cheeks and under her eyes which had made her face vaguely skeletal seemed to have filled out. In the dim light of the solitary bulb which hung over the washbasin, she looked a different person, a slightly younger version of herself. With a start, she realised what it was. It was the lack of the frown lines that punctuated her forehead, the pinched downward droop of her lips which had corrected itself to a preternatural horizontality.

She wiped her face with the scrap of a hand towel kept next to the basin, tied her hair with quick, practised movements into a low knot. When all else is gone, the only thing a human being can do is try to be presentable. When she emerged from the bathroom, still shaky but a little more in control of herself, he was sitting in a chair by the window, looking out into the nothingness.

While she had been in the bathroom, someone had entered and laid the small table with two melamine plates, a far cry from the Wedgewood she'd been served tea with on her first day at the house, dented cutlery that comprised two mismatched spoons and a container in which what seemed like a kedgeree lay, cold, congealed and unappetising. He was eating a sandwich which he didn't offer her. It wouldn't have been doused in whatever narcotic it was that would inevitably knock her out after eating it.

'Come,' he beckoned graciously, 'Let's eat dinner. You must be hungry.'

And so she was, despite the lack of appetising fare. Strangely enough, the impossible situation she seemed to be in had made her ravenously hungry, so hungry that she ate without speaking a word. He looked on at her like an owner might look indulgently upon a favourite pet, offering her his pristine handkerchief when she sneezed and wiped her nose roughly with the back of her sleeve. When the soporific additive took hold on her, in the midst of her asking him why he was confining her here in this place, it lulled her at first into a pleasant high, where she felt vaguely intoxicated and garrulous.

'Why are you doing this?' she slurred, feeling her tongue getting heavy again. 'Why?' His face began swimming in front of her eyes, and perhaps the room was lurching independently of her vision.

'Doing what? I'm just keeping you with me. I thought you liked being with me. You seemed happy enough the first few days. You know this is what you want too.'

'My children need me,' she said, a single tear beginning to work its way down the side of her left cheek.

'No, they don't. No one needs you, Aisha. The faster you understand that the better. I can make it easier for you. Give me what I want. And you are free to go.'

'Will you really let me go if I sell you the kothi?'

'I will. I will also help you get back on your feet, and live a life away from your husband. Don't you want that?'

It was tempting. She needed her children. What about her children? He put a finger under her chin and tilted her face up so she was gazing at him.

'I've figured everything out, now just trust me. It just began with me wanting to convince you to sell the kothi to me. I was quite fed up of your dithering over whether you wanted to sell it or not. Dealing with your husband was difficult, he had his own agenda, I realised, and it involved getting you committed into an asylum the moment the sale went through. He told me it was you who was stalling the sale. Then he said I could send across the papers and a cheque for the token amount. I did, and he came back saying you were in no condition to sign or to even come for a meeting. And then, that got me curious about you…'

His voice trailed off.

'Bring my kids to me and let me go.'

He grabbed her and kissed her hard. 'I will. But first I will make sure you are capable of being on your own. You can't be left alone right now, you know that. You can't take the responsibility of two children. They are safer without you.'

'Why are you doing this?'

'I don't know,' he replied. 'Maybe because I don't want to see you descend into the hell my sister did. I couldn't save her. I want to save you.'

'What if I don't want to be saved?'

It was getting difficult to speak. She fell into a silence.

There was a long silence during which neither of them moved a muscle. He then stood up and held a hand out for her. She took it and rose, feeling his arms go around her, holding her tight, and unwittingly, her arms went around him too, each holding on to the other with the despair that abandonment brings. She clung onto him, in sudden panic, that if she left him she would drown, and perhaps he felt the same.

'Now,' he whispered into her ear, 'Just trust me, okay.'

She nodded, and slumped back into her chair feeling herself drifting into dark oblivion.

He stood up and cleared the table efficiently, scraping the plates clean, putting the leftovers in a little plastic bag, settling everything on the tray it had come in on and carefully walking up to the door and placing it outside. The door was open, she realised. She could push past him and run out if she wanted to. The room began to sway independent of her. She felt unequal to rising and making a dash for it while the door was open. Her chance passed. He closed the door carefully, clicking it shut.

The world around her was spinning too rapidly for her to do anything but remain seated and hold on to the armrests of the chair she was in. Daljeet sat next to her, and looked deep into her eyes with a tenderness that soaked through her. It felt like he wasn't looking at her but into her. He stroked her head as she felt her eyes close, and the velvet blaze of the darkness overtake her all over again.

'Sleep now,' she heard his voice say, 'Sleep well.' The world, when it went out, was a ball of light in her head, an eye-piercing brightness that had her walking through the house of her childhood. She was with her mother, holding her soft hand. The musky perfume her mother had specially made for herself by the perfumer in the old city, cloying and reassuring, swarmed into her nostrils. It blotted out everything, save the tears that began rolling, without her knowing, down her cheeks.

Book 2

1

Prithvi

He should have probably seen it coming, but he didn't. All those years of living with her madness, of never knowing what to expect when he walked into the house every evening. Of telling the children to let him know immediately if she had a meltdown, and to lock themselves into their room until he returned. Tolerating her insane jealousy, her insistence that he was cheating on her. Her steadfast refusal to have sex with him after that one day, when he couldn't respond, what with exhaustion and project deadlines.

She'd been rolling towards a high. He knew; he could see it. He shouldn't have lost his temper that night, but sometimes he just couldn't control himself—she'd been through all his emails, rifled through his drawers, set a tap on his phone lines, called at the office, and abused his PA for what she'd suspected was a sexual relationship between him and his PA.

He'd done all he could. He had taken her to the best psychiatrists he could afford, got her appointments for therapy, taken her for the first few sessions, hired full-time household help to keep things running. But, it all came to naught. She would skip her medication, throw out the hired help, and sink right back into the same cycle of highs and lows. He was exhausted. Some days he wished she would slit her wrists as she kept threatening to do so, and relieve him of the unceasing stress. At others, he loved her and wanted her back, the high-spirited, exuberant girl he had married.

It would never have been easy, marrying her, he always knew. She was fragile, high-strung, the mental issues barely smoothened over by the ivory smooth skin, and the sharp hauteur of her aquiline features. She wasn't meant for him. She was too high-bred, too detached, having lived out her childhood in the impersonality of a boarding school. He was a small-town boy, who had made it to college in the big city on the strength of a sports scholarship. He'd boxed for the state, right up to the national level, until he'd decided that academics would keep him fed where sports wouldn't. His mother was unlettered, but perhaps the clearest thinker he'd ever known. She'd taken one look at Aisha when he'd taken her home to introduce her to the family, and told him he was making a mistake. 'That girl needs more taking care of than she will ever take care of you.'

But love does not listen to reason nor comprehend that anything more would be demanded except the ability to love. He paid no heed to his mother. All was well for a few years. Then the children were born. It first began when Maya was still a baby. Aryan's birth completely set her off the charts in her ricocheting moods and pendulum-like behaviour. And nothing ever made sense in their house ever again.

For the first three days, she'd called home. Told the kids she was stuck in the main town. She had messaged him. Then there was no news. He had called friends in town to keep a watch out for her. One had spotted her at the store, and hadn't seen her since. She would return, he knew. He would go in search of her, if she didn't, though he was sorely tempted not to. She was the millstone his fate was tethered to, he had no option but to go searching for her, and go down in his search for her.

She hadn't called him, he hadn't called her. It had been a standoff, tacitly acknowledging that there was nothing to speak about anymore. He knew she was safe and alive, and hadn't just disappeared again this time. She did that a lot. Disappearing, wanting to be found.

He'd got a call from the police two days later to identify a wallet they had found, with her driving licence, placed carefully at a point on the road, just before the collapsed bridge, over a swirling rapid current river that roared below it. It had taken her five days to decide she was never coming back. He didn't know whether to mourn or to be relieved that it had ended.

There was a note in the wallet, scribbled hastily on a foolscap sheet torn from a child's school notebook, the handwriting within hurried, uneven, incoherent. 'I am ending my life,' it said. 'No one is to be blamed. I am tired of my illness.' It was signed Aisha Thakur.

Was it her handwriting, they asked him. He couldn't be sure. They took samples of her handwriting from the home to match in order to arrive at a conclusion. It could be hers, they concluded.

There was no body. But they had an eyewitness.

'A local shepherd says he saw a woman, wearing trousers and a sweater, keep this wallet by the side of the bridge and jump. He was the one who told us about it and handed us this wallet with the note,' said the inspector handling the case. 'Of course there was nothing of value in the wallet anymore. All the money had been emptied out. We can only assume she's dead and the body has been carried away by the river. If we hear of anything or find anything, we'll let you know. If the body gets washed up downstream, we will get notified, and let you know. No one remembers having seen her walking down the road to the bridge, but then there are not many people who live near that bend. But they do remember seeing her in the market five days ago. The grocery store owner in the main market does recall that she visited the store.'

No one would try to kill her. He might have done so, he thought to himself, but someone else or fate had beaten him to it. 'It could be suicide,' he said finally, having made up his mind. 'She was quite unwell. And she wasn't getting any better.'

'We will organise a search team, get some local divers to check the spot where she jumped, and downstream for the body. There is no telling how far the river would have carried the body and when it would get washed up.'

He nodded, closing his eyes at the thought of her being fished out from the water, stone cold, slimy with rot, the flesh putrid beneath his touch, his fingers sinking to the bone as he touched her. But they did not find a body; the river had claimed it for its own, the fish nibbling at it, until they exposed bone. The skin decomposing and falling off, rotting green, slimy, stuck on the jagged edge of a rock, below the rushing water. She was dead. There was a finality to that thought which made him hold onto it and savour it. It was over, his marriage. He was finally free of her. Why couldn't she have done it earlier, he wondered. It was so perfect a solution. He ignored the strange, sudden pang of grief that would strike him in the ribs unawares, making his breath catch and his body double over with a pain that wasn't physical.

'She was last seen talking to a tall man, with light brown eyes. Would you know this person?' the inspector asked a couple of days later. Prithvi had visited the police station to check whether he could have her declared dead, and a death certificate issued.

He shook his head. She had no contact with people he did not know. He kept a tight watch on her, it was better that way. Despite that, she had broken out a couple of times, and run away, but had left enough trails so she could be traced and brought back.

But there was the lingering disquiet, the unanswered questions. Who was the man she was last seen with? Did he have anything to do with her disappearance?

Then the blast of inexplicable suspicion. Was it a man she was having an affair with? Did she check into any of the anonymous lodges on Mall Road and spend the afternoon with him? Was that why she never allowed him to touch her anymore? The reason she slept on the edge of the bed, her back towards him, the revulsion to his touch evident in the way her body clung to the thinnest sliver of the edge.

He felt his intestines knot up and the bile rise in his throat. He felt jealousy, he realised, with a faint shock that almost made him reel. He was more jealous, now that his dead wife was seen wandering around town with a stranger, than sad at the fact that she was dead. He was also, he realised with a sudden awkwardness, faintly aroused at the thought of his dead wife fornicating with a faceless man.

Did he know who the man was, the police inspector, SD Pant, asked him again. No, he had no clue who that man was, he replied, noticing the sudden smirk and empathy that mingled in the eyes of the policeman. There was perhaps nothing as humiliating as being perceived a cuckold by another man.

'You do realise she cannot be declared dead unless we either have a body or she is missing for over seven years. So right now, your wife is just missing/presumed dead. We have to wait and see what turns up in the search.'

Nothing did. It was a half-hearted search anyway, with local divers hesitant to enter the depths of the raging river. They gave up after two days. Bodies, the police inspector told him, could travel great distances.

'She could turn up on the banks down in the plains. Of course, by then, the body would be completely decomposed; so there would be no way of us being sure it could be your wife. Do you have her dental records?'

He didn't pressurise them to continue the search any further. The property would have to lie in limbo for seven years, until she was declared legally dead. Or perhaps, he could dispose it, he did have the power of attorney to it. And he hadn't yet reported her missing, or notified her attorneys about her going missing.

For a brief, sharp moment, guilt struck him hard in the solar plexus, knocking the wind out of him. He hadn't reported her missing, he thought. If her wallet with her driver's licence hadn't been found, they would have never known what had happened to her. He hadn't bothered to track her down in the five days that she was away. Where had she been, why had she suddenly decided to jump? He would never know.

He had a small havan done for her soul, by an indifferent priest, who didn't know her, and who didn't realise that she was not a Hindu. Neither by birth nor by conversion after marriage. The ritual was more a cleansing for Prithvi, a safeguard against her returning from the other world, and demanding to be taken back into their lives. Would she find peace, he wondered, in death? Or would she be condemned to forever be scrambling up the sides of the steep mountains, trying to cross over to the other side of the broken road, where her home and her children awaited her?

Where were the rest of her things, her handbag, her car keys? Where had she been for almost a week before she had decided to take her life? What had happened with her in that week, he wondered briefly, idling over these questions.

A widower. It had a sense of release to it. He rolled the word over in his mind and decided he liked the sound of it. If they found her body, he told himself, he would have had her cremated and taken her ashes to her ancestral house and have it buried in the grounds there, under the shadow of the mango tree she'd loved to climb as a child. She would have wanted to be buried there. It was an odd moment of sentimentality that scared him when it surfaced.

The children were rather accepting that their mother would never be coming back.

Maya insisted that he give Aisha's clothes away to a charity. 'What is the point of keeping it all locked up?' she said, in her practical do-gooder tone. She had recovered from the death of her mother rather swiftly.

Aryan hadn't. He had begun acting out, throwing tantrums, screaming at Heer when she tried to bring him to line, yelling, 'You're not my mother.'

Heer. She had taken over the house, and Prithvi was grateful for it. Perhaps she had come into their lives to take over from Aisha. Everything did happen for the best. She had nowhere to go to, and they had no one to take care of them. She slid into the vacant spot left by Aisha with the practised ease of a professional interloper. The kids were taken care of, the house was cared for, there was food on the table. She had been only too pleased to take over all the duties that Aisha managed. Even the duties Aisha had long given up.

She was a little sloppy. Not everyone would be as obsessed as Aisha was about disinfecting every surface thrice, and arranging jars in exactly the same order, by size and colour. And then there was her washing up, the way she wore disposable surgical gloves, washed and scrubbed every dish, and then dipped them in boiling water. The sight of the piles of dishes in the sink waiting to be washed up, seemed like a harkening back to normality, of disarray, of life being lived in the vertices of the housework that could wait.

And then there was the sex. It was inevitable, he told himself, for a man who had been deprived for so long. Heer had moved into his bedroom the day after he had received the call from the police, and returned home with the wallet. If the kids were displeased with this arrangement, they didn't show it.

He'd been attracted to her the moment he had seen her. The day he'd reached home to find Aisha gone had been the day he'd become her sister's lover. It was strange how he hadn't resisted the moves she made, and how he hadn't thought about the possible reasons for her actions.

He hadn't asked her how she knew what she knew. He was just grateful that she was one of those women who had no qualms about asking to be pleasured in the way they wanted it, and was seemingly insatiable. But then Aisha had been the same when they started out. You could never tell with a woman, he thought, you could never know whether they would stay who they were when you started out or morph into a complete stranger.

Ever since Heer had taken over the house and slipped into his bed, he kept regular hours. She'd made her move on him the second day that Aisha was away, the day she had called to tell the kids she was stuck with no available mode of transport, and she would be home soon.

That night, it had been raining off and on. The power supply hadn't been restored and she had put the kids to sleep. When the key had turned in the front door, she was ready for him.

He was painstakingly polite, keeping his things in order, noting her attempts to keep the place tidy. 'Have you had dinner?' she asked him politely, getting up from the sofa where she had been reading a book. *50 Shades of Grey*. He had often wondered often why Aisha had ordered it. Was there a hidden side to her?

Noticing his eyes on the book, she smiled. Her eyes were full of seduction and promise. They dissolved iron-clad resolutions not to be seduced by women who were his wife's half sisters no matter that they were wearing the sheerest of t-shirts which revealed they had no innerwear within.

'I hope you don't mind, but I've always found erotica most fascinating.'

'Of course not, feel free to read whatever takes your fancy.'

'So, did you and Aisha try any of the stuff from the book?'

The conversation was veering alarmingly into the territory of the forbidden.

'No, we didn't.'

'Would you like to?'

His mouth went dry.

She moved closer to him, close enough so she could smell the day's sweat on his body, close enough so he could feel the heat of her body barely centimetres away from him, her nipples dangerously perky in the slight chill of the pre-autumnal night. His body surged involuntarily in response to her nearness.

'Not really,' he replied, determined not to get into a complicated situation.

'There's a lot here that would take my fancy,' she replied, looking straight into his eyes, 'but unfortunately, none of it is in a book.' She raised a hand and traced his jaw line. Her touch was feather soft and felt like a current through his skin.

He took a step back. The children could come out of their rooms at any moment. And Aisha, was she back? He hadn't bothered to check.

He wasn't bad looking, she thought, this man with the tired eyes, and jowls that had just about begun softening his jaw. He had crinkles around his eyes.

Her nipples grazed his chest through the t-shirt she was wearing, as she took a couple of steps forward.

'I don't think…' he began, with an unsure voice, but she silenced him by putting a determined hand to his lips and putting another hand to where his body betrayed his response. He closed his eyes as her fingers expertly navigated the zipper and took hold of what had only felt his own fingers moving up and down its length in the privacy of the bathroom for the past many years.

'You want me.' It wasn't a question or a statement. It was a fact stated simply, and he didn't deny it. He had wanted her since the day before when she had come down the stairs in a nightshirt. He had, for the flash of a moment, felt it was Aisha all over again, when she was younger, when the kids hadn't been born and when all her issues with her body hadn't warped her.

The sex, on the kitchen counter, was hurried and explosive. Then she led him up to the bedroom he had shared with Aisha. Her body was Aisha's, before she had the children. Lean and leggy, with the breasts firm and high, the stomach unlined by the silvery lines that crawled across the surface. She rose early, before daybreak, and went back into the guest room where she should have slept. When he went down for breakfast, she was completely neutral and polite.

'Would you like some toast?' she asked, careful to not be within touching distance of him, with the kids at the table. Maya stared at them, sniffing out with her adolescent antennae the stench of forbidden sex that wafted between the two of them. It had never left them, the smell of sex, the musky, indefinable aroma of the illicit that lingered. Despite the pains they took to ensure they were never improper in front of the kids, it was obvious that the kids knew.

Heer did her best to replace Aisha in every way she could, but she couldn't wipe out the memories, or stop a little boy from hugging his pillow at night and hoping that when he woke in the morning, his mother would be in the kitchen. He would, once again, smell the morning aroma of breakfast he associated with her, as he stumbled down the stairs, sleep in his eyes, his teeth unbrushed, his day beginning with him wrapping his arms around his mother's hips and resting his cheek against the soft pillow of her hurried, morning embrace.

He liked to remember the good days. The bad days were dark rooms with the curtains drawn and his mother lying in bed, unbathed. The days his father had to physically lift her and sponge her clean, and put food into her throat. He didn't want to think of the terrible days when they had to lock themselves into their room, until their father came home.

It wasn't Heer's fault Aryan didn't like her, Prithvi told himself. It was natural that he would resent her, an intruder who had displaced his mother. But his mother had displaced herself. She was the one who had jumped. She was the one who hadn't wanted to return. How could you tell a little boy that? Or that his mother had preferred death to life with him? Or that he was probably better off with his mother dead than alive?

To Prithvi, it was flattering that a young woman as beautiful as Heer would find him attractive. He had thought himself unappealing, now that his hair was more pepper and salt and thinning slightly at the crown. The days passed, heavy and placid under the blanket of a carefully established routine. The children took to staying in their rooms more often than not, and even eating while watching the television. Aisha would have never allowed it.

Heer tried to keep the house clean, the way it was when Aisha was around, but she wasn't as obsessed.

Every day, she would wait till Prithvi left for the institute and call, 'Today?' she would ask.

'Not today,' the voice would reply.

Sometimes, she genuinely felt a caring for this man, confused and wanting love. There were nights he slept holding onto her with a fierceness that didn't let her go, until the morning. At others, he tried to reconcile his lust and selfishness with the sudden onslaught of grief at Aisha's death.

Those days he would be standoffish and distant, even irritable. She learnt quickly not to intrude on him, and let him be. He would be back to normal in a day or two. Craving affection. Seducing him had not been part of the deal. All she was supposed to do was to get herself into the house and do what she was supposed to. It was unplanned, the becoming lovers with him.

Not that she regretted it. It would have been difficult staying all these days without sex to keep her going. And it would end soon enough.

Only those infernal, difficult children were making the stint unbearable. One particularly difficult morning, Aryan had, on checking the contents of his lunch box, asked for canteen money. Prithvi refused.

'Eat what has been packed for you, do you think money grows on trees?'

'This is my mother's money that bought this house you're living in,' Maya yelled, startling Heer. Her voice was high-pitched, and stretched. Prithvi looked at her in shock.

Had she inherited the madness from her mother, he wondered. How long would it take before she began unravelling?

'You didn't even wait for my mother to die before you began fucking my dad.'

Prithvi slapped Maya hard and told her to watch her language.

'I hate you, you whore,' Maya spat, grabbing her school bag with one hand and Aryan with the other, and ran out of the house to the start of the road where the bus still had a good twenty minutes to arrive. Heer was shaking with the venom of the onslaught she had just faced.

For that long, heavy moment while he was standing between the two antagonistic sides, Prithvi had a sudden sinking sensation that perhaps what had irrevocably changed was that he was no longer on the side of his own children. Was this the helplessness of fathers through history, when the stepmother arrived? Was this how he alienated himself from his own children?

When he saw them clamber onto the bus which had arrived honking crazily, he'd turned to Heer, who was sitting on the sofa and sobbing softly. 'I'm sorry,' he said awkwardly. 'I'm apologising for her. She shouldn't have said what she did.'

She looked up at him, her eyes caught like a deer's in the

headlights. 'I don't blame her. It must be difficult for the children too.'

For a moment, he was glad she was so understanding and mature about it.

'She'll come around. She liked you before her mother went away. It's just that she can't see you in her mother's place.'

'Am I in her mother's place, Prithvi?'

She stood up and looked at him directly.

He had no reply.

Heer could never be Aisha. She didn't have the temperament that Aisha did, nor her fine features. Nor the ability to have him bewitched.

'Let's just face it, I'm an inconvenience.'

'Don't be ridiculous. You're helping me deal with this.'

'By sleeping with you.'

Her voice was flat. She needed no validation.

'The children will come round,' he said. They would. They had no option.

'Wouldn't it be better if they went to boarding school? Distance might make it easier. And I'm not very good at playing mom.'

Boarding school. He'd always dangled that threat over Aisha to keep her taking her medicines.

'I can't put the kids in boarding school.'

For a moment he felt like someone knee high had butted him in the soft parts of the abdomen. He had wanted to put the kids in boarding school when Aisha was alive, but that was only because he feared, occasionally, for their safety.

'Why not? They will be well taken care of, much better than I can manage. And it will be good for them. I grew up in a boarding school too, it really isn't as bad as most people think.'

He kept silent.

She paused. 'I don't think I can continue staying here if they're here. Maya resents me. There would be too much of conflict every day. The only other option is to put them into boarding school.'

He would have to negotiate this gently, he realised, he couldn't do without what she had brought back into his life again, the feel of a warm body moving responsively under his, a slick, grabbing wetness that pulled him in and left him drained.

'I can't do that,' he said, his voice dangerously soft.

'Of course you can,' she insisted, her eyes glinting, her voice also dipping, their conversation guarded, the thrust and parry of familiar argument not yet part of their lexicon. They had been together too little a while to have settled into patterns of argument, escalation and resolution. She knew they would be together for too little a time for it to reach that level of familiarity.

There seemed to be no appropriate response to give her. He could put the children into boarding school. It would be immensely practical a solution and made sense. But he didn't have the heart to keep them away from him. They were all he had now that Aisha was gone.

'Trust me, it will be good for the children. At least think about it?'

For a moment, his eyes flashed fire. She remembered the first night she had met him when the argument with Aisha had resulted in her splitting her lip open and backed away despite herself. Had Prithvi hit Aisha? Had she tripped and fallen? She'd opened the door of the bedroom to find Aisha already down on the ground.

It had been a decision he had been toying with for a while, this just expedited it, perhaps it was for the best.

He called up the few influential people he knew, and pleaded his case. Within a couple of hours, he had received confirmation that he could move the kids into the hostel of a reputed school in the area as full-time boarders that very weekend.

It was perhaps the most difficult decision he took. Part of

him felt he was abandoning his children and they would never be his again. And the painstakingly rational part of him argued that this was for the best. The kids would be happier at hostel than at home. 'Maya, Aryan, I need to speak with you.'

The kids shuffled to where their father sat on the sofa and stood in front of him. They dreaded what was to come, ready to flee at the slightest hint of him losing his temper. Though they knew he loved them, they feared his hands that moved when he got annoyed. His temper was mercurial. Only now, there was no mom to shield them from him.

Prithvi told the kids he would be moving them to a boarding school the next weekend, because he was planning to move out to Delhi. Now that Aisha wasn't around he was seriously contemplating escalating his career. He was applying for a position in a research institute there, and he was certain of an appointment. In fact, they had approached him a couple of times but he had been the one who had turned down the offer because he hadn't wanted to upset their mother by moving. Maya's face crumbled into a heap of unshed tears.

'It is for the best, your mother is no longer around to take care of both of you,' he said, the guilt making his tongue heavier than the scotch he'd just downed.

'I have too busy and hectic a schedule. In a couple of years, you will be out of school, Maya, and Aryan needs to get more independent. He needs to become a man.'

'And what about what we want, Dad?' Maya asked, her voice quivering. Prithvi got up heavily from his chair and poured himself another drink. The amber of the liquid reflected the golden glow of the light in the ceilings.

'Maya, what you want doesn't matter, I have to see what is practical for the two of you. And this is the only solution I can think of. I should have put you into boarding school a long while back, but your mother wouldn't let me. It would have been for your own good, you wouldn't have had to see your mother when she was in one of her states.'

'Even when she was in one of her states, Mom wanted us with her. That's why. She loved us.'

'I love you too, Maya. Both of you. I love you more than I love anything in the world.'

'Then why are you sending us away from you, Dad? Is it because of her?' spat Maya. Heer, who had been studiedly watching television in the lounge, pretending not to be listening in, turned around sharply at this. Prithvi noted the movement from the corner of his eye, but didn't respond.

'No, Heer had nothing to do with this, it is completely my decision.'

Heer turned her head back towards the television, her eyes on the screen but her entire body listening in.

Maya looked at her swiftly, an expression in her eyes that would need antidote if it could pierce skin. She was blinking her eyes hard, terrified to let a tear spill at the thought of their mother, now not even a spectral presence from beyond the grave.

'I would be at ease knowing that you are around there to look after Aryan, and I'll be a few hours away if ever there's an emergency. You'll love it at school as a boarder.'

Maya pulled Aryan to her side, holding him with a protective arm that effectively excluded Prithvi from its embrace.

'So, Dad, now that you don't want us anymore, we should just call ourselves orphans.' And she turned on her heel to go to her room, dragging a puzzled Aryan behind her.

2

Heer brought up the topic of the kothi a week later. It was a Saturday evening.

'So, what are you planning to do about the kothi?' she asked him, as he lay sprawled in post-coital bliss. His mood was still clouded with the sullen faces of the children as he'd dropped them off at the boarding school dormitory that morning.

'I am doing nothing about it. I can't. Aisha is not legally dead yet. And by right it will go to Aryan and Maya eventually. I need to start getting the papers in order. It takes seven years for a missing person to be declared legally dead, but since we do have a suicide note and a witness who claims he saw her jump, perhaps I could push for a death certificate to be issued.'

He didn't want to discuss the topic with her. She had no right to it. It was the children's, now that Aisha was dead. But he had to get cracking on getting the paperwork in place.

And it seemed strange that she took so much interest in the kothi, and that Aisha had disappeared just when she had arrived. A niggling part of his mind wondered if she had had anything to do with Aisha's suicide. Had she said something that had driven her to it? After all, Aisha had been on an even keel. She was far from suicidal when he last saw her. But one never knew.

He'd sat on it for a couple of weeks now. Whether through sloth or the mistaken apprehension that Aisha would be back, he did not know. But what he did know was that Heer had no legal right to Aisha's property. That was for the children. And as long as they were minors, he was in charge of it. He was the custodian of all the property she had to her name, the sprawling kothi with its many outhouses that came from her father, and the patches of land that came to her from her mother's side of the family. Her mother's share of her family property was bequeathed to her by a father who had carved out equal shares of his property to be shared between his three daughters.

Aisha had been in talks with a few hotel chains that wanted to take over the kothi and convert it into a luxury resort and spa. She kept vacillating between wanting to sell it and wanting to keep it. She had been reluctant to take a decision until she was able to think it through rationally. Prithvi had told her to sell it, the money would have been enough to keep them in luxury till the end of their days. But she did not consider his advice, convinced that he had some ulterior motive.

Now, his wife was dead. It hit him like a sledgehammer. He was free. Or was he?

There was Heer. Did he enjoy having her around? He didn't know yet. Was he in love with her? Definitely not. And, he was too old for infatuations. It was probably just the combination of convenient lust close at home that had created this awkward relationship of no emotion between either of them. It could disintegrate any moment. It was so fragile, existing as it did on the skeletal remains of a dead woman's despair.

If Aisha had agreed to sell the kothi, they could have lived off the interest comfortably for the rest of their lives. He could have stayed home and cared for her like she needed to be cared, full time. He could have nursed her back to complete sanity.

Heer propped herself up on one elbow so her breasts fell gently onto his chest, it was one of the things about her that drove him crazy. She never felt the need to spring back into fully clothed demureness after sex, something that Aisha was particular about.

'What if the doorbell rings, what if the house catches fire and we have to run out in a rush…' she would say.

With Heer it was always about the body. She had a beautiful body and was aware of it. She knew how to use it. There was no shame in her nakedness.

The conversation about the kothi was still not over. Heer was looking at him intently. 'Actually, it was my father's property, it should have been willed down to both of us equally.'

Prithvi felt a cold slither of disquiet curl around his chest and grip his heart. He looked at her, this woman, who lay next to him like a benediction and a curse rolled all into one.

'But then I'm illegitimate. My father left us nothing. You can help me get what is rightfully mine.'

There was a brief silence, one he did not know how to punctuate. She turned onto her back, crossing her legs, resting her hands on her belly, staring up at the ceiling, her breasts falling gently to either side of her body.

'But you won't, because you want it all for yourself.'

He kept quiet. To agree or disagree was irrelevant. It wasn't his to have her name added to the property. That had been her father's prerogative. Or Aisha's. Neither of them were around anymore to make that decision.

'Why did you stay back here, Heer? Why did you seduce me that night?'

'Because I wanted to.'

There was no explanation nor apology.

'Did you want to seduce me, or did you want to stay back?'

'Both, I guess.'

'Why would you want to seduce me? I was a married man, twice your age.'

'You're an attractive man, and I could see you wanted me. There was that expression in your eyes. And I really need a place to stay for a while. Honestly, this is convenient.'

It was admirable. Her frankness. As long as there was no emotionality involved. It was just convenient. He could deal with being convenient. For now.

She continued.

'I'm broke. I have no job. I have no home to go back to. There is a house, but it's mortgaged, I don't know how to repay the loans. You have to help me. Get me some money from the property, pay me my share and I'll leave.'

The extortion had begun. She would not leave easily. He should have guessed this was coming.

He turned to her, propping himself up on his arm, running his other hand along the length and breadth of her body in a conciliatory manner. His fingers found their way back into the moistness he had just vacated, slick with evidence of his pleasure. She pulled his fingers away sharply.

'Why would I want you to leave? You are convenient for me too.'

He had to delay these demands, until he could manage to either get rid of her, or sell the property without her knowing. He needed to plan it out carefully.

She closed her eyes, he drew her again to him, a satiation of the body that wouldn't quiet the loneliness in his chest. The moment passed. The day passed. She hadn't forgotten their discussion and had no intention of letting it go. About three days after that, she stood before him, her hands on her hips. 'You have no plans of selling the kothi, do you?'

Her tone sounded exactly like Aisha's before she sank into the quicksand of her uneven mind. He felt the unease begin in his chest, a fluttering discomfort that he had ignored whenever it had cropped up. He rubbed his chest slowly, waiting for it to subside.

She wasn't waiting for an answer.

'What about you sell it to those folks you said wanted to make a resort there, and give me half the money?'

'I have no intention of selling it, and even if I did, why would I give you half the money?'

She looked at him and smiled slowly.

'Because if you don't, I will file a rape case against you.'

His heart slammed into his chest and contracted with an agonising spasm that knocked the breath out of him. He should have seen this coming. He was a fool. A fool who had been misled by his penis.

'You can't do that. Whatever happened between us was completely consensual.'

'That's what you think. I can always file rape and breach of promise to marry. I can say your affair with me drove Aisha appa to suicide.'

He had to brazen it out.

'To begin with I have no intention of selling the kothi. I can't sell it anyway because Aisha is still missing, presumed dead. So that part of your plan won't work. We don't have a death certificate and even though I hold the power of attorney, everything stays in limbo until a death certificate is issued. Till then it remains unsold.'

She looked at him with barely concealed irritation. 'Find a solution. I want that money. Or I can make things very unpleasant for you.'

He looked back at her, his expression studiedly even.

'It was completely your choice to stay back here with me, I didn't hold you back or ask you to stay back. You yourself said that it was just convenient for you. It has been convenient for both of us, I admit.'

'Did you seriously think I was in it for love? Or that I had seriously come out here to connect with my long lost sister. I cared a damn about her and her mother. They never bothered about us all these years. I just came to get what was rightfully mine.'

He sighed. 'I'm sorry. But the property is not rightfully yours. You are not Aisha's father's legitimate child. She was. She was the inheritor.'

She stomped the floor like a child.

She looked at him straight in the eye while saying this, he looked straight back at her, unafraid that his eyes would reveal that she was speaking the truth. 'I know that. I remind you of her, don't I, even when we're making love?'

He took a deep breath.

'I don't make love to you, Heer. I fuck you.'

She shrugged her shoulders.

'Playing with semantics doesn't suit you. Love-making or fucking. Both are the same to me. And that's rich of you to say, given you got neither love-making nor fucking with your wife.'

She had noted the mattress on the bed, raised in the centre, sunken at both sides. It was the first thing she insisted they changed when she moved into the bedroom, the misshapen mattress. Prithvi and Aisha had never moved into separate beds, they had kept up the pretence of the marriage. Perhaps there were a few sharp shards of hope that they would eventually bridge the seemingly interminable gap between the two of them.

'Whatever the issues Aisha and I had, died when she did. Stop the digging. Let the dead stay dead, Heer. Can we stop the analysing of everything?'

'You are the one who over-analyses,' she laughed, 'Not me. I just state what I see. You see your dead wife in me. You don't want to give me my share of the proceeds of the sale.'

'I'm not selling it. It isn't mine to sell. It now belongs to the kids, I cannot sell anything off without asking the children. It is their mother's ancestral home after all. And they are too young to decide. Who knows, when they're older, they might resent me for selling off their inheritance.'

'So ask them the next time you meet them or call them. Anyway, it is falling to pieces and you might just not get anything for it by the time you actually decide to sell it. And I'm going nowhere without my share. You have a month. Consider this a warning.'

He turned away, ending the conversation, moving into his study and closing the door. He switched on a table lamp, noting the thin layer of dust that had settled on the side tables, the random disarray in which he had kept things when Aisha was around, to check if she was snooping through his stuff, now genuinely undisturbed.

At the back of his mind, he wondered how Heer knew that it was falling to pieces. He put his head down on his desk and felt wet, warm tears flow out of his eyes onto the polished surface of the wood. He hadn't mourned Aisha. Perhaps the tears he couldn't stop right now were for Aisha.

A day after that conversation, he drove out to meet the children. Maya flung herself at him and sobbed her heart out. She was looking fragile, her face pinched and pale, her wrists knobbly. 'I hate her, Dad,' she gasped, between huge gulping sobs that made the teachers walking past the garden bench where they were sitting look at them curiously. 'I hate that she's taken you away from us. I hate that because of her we had to go into boarding school. I hate that she broke our family up.'

'Heer didn't do that, Maya. It isn't fair to blame it on her.'

'I'm not, Pappa. I'm blaming Mom. She had no business committing suicide and leaving us behind.'

Prithvi took the children to their favourite restaurant for lunch, where Aryan ordered the mutton biryani, which was his standard order, and Maya toyed with the dal makhni and roti she had ordered, moving the dal around, without raising any morsels to her mouth. She was looking skeletal, Prithvi noted, her cheeks hollowed out to gauntness, pale, bruise-like blue shadows under her eyes, a haunted expression that made her look wraithlike.

'Why aren't you eating your food, Maya?'

Aryan piped up, 'Give it to me, she's on a diet, she's trying to become thin.'

Prithvi could see only skin and bone where his radiant daughter had once been. 'You've lost enough weight, you don't need to lose anymore, Maya.' His voice was soft and gentle. Maya looked up in alarm. His voice going all soft and hushed had always been the first sign of a blowout. Perhaps it had been the stress of handling their mother that had got to him then, she rationalised. It couldn't have been easy being married to her mother. He had been a good father. Most of the time, he had. Had he been a good husband? It had never occurred to her to ask.

'Dad,' she asked, 'Do you think Mom jumped or was pushed off?' It was a question she asked herself a million times a day and still had no answers to, and knew she was nowhere close to getting an answer that would give her the closure she longed for. The absence of a mother was like a shard of glass lodged into one's heart that stabbed the soul with every beat.

'Maya, I really don't know. I try not to think about it.'

'Could she have been pushed off… who would have pushed her off? Why would she jump off, Dad? Why would she leave us alone?'

Prithvi reached out and put his arm around his daughter's shoulders which were heaving with sobs that could not emerge. He could feel her shoulder bones beneath the thin cardigan she had on. She felt like a hatchling in his grasp. A sudden rough gesture, he felt, could snap her bones like chalk.

'Mom wasn't well, you know that, Maya. She'd tried to commit suicide before. And she had not been taking her medicines, you know that too. I tried to make sure she did, but she was convinced I was trying to drug her needlessly. She was taking some other stuff that did nothing for her. It just gave her a high. God knows where she got that from, and how it reached her. She had already gone far, far away from us before she actually jumped. She was already too far for us to bring her back.'

The three of them sat in silence. Aryan focused all his energies on making bubbling sounds with his straw and his strawberry milk shake. Prithvi looked at the wall, noting the peeling wall paper, the patchy, gilded cornices, the wooden shutters to the windows which were in dire need of a quick coat of polish. The restaurant, like him, was past its prime, and the little efforts to keep it presentable just accentuated how decrepit it really was.

'You did love Mom once upon a time, didn't you, Dad? What made you stop?'

Aryan had stopped making gurgling sounds with the straw and was now shovelling food into his mouth. He stopped, astounded, when he saw his father fight to find the words to reply.

Prithvi blinked rapidly. His eyes were moist. Not one tear spilled though. He took the napkin and turned his head away to sneeze. Or pretend to sneeze.

Aryan craned his neck to look at Prithvi.

'Pappa, are you crying? Maya, look Pappa is crying.'

Maya, who had been sitting next to Prithvi, turned to look at her father's face.

Prithvi shook his head and looked away, blinking furiously. 'Don't be ridiculous, something's gone into my eye.'

'Don't be silly, Aryan, you know Pappa never cries,' Maya continued, pushing her luck. 'You haven't answered my question, Dad. What made you stop loving Mom?'

'I don't think I ever stopped loving your mother. I think she stopped loving me.'

Maya was quiet, she looked down at her plate for a long moment while the answer played itself out in her mind.

'I think we all stopped loving each other.'

Aryan who had been peering at a space behind them started up and jumped to his feet. 'Mom,' he yelled, dashing out towards a figure getting into an SUV with dark tinted windows parked just outside the restaurant. The vehicle zoomed off, scattering unwary pedestrians in its wake. He ran out of the restaurant before Prithvi could restrain him. 'Mom, Mom…' His voice trailed off, as his face crumpled into sobs that heaved his scrawny chest soundlessly.

The SUV had disappeared down the snaking road. They would never be able to follow had they tried.

Maya ran to him and brought him back to the table. Prithvi realised that Maya had been compelled to grow up overnight; she was almost maternal in the way she dealt with Aryan. 'Don't be silly, Aryan, Mom's dead. If Mom was alive and well, why would she not come back to us? Why would she have left us?'

Aryan's face was determined, his lower lip pouting out in the stubborn way it did when he was being pigheaded. 'But it was Mom. I saw her. She was sitting there, behind the pillar, she was watching us. And when I smiled at her she got up and went away before I could call out to her.'

Prithvi drew his chair close to Aryan's and hugged him in the awkward way fathers do, when their boys grow up into almost adolescents, and boundaries subtly get rearranged.

His voice lowered itself to gentleness. 'Son, your mother is dead. Someone saw her jumping off the bridge into the river, the river was in spate, there is no way she could have survived the jump, she didn't know how to swim, you know that. You must have imagined her.'

'I didn't. She's looking happy.'

'Perhaps it was her, Aryan,' Maya decided to humour him.

'Maybe she's watching over us from wherever she is. And maybe she is happy now.'

'I wasn't imagining it, she wasn't a ghost, okay,' Aryan stormed. 'It was her. She was sitting there behind the pillar. She was looking at us, her face was wrapped in a scarf and she had dark glasses on. And when I looked up at her, she got up and ran out quickly. Let's find her.'

'How can we find her, Aryan? Don't be silly. Your mother is dead. You probably saw someone who looks similar.'

Aryan stood up and walked to the chair where the mystery woman had been sitting, unnoticed by them. He picked up something that had been left on the table—a crumpled piece of paper, with something scribbled on it. He opened it, smoothed it out. It was a bill. 'See, it is for a chocolate milk shake. Mom always had chocolate milk shakes whenever we came here. Now do you believe me? It was her. I know it, I saw her…' His voice rose in decibels.

The ashtray at the table had a cigarette stubbed out hastily in it, in the fierce manner Aisha would stub out her cigarettes when they refused to calm her down. The tip was smeared with the remnants of a bright pink lipstick. It was a shade Aisha had preferred back in the day when she used lipstick regularly. It couldn't be her, could it? Prithvi shook his head. She was dead. Or was she? What if Aryan had not imagined it, what if she had faked her death, for whatever reason?

Had it really been her, he wondered now, the one the shepherd said he saw jumping off the bridge. The wallet that had been found devoid of all money and cards, with just the suicide note tucked into it, was a plain black one which was probably stocked at a thousand leather goods stores targeting tourists in the hill stations around here.

It had been bought, he remembered vaguely, at the bustling Tibetan market just at the end of the mall road, right here, on the last trip they had made as a family. Nondescript, functional and self-effacing, the wallet embodied all that Aisha had become over the years. There was nothing in the wallet except her driving licence and her blood donor card. And of course the suicide note. Perhaps it was planted in the wallet. Why had everything been removed from the wallet, except the identification cards and the suicide note? Where were the bank cards?

'It was a white Toyota Fortuner,' Aryan informed him, his obsession with SUVs coming in handy.

Aryan sighed, his face crumpling into an expression of unbearable sadness that made Prithvi's heart shatter into jagged pieces.

'And, Pappa, you know what really hurt the most? Mom didn't even wave goodbye to me.'

3

By the time Prithvi dropped the children back to their respective dorms, and started his journey home, it was dark. The road was unlit, treacherous, the beeping of the horns from oncoming traffic punctuating his thoughts. He had stopped at the spot from where Aisha had jumped, and looked down from the repaired bridge, into the darkness for some time. He could hear the sound of the water gushing far below.

The flickering light of the television lit the den, as he turned the key in the lock and stepped into the dim light of the passageway.

'Where have you been all day?' she asked, without turning her head to look at him. Barely had he stepped into the house. She was studiedly indifferent to his comings and goings. Initially it had been a relief from Aisha demanding a minute-by-minute account of his whereabouts during her manic phases, calling him at work with her words tumbling into incoherence, her thoughts colliding into each other, before she could articulate them.

'I told you I was going to see the kids.'

He tossed the car keys into the key basket on the side table in the lobby, took his shoes off carefully and put them in the shoe cabinet, careful not to muck up the floor, and walked towards where she was sitting, her face, with all its beautiful, razor-sharp planes, now a mask of thunder, her eyes little chips of smudged ice.

'How are they?'

'They're fine,' he sighed, and began climbing the stairs to go to his bedroom. It would be rather ambitious of him to expect her to have any affection for his children. She didn't have any for him or her sister to begin with. Sending the kids off to the boarding school was perhaps the best decision he had taken. As he felt the warm wood of the banister beneath his hand curve as he turned the landing, he wondered if he should have done that earlier, if sending the children away would have allowed him to take better care of Aisha.

He sighed deeply and turned towards the stairs to go up to the bedroom. 'I'm going to bed.'

'Good night,' she said, with no emotion in her voice. He wondered if she would ever move out. Or if she would follow through on her threats, if he didn't pay her. He had no doubt that she would. Hadn't he always told Aisha to never open the door to a stranger? He wished she had paid heed to him. He stopped, turned around and went back down.

'The strangest thing happened today,' he said, sitting in the sofa opposite her. There was a tenuous truce between the two of them that he didn't want to break until he had figured out how to extricate himself from this mess he had gotten into with minimum collateral damage.

'What?' she asked, her eyes not moving from the screen.

'I was with the kids at Ambassador, that's a restaurant in the main mall road. We had almost finished our lunch when Aryan suddenly got up and ran to the entrance saying he'd seen Aisha sitting at the same restaurant, watching us. And he insisted she had gotten into a car which then just sped away at top speed.'

She started and turned to him, her expression inscrutable, even wary. 'Interesting. What made him think it could be Aisha?'

'Probably someone who looked similar,' he replied, unwittingly editing the information about the chocolate milk shake, the tip of the straw tinged with the pink lipstick. Velvet Rose, the name of the shade came to him unbidden, residual among memories of shopping in stores for that one particular shade, and the resultant dismay when she couldn't find it. Could it have been Aisha, he had been mulling over it all the way home. Why would she pretend to have committed suicide and then stay so close to where they lived, when most people in the market of the small town would easily recognise her? Aryan must have been imagining things, his mother in the form of another casual visitor. That was the only explanation he could come up with.

She turned back to the television. On the movies channel, a rerun of a Harry Potter movie had Voldemort confronting Harry over the Triwizard cup having summarily dispatched Cedric Diggory to the land of the dead. Her eyes barely flickered as she watched the screen. He got up again to go.

'Did you see her?' she asked, 'Do you think it could be Aisha?'

He looked at her face, wondering if it was insecurity about a possibility of his wife coming back into his life that made her ask this.

'Truthfully, I don't know. And I hope not.'

Her expression shuttered down into neutrality. 'I've been thinking I should be getting back to Delhi,' she said.

'It is your call,' said Prithvi, his voice heavy and tired. 'It was your call to stay, and now yours to leave. You know I can't stop you.'

'Well then, I think I will leave in a few days.'

'I'm not stopping you,' he replied, realising that all the time he had been hunting for Aisha in her, and found nothing but the warmth of another body and the chill of a soul he couldn't touch. She looked up at him from her spot on the sofa, and for a moment, a brief moment, it was Aisha in front of him, her face set in hard angry lines, her eyes blank holes of nothingness, his betrayal real, tangible and humiliating.

'Pay me my money.'

'I don't owe you any money.'

She stood up with a sudden gesture and slapped him hard, her expression ugly, her breathing ragged and hard.

'You're done with me now, is it? You think you can dispose of me so easily, do you?'

He held her hands, gently, knowing that if he used force, he could bruise her. Her skin was so pale, any imprint showed almost immediately. She calmed down, panting heavily, and disengaged her hands from his, with a disgusted expression.

Her hair had come unravelled, and was hanging all over her face, like an impenetrable wall. It gave her a maniacal look that scared him. For a moment, a terrifying moment, he had thought it was Aisha in front of him, Aisha in the days when she had just begun her descent into the personal hell of her mind, when her temper was beginning to burst out of her feeble attempts to control it, and would overpower her, turning her into a violent, terrifying force that nothing except physical restraint could calm down. And then there was the medication to keep her stable. Regular medication that she needed to take but occasionally flushed down the commode because she felt she didn't need it.

'I'm sorry, I didn't mean to hit you, all I need is money,' she said in a strange, flat voice. He left her hands and put his arms around her, smelling in the fragrance of her.

'I can give you some money to help you. Not much, but it should be enough to keep you going for a couple of months till you find a job.'

'Fuck-off money,' she said drily.

'Call it whatever you like.'

'I'm not going off with a handful of guilt money. I'm going to take what is due to me.'

'That's my offer. Take it or leave it.'

She walked off. After their argument, she had moved into the children's bedroom. How could he get her out of the house, he wondered.

He went into the kitchen, and checked the fridge. There was no dinner. He'd expected it.

Aisha would have had dinner ready, he told himself. Unless, of course, she was in one of her phases, when she would have chased him around the house with the meat cleaver.

Heer settled herself back on the sofa and made no move to rustle up anything he could eat. He wasn't very hungry but the need to do something made him move down to the kitchen to forage the contents of the refrigerator for something, anything, he could eat.

It was October. It would begin to get a bit chilly in the nights, by the end of the month. Right now the leaves were turning into a blaze of red, brown and gold, carpeting the hillsides like so many unanswered prayers, to be trampled upon by mortality.

He found himself some bread, unyielding from staleness and a slice of cheese, and heated both in the microwave so the cheese melted over the bread, softening it into edibility, and chomped through it. The kitchen sink had dirty utensils which meant a meal had been cooked. He pressed the lever to lift the lid of the dustbin from a vague sense of curiosity and found an entire meal ruthlessly discarded in there.

He went into the bedroom, changed into his night clothes, and pulled the covers down, as he got into bed. It had been a tiring day, and then there was Aryan's strange insistence that he had seen Aisha in the café. It had completely unnerved him.

A little while later, he felt her walking into the children's bedroom, her footsteps light as always and barely audible. The door to the connected bathroom opened, there was the soft sound of a stream of urine hitting water followed by the flush. The sound of teeth being brushed, the splashing of water on a face, the odd silence of nothing discernible happening.

Aisha never entered the bedroom when he was awake, she would spend her time scrubbing the various nooks and corners of the house, rearranging the containers in the kitchen, doing something, anything, that would keep her from having to enter the bedroom and confront the possibility that he might be awake and that he might want to have sex. And she would slip away from the bed before he awoke in the mornings. It had been that way for years. Some nights when he ached for the feel of skin, for the warmth of an embrace, he wondered if he should reach out across the humiliating divide of the mattress between the two of them, and touch her. Because he could not touch her with love anymore, he touched her with hate and anger and resentment until touch was forced upon the both of them.

Aisha had gone away. She would never come back, no matter how much he yearned for her.

In the distance, the Himalayan range flared into fluorescence, as its snowy peaks reflected the moonlight back at the velvet sky, split into half by the shimmering strip of the Milky Way.

Sometime, before daybreak, he opened his eyes to see the early light filtering in through the room. He reached out an arm for Heer and found the bed empty. It came back to him. It was six in the morning. He went downstairs after showering, and getting ready for work. Perhaps she would leave today. Perhaps he could convince her to leave.

The cereal box lay unappealingly on the shelf above the kitchen counter. He didn't ask her what was for breakfast. He poured himself a bowl of cereal and milk, ate it without speaking a word, before slamming the door shut behind him.

And with that it was over. Heer dialled a number and waited for it to be answered. She spoke hurriedly into the receiver when it was, and put it down with a soft sigh of what could be relief. It was time to have a bath and get ready for the day ahead. It would be a long day, she knew.

She liked the vastness of the house and the sound of their voices echoing in the emptiness when they quarrelled. It felt like whatever the issue was, it was being repeated by spectral beings who were taking sides. She did not miss the kids and their voices floating around, constantly bickering with each other. It was strange how she had craved for this absolute solitude, and now that she had got it, she was craving for the insanity of a chaotic city again, the crowded roads, the constant honking of the traffic outside her window, the shouts of the street vendors piercing the air, the air that filled her lungs with acridity and made her eyes water. As she waited for the sputtering old geyser to heat the water for a bath, she opened the bathroom cabinet to find a new tube of toothpaste.

The bathroom cabinets were filled with stuff, arranged in a precise order—dental care products, floss, toothpaste tubes still in their cartons, unused, tongue cleaners, bottles of mouth wash. She pulled out a tube of toothpaste. Then she stopped short, and pulled the shelf where she had felt a give. Behind the first layer of the cabinet, there was a second layer, almost invisible on the outside, a hidden shelf. On it were bottles of pills with strange names. She looked at them and turned them around in her hands, wondering what they were, taking them out to the bedroom side table, resolving to Google the brand names and the ingredients. Who had been taking these pills, she wondered. They had been hidden away carefully. She had never seen Prithvi taking anything, but then what he did in the bathroom, she didn't know. And Prithvi wasn't gentle enough to move all the stacks of bottles and cartons without disturbing the careful alignment. Aisha. Aisha had said she was on medication. What was the medication for, she wondered.

Heer rearranged the shelves, realising that Aisha had stocked enough medication to last her for months. Or perhaps, it was medication meant to have been consumed over months, and had been kept there, untouched. When Aisha disappeared, Heer had found the pantry stocked with provisions enough for a couple of months. The shelves had packets of ready-to-eat noodles and pasta enough to feed a small army, and she had fed the kids with little else for the first couple of days, reluctant to actually do any real cooking.

Heer had signed up for a deal when she came here, that of a task to be done and then leave, having handed over what was required from her. But now that Aisha was dead, all deals were off. She sighed. She might as well make the best of the situation she had found herself in. A little extra money extorted from this man would only help. And surely she wouldn't be grudged that, given she'd provided services beyond the call of duty.

She had a quick bath, washed her hair, and padded out in her dressing gown and fluffy slippers to the study, the bottles of medication in her hand.

It took some time for the computer to start up. She had cracked Prithvi's password in the first hour she sat at the computer. It pained her that it was still Aisha's birth date and that he hadn't bothered to change it yet, after all these months. She typed in the names. Long release capsules. Used to treat anxiety disorders, bipolar disorders. Available only on prescription.

She logged in through force of habit into Prithvi's personal email which he never bothered to sign out from. There was nothing new there. Nothing except the occasional spam and work mails. And an email from Aisha. It stopped her in her tracks as she scrolled down the inbox rapidly, her heart thudding against her chest. She clicked on it. It was an empty mail. Sent a week ago. Opened. Who was using Aisha's email account and from where?

Just then, the doorbell rang. She swiftly switched off the

computer and rushed to the door, throwing it open without thinking about using the security phone in the passage area to check who could be at the door. A man stood outside, amazingly handsome, with copper-flecked hair, tawny brown eyes, shoulders so wide they wouldn't almost fit through the door, and hips so slim that his low-slung jeans were almost falling off them. He leaned against the door jamb and smiled slowly at Heer, a smile that was a molten assault of honey and chocolate and sugar bombs mixed together.

Heer dropped the bottle of pills she was still carrying in her hand to the floor, where it shattered noisily, sending the long release capsules skittering around the floor like confused escapees from a prison not of their own making. She didn't notice the glass crunching under her slippers as she took a hesitant step forward and then threw herself into his arms. 'What took you so long?'

He kissed her hard and pulled away, 'There were complications. It's been done now. It is time to go.'

4

When Prithvi returned home that night, the house looked off kilter in a strange way he couldn't quite pinpoint. There was a dim light burning within, while the rest of the house was dark. The huge glass panes of the windows stared at him questioningly as he stared back, their questions going unanswered. Then it struck him, the main door was wide open. Heer really needed to be careful. There were wild animals in these parts. Anything could get in if the door was left open.

He had also received a call from school telling him that they needed him to visit the next day, there had been an incident with Aryan. What incident, they would not specify and were infuriatingly mysterious about.

Damn. He had to visit the school the next day. It wasn't something he was looking forward to. Winter break was coming up, and the kids would be home soon. He wasn't looking forward to that either. His eyes were burning from the incessant time spent before the screen analysing stacks of figures and plotting graphs, basic level work he would rather do himself than entrust to someone who wasn't competent. The tiredness from the day had made him drive rashly through the unlit curving mountain roads on the way home. All he wanted was a good, hot meal and the warmth of a body to sink into before going off to sleep.

The house was empty, he realised. A few seconds later, he realised there was no response to his opening the door with his key and slamming the door shut. The human presence that gives a space its life was missing. The air within was still, predatory.

'Heer,' he called, low at first, expecting her to call back from the bedroom where she might have drifted off to sleep, or from the couch in the den, where she would be watching television. The cushions on the couch were scattered down on the floor and the couch was empty. The house had the absolute stillness of a space waiting for a human to enter and move the air molecules with breath, movement, dead skin cells scattering like a microscopic shower.

He put his laptop down on the breakfast counter, where Aisha had always hated it being, and where he would perversely put it down to get a rise, a reaction out of her, and called out again. 'Hello? I'm home.' His voice rose a few decibels. Silence greeted him in return. The lights were off throughout the house except for the landing on the stairs. He went through the rooms, looking for her. All the rooms were empty, the yawning kind of emptiness that denotes a leave-taking rather than a temporary parting. He opened the wardrobe in the bedroom to which Heer had moved her clothes, after burning up all of Aisha's that had been left behind after the giving away, in an insane moment when they were burning the leaves in the garden a few months ago. It was empty.

The few clothes she had carefully stacked in the shelves were gone, the dressing table was cleared of all her lotions and potions and makeup that she didn't need, and looked much better without.

Heer had gone, she had warned him she would go, and now, she was gone. He had wanted her to go, but didn't actually expect her to. A curious sense of relief washed over him.

'Aisha,' he groaned out to a cold, unhearing house, arranged unsympathetically in the disarray of neglect, sinking down, unwittingly to his knees on the hard, unwelcoming ground. 'Aisha,' he called over and over again, until he realised he would never get an answer, no matter how much he called her. His voice echoed back at him from the damp, cold, stone walls that he had encased their lives in.

An hour later, he was at the police station up in town filing a missing person complaint for Heer. He furnished all the details about her that he knew, realising how little he knew about her. He didn't even have her photograph. He had clicked none from his phone. Nothing, except her name and that she was Aisha's half sister. He had no previous address nor phone numbers for her, nor the contact details of anyone who might have been part of her life, before she came into his. It had never bothered him earlier, this blank slate with which he had accepted her. It did now.

He was doing this, he told himself, just to be on the safe side. In case she decided to follow through on her threat to frame him in a false case.

The police inspector who took down the complaint was the same who had informed him about his wife's wallet being found. SD Pant was a small, round-eyed man who seemed to be bursting out of his uniform, with both curiosity and avoirdupois, and what seemed to be a carefully controlled streak of irritation, which promised to degenerate into rage at the slightest provocation.

'So, this lady, your wife's half sister, was now staying at your house after your wife died.'

He was noting, no doubt, and too polite to comment on it, the fact that Prithvi was in a state of complete disarray, a stark contrast from the calmness with which he had identified his wife's wallet, and completed all the formalities when they had last met.

'She was staying with you from before your wife went missing, you say?' he repeated.

Prithvi explained patiently how his wife and her half sister had had no contact for years and how Heer had landed up at their doorstep a couple of days before Aisha went missing.

'You didn't file a missing complaint for your wife,' the inspector stated baldly.

Prithvi explained that it had been a time when great calamity had struck the area and that his wife had called home to say she was safe and would be coming back when she could, but then had dropped off the radar and before he could have even filed a complaint, they had found her wallet with the suicide note in it. 'She had been calling home, she was safe she said, and the roads had been hit by landslides. There was no sense in trying to go find her in that chaos.'

'Even then,' replied the smug man, complacent in the authority vested in his uniform, 'I found it rather strange that you were not concerned about the whereabouts of your missing wife for over a week, but yet the moment this lady, her sister, goes missing, you rush to file a complaint.'

Prithvi shrugged, he was not about to get into a discussion with a man he barely knew about the whys and the wherefores of what was the rationale behind his decisions. He had long locked whatever little guilt he had suffered over Aisha's death, into a remote corner of his mind, and it lay there, silent, unobtrusive in his daily functioning.

'Are her clothes and things still at home? Were there signs of forced entry, a struggle?'

'No,' Prithvi admitted. 'All her clothes and things are gone and there is no sign of forced entry. I did find the door wide open though when I reached home, which was highly unusual.'

The tiny man looked pensive. He tapped at the faded surface of the sunmica-topped table which was slightly sagging beneath piles of files, stacked precariously against the wall.

'If her things are gone along with her, it could be that she has left of her own volition. But if you say there seems to be something missing, this might be worth looking into.'

'Actually, I didn't check if anything was missing.'

In a sudden swift move that Prithvi would have never thought him capable of given his girth, the inspector rose from his chair, picked his jacket slung over the back of his chair and moved out, gesturing to a constable to accompany them. 'Let's go to your house and have a look, shall we?'

The drive to the house, with the police jeep following Prithvi's car, was quick.

The gate, still unrepaired after months of the tree crashing down on it, swung erratically with the wind that blew in brave gusts through the space that the huge tree had once occupied. The lights in the house were still on. A bulb in the kitchen flickered in quiet expectancy. The upstairs windows blazed with the fury of uncertain waiting.

SD Pant hopped out of his jeep and rushed in through the gate, followed obsequiously by the constable who held an umbrella open over his senior's head to keep him from the light drizzle that had started coming down. It would blow away soon enough, but the droplets as they felt now, were piercingly cold.

'Where are the children?' he asked. Catching Prithvi's puzzled gaze, he pointed at the pictures framed on the wall, kept on the side tables, the layer of dust on the photo frames telling their own story of neglect and abandonment, one that Prithvi had wilfully ignored.

'I put them in boarding school after their mother died. It was just more convenient.'

'Convenient?' repeated the inspector, rolling the word on his tongue for taste. 'Yes, it would have been convenient surely, but were the children happy with the arrangement?'

'They didn't have a choice,' Prithvi replied, as honestly as he could. 'I am at work all day, and I wasn't really sure if they would be cared for well.'

The inspector moved swiftly through the house, taking in the place. Prithvi saw his home, after months, through a stranger's eyes, and was suddenly embarrassed of the shabbiness that was evident now. Once upon a time, the house had sparkled so ferociously when the lights were switched on that it used to dazzle one's eyes. Now, there was a dull patina of dirt that covered whatever one laid one's eyes on.

'Is there a possibility that someone would try to kidnap her?'

'None that I know of,' Prithvi replied, honestly. He did not know much of her life before she came here, and hadn't been bothered to ask her about it. All he knew was that she lived in Delhi, and she shared a flat with a roommate. Of the roommate, she had mentioned nothing. He had asked nothing. As far as he was concerned, she came to him a tabula rasa.

SD Pant stopped at the porch, looked down on the ground, noted something in a little notepad he was carrying. He looked up at the unseeing CCTV camera fitted on the porch. 'Where is the footage from this?'

Prithvi sighed. 'I'd installed it when my wife was… unwell, just in case she did something to herself. When she died, I switched it off.' The inspector shrugged and went up into the bedroom. The bed was in complete disarray. The pillows were scattered on the ground. He raised an eyebrow at Prithvi, and continued without comment. He browsed through the cupboard where Heer's clothes had been kept.

'Was she sharing your bedroom?'

'Yes.'

'You were having a relationship with her?'

'Yes.'

'Is that why your wife committed suicide?'

'No, we got into a relationship after my wife committed suicide. And it was over.'

'If it was over, she would have left of her own volition. Why are you filing a missing person's complaint?'

'Because she didn't inform me she would be leaving.'

He didn't think she would leave so easily, without any money. She had been so insistent on the money. Would he really be rid of her that easily? He didn't think so. There had to be more to it. And he had to play safe.

'What about your wife's jewellery?'

'Nothing was kept at home, everything was in the locker in the bank in town. You see, we don't really socialise here, so there wasn't much opportunity for her to wear it. And she wasn't a woman who was very fond of jewellery. She barely bothered to wear earrings or bangles. At the max, she wore a couple of rings on her fingers and a thin chain around her neck.'

'Anything else you think could be missing?'

Prithvi shook his head to indicate a negative.

The inspector politely opened Prithvi's cupboard, looked into the morass of the unsorted piles of clothes and the few ironed-for-work shirts and trousers which were hung up, and closed it carefully.

'In any case, if you find something missing, do let us know. But, your wife's sister,' he paused meaningfully after he said that, 'is an adult. She seems to have gone of her own will, there are no signs of struggle, no breaking in and entering, her bag seems to have been packed quickly but thoroughly, she seems to have left nothing behind nor taken anything that didn't belong to her with her. I am confused, Mr Thakur. Is there something you are not telling us? Did you have a fight or was there something that was troubling her that could make her leave?'

Prithvi shook his head again, to indicate a negative.

'Have you checked in Delhi, where she lived?'

'She didn't have a home in Delhi, in the sense, she lived as a paying guest,' Prithvi replied.

'Where did she live in Delhi, have you called there?'

'I don't know where she lived, I didn't check.'

'Was she pregnant?'

'I don't think so,' Prithvi answered, his voice flat and matter of fact.

The inspector cast a cursory eye up and down on him and whistled. 'Badhaiyaan. Here we can't manage one wife, and you have a stepney before your first wife has even been declared legally dead.' He muttered something in the colloquial about wife's sisters being half wives in an aside to the junior who was standing a step behind him, poker faced, but who obediently tittered in response to his senior's wisecracks.

The inspector shrugged, his eyes looked over Prithvi in a gaze that was cool and appraising. This had once been a handsome man. His eyes looked tired and his face was haunted with what seemed like agony.

The inspector looked with interest at the door, and down at the porch where he shone a torch he was carrying for a better look at something that had caught his attention, and then at the path outside leading from the gate to the porch.

'Were you expecting any guests?'

'No.'

'Why did your wife's suicide not disturb you? Why are you so much more concerned about a missing woman who seems to have gone back to where she came from?'

The silence hung around undisturbed for a long moment that spiralled into infinite other moments.

'My wife was unwell, mentally. It was very…' Prithvi paused, waiting for the exact word that denoted the hopelessness and helplessness of being married to someone who was no longer the person one had fallen in love with' '… difficult.'

'Interesting that you didn't mention this when your wife's suicide note was found. Was she under treatment from a psychiatrist?'

Prithvi nodded in reply.

'Well then, do give me the details of the doctor she was consulting, I think I would like to have a word with him. Or her.'

Prithvi took a piece of paper from the notepad next to the phone, checked the number on his mobile and scribbled it down for the inspector. Dr Vishwanath Lal. A young Delhi-based psychiatrist, who did monthly visits on the last weekend of the month at a polyclinic in town. Prithvi had accompanied Aisha to her monthly sessions, they had done family therapy sessions. He'd begged her to stop dosing herself with the uppers she procured on the sly from a supplier in Delhi. She promised she would stop, but she didn't.

Prithvi had maintained her mood charts, noted when she was about to have an episode, whether medications needed to be tweaked, and been in touch with the psychiatrist regularly about any concerns. But she had missed her last session. Prithvi had been travelling for a conference, and she just hadn't shown up. When he had called to check, she had been dismissive about it.

It had been like struggling with a tantrum-throwing toddler to get her to take her medicines most times. What could he tell the inspector about his marriage that he would be able to understand? Would he be able to understand how scary it was to see his wife at the brink of terrifying insanity, and how difficult it was to bring her back, gently, forcefully, day by day, to a modicum of functionality, despite her believing that he was trying to control her.

The inspector then spoke, after a bit of wandering around the room, lifting things, examining pictures on the wall, almost like he was on a social visit rather than an official, investigative one.

'Did your wife's sister normally have visitors when you were not at home?'

'We are very isolated out here, and few people drive all the way. She had no immediate relatives. My only sister lives in Delhi and rarely visits us, and the neighbours have not really been very friendly since…' His voice trailed off.

He realised that he had had no visitors here ever since Aryan and Maya had left for boarding school. No friends dropped in after school, no neighbours down the lane came by with a freshly baked cake or a basket of vegetables pulled out from the patch behind their kitchens. In fact, their own kitchen garden had gone to seed, and was a riot of crabgrass and weeds.

The house had subtly converted itself into a sterile mausoleum where the two of them—Heer and Prithvi—played out their roles after sunset every day. He had no idea of what she would do with her day. As long as there was a meal on the table, his clothes laundered and ironed for the next morning and her body in bed with him in the night, her legs opened and unresisting, he hadn't tried to understand what she did with her day, stuck in this outpost. Aisha had the kids to keep her busy, and the demons in her head to keep her occupied when the kids did not. What had Heer had to fill up her day except the sterility of nothingness?

The inspector pointed at the floorboards near the porch, there were indistinct foot marks clearly visible in the layer of dust. Prithvi noticed that the porch was littered with dead leaves. Aisha would have gathered up and burnt them in the grate placed at the end of the yard before the feet could even crunch on them. Somewhere in the dark, a howl pierced the slowly drifting wind. A wild dog, a wolf, it could be anything here. It was a howl that was unearthly, like a disembodied spirit was roaming the ethers, seeking vengeance from those who had wronged it.

'Those footprints, the foot size doesn't match yours. Nor

mine. Nor I presume would your wife's sister be wearing such huge boots coming in from outside. The prints end at the door mat, where I think the feet were either wiped clean or the shoes were removed and kept to one side. But these are very big feet. At least a size eleven. You must be a size nine. What was her foot size?'

Prithvi felt an alarming thudding begin in his chest cavity, the boom echoing in his ears. He didn't know her foot size.

'She was a tall woman, five foot seven… eight… but I would put her shoe size at a nine at the max. Definitely not a size eleven,' he answered.

'Anyway,' said the inspector, turning away from the porch to his vehicle which was parked beyond the gate, 'I will put out a missing alert for your wife's sister and hopefully she will be found soon. If she isn't found, then perhaps we could start looking into whether it is abduction or a possible homicide. As of this moment though, I think she has gone willingly, wherever she has gone. Have you checked with people who know her?'

'I don't know any of them,' he admitted.

'Okay, I will be in touch if I hear anything.'

He saw the inspector out and then sat down heavily on the couch in the day room, after pouring himself a stiff peg of scotch on the rocks. Someone had come into the house today, and been welcomed in. Heer would have been able to see who it was from the safety grate, from the peephole, and had opened the door for that person to let him in. It would have been a man, Prithvi knew, the size of those shoe prints was a giveaway.

Who could it have been, he wondered? She had never mentioned her past, he had never asked her. After all what is the present but a constant escaping from the pursuing footsteps of a dogged past.

A thought struck him out of the blue, and he rushed to the bedroom. The safe was locked, he noted with a deep, relieved breath, but still he pressed the combination with trembling fingers. Something was amiss, and he had been silly not to realise it. The carefully filed papers of his appointment letters, degrees, certificates were all in place, as were his birth certificate and passport, and the children's papers, but everything else was missing. Everything, he realised, as he sank with a thud to the adjoining bed, related to Aisha. Aisha's certificates, passport, Aadhar card, the blue plastic folders with all the documents of Aisha's ancestral home and the little patches of land that had come down to her from her mother. These, with the folder containing the power of attorney giving him legal authority to deal on behalf of Aisha for all the property, were all gone. Had Heer taken these or had they gone missing earlier? Did Aisha have something to do with their disappearance? He didn't know. He had never checked, he had just assumed they would be there and that he would eventually, some day, go across, once Aisha's death was substantiated with a death certificate and conclude the half-begun negotiations that involved a resort chain taking over the property, and converting it into a luxury heritage spa destination.

And there was something else that was not quite right about the room, something he couldn't quite put his finger on. He went into the bathroom, splashed some water on his face and looked at himself in the mirror. It was then that he spotted it. The bed sheet was in complete disarray, the dark sheet had two distinct dried whitish patches which could only be semen stains.

He sat heavily on the messy bed, as he looked at the stains on them again. He had switched on all the lights in the bedroom. He then ripped the sheets off and dumped them into the laundry basket. Whoever had entered the house after he had left home, with the foot size larger than his, had had sex with Heer without using a condom. Something she had always insisted he use with her, after the first time. Someone had been welcomed into the home, someone Heer knew, someone she was comfortable with, someone she had taken into the bedroom she shared with Prithvi. It felt like a violation, a red curtain fell over his eyeballs; the emptiness of the house mocked him. He screamed out loud, a wild scream that echoed through the rooms, the lack of a corresponding human voice making him realise that he was now completely alone.

She had gone away, back to wherever it was she came from, back to whoever it was she had run away from when she had come here that afternoon, dripping wet from the incessant rain. And she had taken away with her, more than her clothes, her belongings and her presence. She had taken away his children, their papers and the property papers from the locker in the bedroom. She had figured out the combination, though he had always been careful not to open it in her presence. Or maybe someone had told her the combination to the safe. Who could that someone be? Why would Heer do this? What did she stand to gain, after a couple of months of being in a sexual relationship with him, except a fistful of papers she could do nothing gainful with? Or could she? He fretted, wondering how he was to trace, and how he needed to get those papers back, for Aryan and Maya. Or at the very least, go to Aisha's home town and get all property transactions halted until a fresh set of documents could be drawn up.

It was then that his phone pinged. A message from an unknown number.

'Prithvi,' it said, without preamble, with the authority of a discarded familiarity. 'It was good knowing you.' When he tried the number, he came up against the hard wall of an electronic voice that kept repeating, 'The number you are trying is currently not reachable.'

5

The night was marked with little sleep, and what he got of it was fitful and disturbed. Dreams haunted him, with Aisha knocking on the door, the rotting flesh falling off her body, demanding to see her children, demanding he embrace her, forcing her putrid lips on his.

The morning was dull. Its paleness momentarily unnerved him, and then he remembered, the missing Heer, and with her, the missing documents. And the message from the unknown number which was switched off now, and had been ever since he had received that message. What was she planning to do with those papers she had taken away? He had to stop her before she got things done. He had to go to Aisha's lawyer and get a stay on any transactions made with those papers. But then he didn't know whether she had taken those away or if it had been Aisha who had done so. Had Aisha planned this—taking her papers away, staging her suicide, planting Heer in the house to keep him distracted? Would she have been coherent enough to plan it all? It didn't make sense.

He threw together some clothes into a duffel bag and drove across to the school to meet the children. They needed to know he was going off for a few days to ensure that the property hadn't been disposed without his consent.

The school was, as always, a bustle of young, bridled energy. Basketball was being played out in the quad as he crossed it, making him long, palpably for the days of his youth.

Aryan's class teacher was a compact lady with neat hair. She wore a pair of trousers and a cardigan that spoke of thriftiness, with the evidence of a painstaking hand darning and holding it together, where it had begun to fray. What did humans have to do to hold themselves together when they begin to disintegrate, he wondered? What had led Aisha to completely unravel, despite the medication and the therapy and all the love? Mrs Paulouse came hurriedly into the little ante room, off the main reception where parents were called in for discussions with the staff.

'I would like to let you know that we think your son hasn't yet got over the shock of his mother's passing away and probably needs counselling. We had an incident yesterday…'

'An incident?'

She paused and looked at him directly.

'Well, he tried to run out of the main gate saying his mother had called him, and she was waiting for him there.'

Prithvi felt his heart stop beating for a fraction of a second. And when it began beating again, there was a skip in its beat that would be indiscernible to anyone's ears, except his own.

'Luckily the security staff apprehended him at the gate. You need to talk to him and explain that his mother is dead and that he cannot just go wandering off, or sneaking out to meet her. The school will not be responsible, if he does so again.'

Prithvi nodded, and said he would speak about it to Aryan.

'We need your permission and signature on these papers to allow the school counsellor to take sessions with him.'

He signed the papers put in front of him without reading them.

'Has there been any history of mental issues in the family?'

Prithvi breathed in deeply and looked at his hands gripping the edge of the chair he was seated in. His knuckles were taut, white. The lie came easily. 'No. Not that I know of. Why do you ask?'

She gave him a long, hard look, and then nodded unexpectedly, an apologetic smile springing to her lips. After all, the mother of his children had committed suicide; it had been an insensitive question to ask.

'It might not be true, but the school doctor suspects Maya has an eating disorder. It could be just a suspicion but we would like your consent to counsel her too.'

He nodded. There were some more papers to sign. His children had begun to unravel too. With Aisha's going, all his life was unravelling.

The kids came in. Maya looked taut and stretched, the hostility emanating off her in waves. Aryan looked shamefaced. The teacher smiled apologetically at both of them and excused herself, bustling off with the air of permanent busy-ness that seemed to hang over her even when she was standing still. If they found it odd that their father would visit them again barely a few days after he had taken them out to lunch on the weekend, they didn't mention it.

'Let's go for a walk,' he told them, reluctant to sit in the tiny, cosy parlour with its wood-panelled walls, and the people walking past the open door, looking in curiously.

The lawns were still green and would be frozen over with frost in a little over a month. The kids would be home for the winter break. Before that he needed to sort things out. The children were already wearing their school sweaters and woollen socks, he noted. He had needed to rustle up a long list of school supplies singlehandedly, when he'd decided to have them join as full-time boarders. Now he wondered if it was really enough for them to survive on their own, without Aisha to ensure that they wore their thermal inners, and layered up appropriately before stepping out. He would take the month off to spend time with them during winter break, he decided. They hadn't even had a chance to grieve for Aisha together, as a family. Perhaps, that was just what Aryan needed, closure.

'What is this about you trying to run out of the school gates, Aryan?' he asked gently, putting his arm around his son's shoulder, watching his face, such a gentle blend of features from both him and Aisha. This manling, with his hazel eyes and firm jaw.

'I told them Mom had told me to meet her at the gate. She called me. She told me to bring Maya with me, and meet her at eight sharp at the main gate, when the guards were changing duty, but Maya refused to come, and I got late and they caught me.'

'Aryan, you need to stop believing these pranks, surely someone was pulling a prank on you. Mom is dead.'

'No, no, I recognise Mom's voice, Dad,' Aryan kicked an errant pebble in their path, as they strolled through the campus. 'I told you I saw Mom that day. She's alive.'

'If she was alive, Aryan, why isn't she coming back to us?'

'To you, Dad. She doesn't want to come back to you.'

Prithvi swayed on his feet from the impact of those words. Luckily, a park bench was conveniently placed at the side of the path and he sat down hurriedly on it.

'Why would you think that, Aryan?' he asked.

'She told me. She told me she's doing this to get away from you because you were going to kill her. And that you would have killed us too.'

Maya gasped and grabbed Aryan by the shoulders. 'What are you saying, Aryan? Have you gone mad?'

'That's what Mom told me.' His voice was stubborn, intractable, confused.

The soft wind blowing through the deodars, crisp and clear, drilled its way into Prithvi's cranium with a sibilant hiss that was menacing.

'Do you believe her, even if you had spoken to her? Do you think I could do that? Why would I want to kill you, I love you. And Maya. And I loved your mother too.'

Aryan looked up at his father, with eyes that were no longer sure, but were brimming with confusion.

'That's what Mom told me, Dad. That you wanted us all gone so you could get married again, and have a new family.'

Prithvi held his head with his hands and groaned with a pain that was visceral.

'Aryan, stop imagining things, your mother is dead. She could not have called you. And even if she did say that, you know she was ill, and she kept imagining things. Do you think I would ever kill you both? You are my life.'

Maya spoke, 'Stop making things up, Aryan. Dad would never do that. You know it.'

'I'm not making things up. I spoke with her.'

'Anyway, we're beginning counselling for you and the next time I'm here, I'm going to take you to meet a doctor who will help you deal with this confusion about your mother.'

Aryan stayed silent and continued scuffing the cobblestones on the path with his shoe.

'Heer has gone,' he told them, watching their faces carefully for a reaction.

'Gone where?' Aryan asked. Maya didn't react, she continued looking at him with eyes which were narrow and suspicious. For a sudden moment, she looked exactly like her mother had.

'Gone away, I don't know where. Perhaps back to Delhi.'

There was no response to this from either of them. They were quiet, politely non-committal. Perhaps it didn't matter to them anymore, they barely knew her anyway. She was, at best, an intruder.

Maya was in a hurry. 'I have riding practice in ten minutes, Dad,' she said, her voice already distant, in the stables with the horses she had begun to love. 'Was there anything specific you wanted to speak with us about?'

'Just this, the school had called me for signatures on consent forms for Aryan's and your counselling sessions.'

'I don't need counselling sessions,' she retorted, her hackles rising instantly.

'Yes, you do, and you must attend them. And yes, I will be going to your mom's hometown to finalise some things about the kothi and the property, I will be back in a few days, hopefully,' he said. 'Make your plans for winter break. I thought we could go to Goa, perhaps.'

'I will drown,' Aryan said solemnly. 'I don't know how to swim.'

'I will teach you to swim,' Prithvi laughed, 'and no one will drown.'

'If mom knew how to swim, she wouldn't have drowned.'

For a moment, there was an aching silence between the three of them.

'Mom wanted to drown, you ninny,' Maya said with the cruel deliberation that adolescence brings. 'And now you better stop imagining mom everywhere, unless you want us to get an ojha to beat you black and blue and get the ghost fantasies out of your head.'

It was overwhelming, the realisation that his children had gone far away from him in the few weeks they had been here. He blinked back the sudden tears that pricked the back of his eyes, demanding their right to be shed. He felt the brokenness seep out of him, and cloak him with its stifling pallor.

He had lost some of his presence, he even looked diminished. When Maya looked at him with her girl-woman eyes, he sensed a scathing appraisal of the figure he presented. The hair at his temples had gone grey and his cheeks looked hollow. He'd aged in the few months since their mother had died. He was no longer a man in his prime, he was a man who looked and sounded defeated.

'You aren't looking well, Pappa,' she said, her voice concerned. 'Are you alright?'

No, he thought to himself, he wasn't, but he couldn't tell the children that.

'I'm fine,' he said, unwilling to confess that he had a sinking feeling that this was the beginning of the end of life as he knew it. 'There's nothing wrong with me.'

'Can we come back home?' Aryan asked. 'I can't watch TV here.'

'Not now. But later perhaps you could go stay with Ritu bua. She would love to have you stay with her now that your mother is not around, and she would take better care of you too. Let me sort things out so I can move to Delhi too, and find a home next to Ritu bua's place,' Prithvi promised, reaching out gently and hugging his son, a rare display of affection, noting how the child's shoulders had become scrawny and birdlike.

The morning had morphed into the lunch hour, the sun was as high in the sky as it could get.

'Dad, I've got to go, or Singh sir will be annoyed. I missed riding class last week too because of drama practice.' Maya, as she had told him, had emerged as a budding equestrian performer, and had discovered a new-found love for horses that made her want to spend all her spare time around the horses in the school stables.

'You go on ahead,' Prithvi waved her off. 'Aryan and I will sit and chat some more.'

Maya started to walk, then stopped abruptly.

'Will you take her back if she returns?'

Prithvi sighed. 'No,' he replied, realising this was not the answer his daughter expected. She sighed impatiently, a sharp exhalation of irritation.

'Not, Heer, Dad, I'm talking about Mom. Would you take her back if she returns?'

Prithvi looked at her with eyes that were suddenly moist. She, too, hadn't accepted her mother was dead. Within the cynical teen carapace was the little girl still hoping that her mother would show up some day.

'You know I would. There's nothing, nothing, I want more than for her to come back. But she's dead, Maya. We have to accept it.'

'You accept it, Dad. It makes it easier for you to sleep around.'

She lobbed the words at him like a grenade, with its pin removed, and ran off in the direction of the stables. The distant, muted clip-clop of hooves had begun echoing down the cobblestone pathways as the riders led the horses out to the small ground at a lower level, where they would be allowed to pick up a little pace.

Aryan sat on the bench next to his father, his shoulders suddenly giving beneath the weight of his father's grief.

'Why did Heer go away?' Aryan asked suddenly. 'I thought she wanted us to go away so she could be alone with you? Isn't that why she sent us away?'

'It wasn't like that,' Prithvi replied. 'I thought it was for the best. You would be cared for well at school. I couldn't expect her to cook and take care of you both.'

'She was very mean to us when you were not around. You chose Heer over us, Dad.' Aryan's voice was soft, and there was a soft undercurrent of wisdom to it. It wasn't any wonder that he sounded bitter, his eyes bright with all the tears he wouldn't allow himself to shed. Boys didn't cry, that was what his father had taught him, even though his mother had been adamant about insisting that he should cry when he felt like it, and laugh when he felt like it.

They sat in companionable silence for a while, until a passing shower threw them back indoors. Prithvi looked at his watch, it was almost lunch time.

'Your mother is dead, Aryan,' Prithvi said as softly as he could. 'And the sooner you accept that the better.'

There was an awkward silence between father and son that only birdsong and voices in the distance pierced.

'Okay, Dad,' he replied. His voice was flat. 'I wasn't imagining Mom though…'

The lunch bell rang. Streams of children poured out of the main school building and rushed towards the huge dining hall which was housed in another building, just off the main grounds. Excited voices, squeals and the sounds of fights breaking out in the quad, filled the air. Aryan spotted some friends and was up in a flash. 'I'm going, Dad, see you later.'

A curious sense of being bereft grabbed hold of Prithvi, as Aryan moved away from him, getting swallowed by the swelling crowd of heads moving like a tide into the dining hall. Then for the briefest second, Aryan stopped and looked down as though contemplating something. He turned around and looked straight into Prithvi's eyes, calling over the heads bobbing past, 'Dad, Mom is not dead. I lied that she called. I met her that very evening after I saw her at Majestic. She was standing at the side gate down the steps behind my dorm. The gate was locked. She told me to come to the main gate in the evening with Maya, and she would get us out but when I went she wasn't there, and I waited…' And then he ran off before Prithvi could stop him.

He wondered if he had heard right, whether Aryan had seen his mother in the flesh or whether he had been imagining it all over, like that afternoon in the restaurant. It was perhaps a dream, which had his mother visiting him and running her spectral hand over his little-boy hair, with the stubborn cowlick that defied combing. Prithvi sat there until the sun moved out of joint and the shade of the school building draped itself around him, carefully, letting the chill of the early afternoon prick itself into where his skin lay open and vulnerable.

He got up and walked to the gates feeling hollowed out, and physically sick. He sat on his haunches by the side of the sloping road leading to where he had parked his car, and threw up the little cornflakes and milk he'd ingested in the morning, before stepping out. The security guard from the gate came rushing up to him, and helped him back to his feet. Another man came up with a bottle of water, helping him to clean himself up. For a moment, he was overwhelmed with gratitude for the gentle helpfulness of strangers in a world where everyone was now a stranger. His hands on the wheel, when he got into the car, were still trembling.

He drove back into town, and stopped at the restaurant, where he had taken the kids for a meal, the last time he had visited them. He had questions to ask. It was an old-style restaurant which had been in existence from the time the hill station was a favourite haunt of the Britishers, seeking an escape from the oppressive heat of Delhi. The décor and the menu had remained pretty much the same over the years, with the wood-panelled walls, the old stained-wood furniture, the original fine-grained leather of the banquettes, now replaced by faux leather in an appallingly bright red.

It was managed by the third generation of owners now. They had diversified into other businesses, including construction and organic farming. The restaurant was still operational as one of their businesses, but didn't get the amount of attention it deserved. The owners barely sat at the counter these days, and the old staff ran the restaurant with the sense of ownership that new recruits rarely had with their place of employment. A familiar face welcomed him; this was a waiter who had been around for almost as many years as they had lived in the mountains and had been visiting the hill station before things deteriorated between him and Aisha.

'Kaisey ho, saabji'? the wizened waiter greeted him, the lines crinkling beneath his eyes and fanning out from its corners down his cheeks as he smiled, a smile of recognition. He steered Prithvi him towards a table he knew they always preferred, to the corner of the restaurant, overlooking the lake spread out across the mall road. 'Will you be dining alone today?' he asked gently. Prithvi replied in the affirmative. *'Aaj bachchey nahi aaye*?'

Prithvi replied politely that they were at school, as full boarders now.

The man shook his head gently. 'Yes, I know. I saw them the last time you were here. You had lunch with them. What surprised me is that your wife sat at another table, the one right at the back. And then she left on her own.'

Prithvi's heart skipped a beat. 'You must be mistaken,' he replied, his voice infused with an iciness that came from the dagger which had pierced his heart. 'My wife is dead. She jumped into the river some days after the floods. The police found a suicide note on the bridge, with her wallet and her personal belongings.'

The weather-beaten and lined face of the waiter crumpled into confusion. 'I'm so sorry to hear that. But I was pretty sure it was her.' He paused, thought for a long moment and shook his head. 'No. It was her. She ordered her usual cold coffee, and asked me for an ashtray. I know you didn't like her smoking. I remember you had had an argument about it once, right here at this table. You strictly instructed me not to get her an ashtray and she'd tipped her ash into an empty glass, blowing smoke in your face. I told her it was strictly no smoking in public now, and she'd replied she would stub it out in a couple of puffs.'

'Did you see her again?' Prithvi asked.

'No, Saabji, that was the only time I saw her, and I was surprised that she sat apart from you and went off on her own. And there was that gentleman in the vehicle outside, waiting for her. I see him around sometimes, but that was the only time I saw her with him.'

'Do you remember anything else, any details about the car, about the person inside, about what time she arrived? It might help me. You see, my son also insisted that the lady sitting at the back the other day was his mother, but my daughter and I were on the side of the seats facing inwards and didn't see her, so we didn't believe him. We thought he was imagining things.'

'That car comes around town very often. If you hang around here in town, you would probably spot him. He stops at the cigarette shop at the corner to pick up cigarettes and then goes to the chemists to buy some medicines. He doesn't live here, but comes here quite often I think.'

'What does he look like, can you describe him?'

'He's tall, much taller than you, good-looking chap. He has thick hair almost till his shoulders, brown hair not black, his family owns the old manor uphill. He's only just started coming here. We don't really know him in town, he keeps to himself...' His voice trailed off as he looked into the distance and squinted, as if trying to recollect something, a trivial detail perhaps, which had meant something to him.

'Do you remember the number of the car, or any other details?'

Aryan had told him it was an SUV. That he remembered clearly. The waiter corroborated the details. A Delhi vehicle, a luxury one, driven around by someone who was familiar with these roads, and who lived here occasionally. He hadn't stepped into the restaurant but had sat outside, watching as Aisha, or her doppelganger, had sat at the back of the restaurant, watching Prithvi and the kids as they lunched. She had left as fleetingly as she had arrived, a whisper of smoke blown into the air. The only trace of her having been there, was the hastily stubbed out cigarette in the ashtray on the table.

Prithvi pushed away the plate before him, the food was making him feel queasy. It was too late for lunch too. Almost evening. The cold fist clenching and unclenching his intestines, had done away with the hunger that had led him to the restaurant. He thanked the waiter for his help and ran to the hole-in-the-wall cigarette store down the road. As usual, it was being propped up by the local louts who lounged around it, waiting for an unsuspecting tourist needing a guide, a hotel, a tourist taxi, a warm body for the night, anything they could supply and make a commission off.

He described the man, with the same words that had been used by the waiter, and the police inspector. He wondered if he should go to the grocery store to get Mr Negi's description. 'Haanji,' said a face that had been crinkled by the high altitude sun into early dotage, 'I've seen this person. *Khandaani admi hai.* His family owns one of the stately houses out on the bend, beyond the ridge. But no one is allowed in. He doesn't hire local staff but gets them from back home.'

That was a long way from the main town. It was a place not easily accessible to the casual tourist, and only someone with purpose or business would attempt the long trek up the winding mountain roads, right to the top of the peaks that cradled this little hill town like two palms cupped together.

'Could someone give me directions to get there, please?'

The gaggle of flotsam and jetsam who had congregated at the cigarette shop looked at him, their expressions blank, coiled, wary. There was something that made them hesitate while dispensing information, he realised, because in normal circumstances, the locals were always more than eager to put themselves out on a limb to help a stranger, whether there was something in it for them or not.

'I could take you there,' the face said, having identified himself as Bhisham Singh. 'But it will cost you.'

The conditions were to have the money paid up front, that Bhisham Singh would not enter the accursed place along with

Prithvi, and if anything happened to Prithvi, Bhisham Singh was not responsible.

'Why would you say that? Is it dangerous?'

The man looked at Prithvi with a gaze that was a mix of curious and compassionate. 'There are strange goings-on in that house. No one who goes in comes out, they say, and ghosts haunt the place. A female voice screams around the grounds in the night. One of my distant relatives' son got a job as a houseboy there. They say he ran away after three months and went to Delhi because of the screams. No one from the locals works there. They say all the staff in the house comes from elsewhere and lives on the premises. When they come down to the market to buy provisions too, they don't speak about the house or the owners.'

Bhisham Singh took himself, and the reek from the amalgamation of coagulated sweat and the detritus of possibly umpteen sessions of drinking himself into a stupor, into the front seat. He had the tremors in his hands. A habitual drinker, one who did not drink to relax himself, but rather one who drank to be himself. His eyes were rheumy. He looked careworn and battered by a lifetime of neglect and dissipation. He folded the notes Prithvi handed him and carefully tucked them into a worn wallet, which seemed to have little else.

'Turn off right,' he commanded, from the main mall road. They turned onto a side road, which went away from the town and climbed higher, past the tumblings of houses stacked one on top of the other. The houses, perched precariously along the side of the road, got thinner and more scattered, until they finally gave way to just landscape with vast tracks of forest, before they curved through the roads a little more until they reached a dead end, where stood a huge gate, closed, impenetrable, ominously threatening.

'There,' he pointed out. 'There is where that man you want lives.'

The path within the gate curved sharply, hiding the house it led to from view. 'Go on, go in and ask for him.'

'What is his name, whom do I ask for?'

Bhisham Singh shook his head, still staring into the distance, chewing on the stub of a beedi he had long smoked out. 'You can ask for the owner of the place, can't you?' he replied with homespun commonsense.

Prithvi got out of the car, looking down the path, hoping to find someone at the gates, but the place seemed deserted. He approached the looming gates warily. It was sunset. The canopy of trees blocked out all sunlight except for a few stray rays that pierced the gaps between the leaves, and straggled down to the strangely well-maintained road.

There was a strange hum at the gates as he approached it, and before he could reach out to touch them, Bhisham Singh yelled out from the spot he was standing at. 'Don't touch them with your hand, use a stick or a branch.'

Prithvi jerked his hand back and realised, that the gates and the walls with their barbed wire in coils on the top, were probably electrified. This wasn't just any old mansion, but a mansion that wanted no one coming in. And probably, more scarily, no one getting out.

He looked around for a bell to summon someone to open the gates, and wondered how to swing them open. In the end, it was quite simple. He picked a fallen twig and gently prodded the gate, it was unlocked, either through oversight or deliberateness. The right gate swung open with a horrifying creak that had the birds nesting down for the night scattering off into the skies again. If anyone was on the grounds, they would have heard the sound of the gate.

He walked inside, his shoes sinking into damp, dew-sodden grass that was running into being overgrown, onto a gravel pathway that curved through the patch of the emerald spread of lawn that was deepening into black, as the late afternoon turned to early evening. The chirping crickets and the occasional call of a bird returning to nest were the only sounds in the air. The house loomed up ahead, on the right, as he turned through the rough gravel path, which was wide enough for a single car to pass on it. It wasn't a house, a more appropriate word would be a mansion. The windows were dark, no lights were lit up within to show anyone on the premises. It seemed abandoned. If there was anyone inhabiting these premises, they seemed to be living underground. There was no sight of the SUV that both the waiter at the restaurant and the good people at the cigarette shop had mentioned, unless there was a garage further down the path, where it would be kept, away from the rain and damp. There seemed to be some outhouses at a distance, where the grounds dipped, perhaps those were for the staff to live in.

Prithvi went up to the front door and rang the bell, the chimes echoed within; he imagined the waves of sound disturbing the dust motes within. There was no answering movement or sound. He rang the bell again. Nothing moved. He turned around, wondering whether he should go check at the outhouse. He could see a short path, further away from the main gate, when he faintly registered the sound of dogs barking that seemed to come to him on a soft blowing wind. The sound came from behind the house. The land sloped down steeply there, and the garden fell away to nothing. The fence, with its barbed wire, ran down until it disappeared from sight. The barking gradually increased, and in a sudden flash he realised that they came from the sudden black movement in the distance. Hounds, black hounds, running at a streak towards him, their strides long and determined, gaining on him, their jaws slavering in anticipation.

He turned swiftly and dashed towards the electrified gate which had swung itself shut behind him and raced towards it, hoping, against hope that they would swing open. The barking grew louder, as the hounds closed in on him. As he reached the gate, the buzzing stopped abruptly and the gates swung open, as if controlled by an unseen hand. He rushed out, the dogs barely metres away from sinking their teeth into the calves of his legs. The moment he stepped out of the gates, they clanged shut automatically, and the dogs stood snarling a little distance away, trained perhaps through bitter experience, not to make contact with the gate.

Bhisham Singh had been lolling against the hood of Prithvi's car, watching disinterestedly while this chase sequence unfolded. 'I told you, didn't I?' he said, as Prithvi walked shakily towards him, his legs trembling from the unaccustomed exercise, feeling the sweat break out on his brow despite the chilly wind of the settling dusk, 'There's something strange about this place and that's why I didn't want to enter. Now you know why.' He put a pinch of the snuff he had been constantly smoothening to his nose and inhaled deeply, with his eyes closed reverentially and gave a shiver before opening his eyes again.

Prithvi sagged against the side of the car, feeling his limbs, quivering with unfamiliar lactic acid build up, begin to cramp painfully. He realised, with a shock, just how unfit he had let himself become.

From the other side of the gate, the black hounds continued to bark and snarl warily, refusing to throw themselves at the gate in a bid to get at them in what would have been very normal animal behaviour. Perhaps they had lost one of their own to the soft hum of the dangerous volts flowing through the metal of those huge gates.

Prithvi looked back at them, knowing that he was now safe, and looked down the pathway, which was now quickly being draped in the velvety darkness that the swift fall of night had brought along. The fog and mist was rolling in quickly, blanketing the trees with wraith fingers that swooped down to caress the road, leaving a trail of dampness on the leaves, on the roads, sending a chill through the thin day jacket that Prithvi had worn when he set out in the morning. The stones which held the mountain back from the side of the road, glistened in the semi dark, the shadows were disappearing into uniform blackness. Nothing human seemed to stir within the gates.

Someone must be within, he knew, someone to keep the dogs fed and bathed. The house looked cared for, someone was switching the electric current on and off at the gates. Prithvi pulled out a cigarette from the almost finished pack in his pocket, and lit it with shaking hands, struggling with the lighter for a couple of times before it deigned to click on.

'Chalein?' Bhisham Singh asked, now chewing on a wad of tobacco, which he spat out inelegantly by the side of the path, in order to free his mouth for conversation.

Prithvi nodded and went reluctantly to the car, lowering himself into the seat when he heard it. A loud scream, followed by a wail that tore the fog apart and clawed into his ears.

It was Aisha's voice. It had to be her voice. It was her voice when she was in one of her states. Or was it his mind playing tricks on him? He didn't know. 'Did you hear that?' he asked Bhisham Singh, who looked back at him blankly. 'Hear what, saab? The only thing I can hear are those dogs growling, let's get out of here before they change their minds and decide to crawl under the gate to get at us.'

6

The speed Prithvi drove at completely rattled the snuff-addled Bhisham Singh, who was finally reduced to sitting with his feet up on the seat clutching onto the handle above the window. Prithvi drove straight to the police station in the centre of town, just off the main mall road.

Inspector SD Pant wasn't in the police station when he entered. He was told that he was out on a call regarding a brawl in the market place, and opted to wait rather than have the junior take down the details for his visit.

When Inspector Pant came in, bristling with suppressed rage in his too-tight uniform and too genial a smile, the staff in the dusty police station snapped to attention. Bhisham Singh sat down on his haunches in a corner of the room, in the manner that those who have had previous run-ins with the law do, making himself inconspicuous, and threw across a casual greeting in the native dialect to the attached prison cell, which had two local criminals sprawled lackadaisically within.

The inspector settled down in his chair with the hand towels carefully draped across the back and turned his attention to Prithvi. 'Haanji, Mr Thakur, what is it now? Have you any further information about your missing sister-in-law? Has she returned, has she contacted you?'

Prithvi gave the information he had gathered, including the message he had received, and concluded with the voice he had heard from the deserted darkness of the mansion. The inspector took the phone number down and asked a constable to forward it to the relevant person to track down the owner of the number.

'We'll find out who owns it soon enough. Don't worry. Now technology is really great,' he said, popping a mint into his mouth, after courteously offering Prithvi one, 'Everything is at the click of a mouse. Forget the specialists, even my son can find out so much just sitting at home on his computer. He puts in a number and finds out the name of the owner on something called True Caller. Do you have True Caller?'

Prithvi shook his head to indicate a negative. The inspector's manner perplexed him. He seemed rather unconcerned about Prithvi's suspicions that his wife was still alive.

Inspector Pant having dispensed with the mint he had in his mouth, now tore open a packet of gutka, and popped the contents into his mouth. Intermittently, he would spray the contents of his mouth into a waste paper basket that doubled as a spittoon, kept at convenient reach beside his desk, while barking at the two residents in the cell to shut their mouths or he would shut it for them.

'Let me get this right, Mr Thakur,' he said, spitting inelegantly into the waste paper basket kept next to his desk, 'You think your wife is still alive, and she is in this house with a man who you describe as taller than you, with hair till his shoulders and brown eyes, but you personally have not seen this man or your wife. Right now, do you want me to investigate your missing sister-in-law or your dead wife? You expect me to march into a private residence on a suspicion that it may have your supposedly dead wife within, and conduct a search of the premises?'

'Yes,' Prithvi replied.

'What warrant would I have to search the premises? Those are powerful people, one cannot actually afford to offend them. They would get me transferred to a village reachable only by foot.'

Prithvi put his head between his hands and breathed deeply. 'I need to find out if my wife is alive,' he replied, the words torn from him.

'Your wife is dead. We saw the suicide note. We haven't found the body, but we have a witness who says he saw her jump. Now you say she is alive without having seen her personally.'

Prithvi nodded.

'Your son claims to have spoken with her. The waiter states that he saw her and recognised her. Why is this all coming up after all these months? If she was indeed alive, why hadn't she shown herself in public earlier?'

Prithvi nodded, wondering about the same. Aisha wouldn't have left the children behind, he knew. She would have climbed mountain cliffs and crossed feral jungles to be with them.

'We have already put out an alert for your sister-in-law. Your wife is missing, presumed dead, so unless we have some substantial evidence to believe she is not, we will not re-open the case on mere hearsay.'

Prithvi sighed. He wasn't sure if he really wanted to find out if Aisha was still alive. He had just about made his peace with her being dead, and the raw gaping hole within him that had been hollowed out with her disappearance had stopped throbbing every time he thought of her.

'I could take you there right now,' he offered, a strange disquiet within him fluttering away, wondering how he would reconcile his acceptance of Aisha's death with her being found. And what if she didn't want to be found this time? Every time she had gone away she had left trails, like pebbles in a forest path.

This time, there were only crumbs for him to follow, crumbs that led to gates that held back monstrous black hounds.

Inspector Pant opened a file on his table, an implied gesture of dismissal. 'Mr Thakur, we are already overburdened with more cases than we can handle. I do sympathise with you. But seriously, two women in your home have gone missing in the past year, and of these, one committed suicide. This doesn't look good for you. If I were you, I would not be frequenting police stations. You do seem, in my eyes, right now, the one with most reason to do away with both. I believe your wife had some substantial property in her name.'

He looked up and directly at Prithvi, as he said that, noting the abrupt recoiling shock with which Prithvi reacted. 'Oh, we have our ways of finding out,' he added. 'We know you say this lady went away with all the property papers from within your safe, but we also know that you called the caretaker of the mansion a few days ago, and informed him that you would be coming down soon to do some transactions and probably finalise a sale.'

Prithvi shook his head in shock. 'I needed to transfer the property papers to my children's name. That was what I planned to go there for, not a sale.'

'I heard differently,' said SD Pant, steepling his fingers under his chin, resting his elbows on the desk, as he looked at Prithvi unwaveringly. His eyes were cold hard pebbles embedded into the podgy expanse of his face.

'I heard you were in conversation with a hotel chain to sell the property. They had plans of converting it into a heritage hotel. Your wife opposed your plan first, so you eliminated her. Just when you thought your path was clear, your sister-in-law butted into the scene. You hadn't factored her in, had you? She refused to let you sell the property. In fact, she wanted you to add her name to the papers.'

A cold sliver of panic pierced Prithvi's gut. Imperceptibly, the atmosphere in the room had changed from one of gratuitous tolerance to a barely-there menacingness.

The inspector smiled a slick, oily smile, and gestured at the constables around, a slight nod that had them place restraining hands on Prithvi's shoulders, intent on keeping him in his seat.

'What is this?' Prithvi asked, confused.

'I'm glad you saved me the trouble of coming to get you, Mr Thakur. Perhaps your biggest mistake was to come to register the missing person's complaint for your girlfriend. It made me reopen the case of your wife's death and ask some more questions. We spoke with your gardener. I learnt something completely different from the story you gave me about your wife's disappearance. Interesting, Mr Thakur, that your gardener would be so relieved to confess his part in the story, and tell us about yours.'

Prithvi started, and rose inadvertently, the constables held him down firmly.

'I don't know what you are talking about!' The constables did not yield the unrelenting pressure on his shoulders. They were tiny, but tough, but not trained fighters. Prithvi knew he could take them down even with his rusty, pugilistic skills.

'I'm sorry, I have to take you into custody for interrogation, Mr Thakur, with regard to a conspiracy to have your wife killed,' said Inspector Pant, the oily smile still in place on his face, as though he was trying to convince Prithvi to stay back for a spot of tea.

In an instinctive reaction, Prithvi sprang to his feet.

The long-forgotten litheness of the university pugilist coming right back to his limbs, a residual memory still lurked within his muscles. He swung a sharp right hook to the surprised constable, who was unfortunately no match for him, either in size or strength. He collapsed in a crumpled heap in the corner of the police station, the blood gushing from his nose which was a pulped mess.

All conversation stopped. Even the drunks in the cell stopped abusing each other, and Bhisham Singh jumped up from his position near the door and moved in to inspect the bleeding collateral that lay sprawled on the floor.

Prithvi didn't wait to see the inevitable pandemonium that would result from his actions. He rushed out of the station, pushing aside the onlookers, got into his car, and inserted the key into the ignition, hoping this wouldn't be one of those moments when it decided to act up. It didn't, thankfully. He swerved the car out at top speed before SD Pant could charge out, his cap in hand, yelling at the lackeys gathered around the one with the nose spouting blood, for ineffectual first aid, to get on the wireless and sound an alert for the car Prithvi was driving off in.

The jeep started behind him at a distance, and he could hear the whine of the siren, which made the people littering the side of the narrow roads fall respectfully to the side, as he drove past. Thankfully, there was almost no traffic, a jam would have done him in. He turned through the lanes and was out of the main town, onto the mountain roads he recognised, thanking his stars that the surrealism of the fluorescent dusk had been dispensed with, and darkness was now an ally. He stopped the car in a deserted path off the road, pulled on the jacket he always carried along in the car in case it got chilly, a woollen cap low over his face, took out the duffel bag always packed and ready in the boot, and stepped onto the path leading back to the main road. He was just in time to see the police jeep whizzing past him, siren at full volume.

He would return for the car when he could. Or the shepherds that roamed these parts with their flock could sell it for scrap, he didn't care. He hailed down a passing state government bus and clambered on, pushing himself into the thick of the crowd, after paying the conductor, and finding a quarter of a seat at the back. He sat down, trying hard to be inconspicuous but standing out in his city man air, amongst the throng of hill people clutching onto the battered suitcases and duffel bags, held together with a prayer and a rope most times.

'Daju,' asked a face to his right, '*Kahaan jaa rahey ho*?' He mumbled something indistinctly, unwilling to get into a conversation because there was nothing to be said. He realised, with a cold clammy hand that clenched his chest, the last he'd taken the property papers out had been over eight months ago. Who had taken them? Had it been Heer or had it been Aisha? Had Aisha actually planned to go missing? If Aisha had indeed planned her disappearance, she would have had ample time to dispose of the property and slip away into another identity. Was that why she was trying to get the children to come with her?

He hopped off the bus at a junction town, and watched it lumber away to Delhi. At the crowded depot, he found himself another that went towards the small town in the middle of the Gangetic plains, with old-world charm and colonial relics, where modern gang wars and caste politics made it a roiling hotbed of communal strife. He would be relatively safe now, he realised, he was out of the state, and coordination between the police departments of various states was not the most efficient. But he had to be careful, stay under the radar as far as possible.

It wasn't what he thought he would ever do, be a fugitive from the law, running and hiding with just the clothes on his back, and a wallet that was rapidly running out of funds, until he could reach an ATM next. He couldn't withdraw from his account too often. The duffel bag had been packed for a trip he was to make from the office directly into Delhi via chopper, for an urgent meeting with government stakeholders in a research project. The trip had got cancelled as urgently as it had been scheduled, and somehow the bag never got unpacked. It had remained in the boot of the car. One of those things one means to get round to doing, but never does. Today, his procrastination had been a life-saver.

By the time the clanking bus pulled into the bus depot in the town he was headed to, he was as grimy and dishevelled as the men he had been travelling with. There was something diminished about him that let him pass scrutiny, that would allow no one on that bus to quite recall any specific details about him, if asked. He had managed successfully to merge with the dispersing crowd.

He walked creakily, his bones and joints cramped and protesting from the lack of movement for the past so many hours. The warm rays of the fading late afternoon sun beat down on him, as the chill from the evening breeze hit his face. He looked at the plethora of dingy lodges lining the road leading out to the city, and wondered if he should stay there or look for a better hotel. Those would need proper credentials to check into.

He decided against the latter. The former would be more anonymous and welcoming, never mind the lack of material comforts. He walked into one of the shops lining the side of the street, through a maze of auto rickshaws and cycle rickshaws parked in the most disorganised organised manner. Then, he went further down the crumbling arcade of shops and bought himself some more basic clothes and stuffed it all into the duffel bag. It had only contained one change of clothes.

He then walked into a decent-looking hotel that seemed to be the least biohazard of the lot on offer, signed in for a room on a scribbled name and address. The decrepit old man behind the counter, his eyes glazed with weariness and his hands shaking with a tremor, was too lackadaisical to be particular. He had always been ready and prepared for this moment, Prithvi realised. He had always known that someday he would have to run to save his life, and never go back to where he came from ever again. He could lie low here in this room, with its peeling wall paint, lurid curtains with red and green flowers. The floral decoration comprised plastic flowers with clear glass dew droplets, covered with a layer of fine dust that had seeped between the droplet and the fake petal, conferring upon the illusion of freshness a patina of neglect. He could stay here until he got everything sorted out. He would return to find Aisha, to get her away from whatever it was that was keeping her away from him and the children. They would be a family again. That's all he had ever wanted.

The room reeked of stale sweat and cheap phenyl, the sheets were yellowed, fraying but clean. The window opened onto a view of grimy rooftops extending into a blur of more rooftops, dotted by satellite dishes scattered in the most haphazard manner. His room was on the top floor. If he looked down, he could see the narrow by-lane which ran alongside the main road the lodge was located on. The road connected the city from the terminus to its intestines, to the chaos of the narrow lanes and by-lanes, where vehicles larger than auto rickshaws didn't dare attempt to enter. In these lanes, the sick were carried out by the able-bodied to the roads, where ambulances waited. Pregnant women stumbled down steep stairways, holding their ballooning bellies, so that the life within knew that every step was a gamble between descent and death.

Prithvi had no clue whether his car had been located, abandoned as it had been at the little turn off the main connecting road. That turn led down the mountain towards a forgotten village, where the villagers had lived for centuries without the luxury of a road leading down to them. They scrambled down the precariously etched path, down the mountainside, holding onto their possessions with the strength and certainty the lack of an alternative gave them.

It was in a similar landscape that Aisha had jumped off if she indeed had; a suspended bridge, the towering coniferous trees looking down on her, silent and unquestioning. She would have careened down swiftly into the deep river gorge, where the tumultuous rapids against the huge boulders that dotted the churning river bed would have smashed her body into pulp. How much courage would it have taken for her to jump knowing she could not swim? Had the blackness of living become scarier than the terror of being swallowed up by the water? Had she really preferred the oblivion of death to coming back home to the children, to him? Had the demons in her head finally taken over?

For a terrible, brief moment, he wondered how she would have felt in those seconds after she had jumped. Had the rocks smashed into her face, first rendering her unconscious, or had her heart stopped beating from the swift fall?

He should have insisted on speaking with that shepherd, on getting all the details he could have got from him. Death unwitnessed was a different demon from the death that unfolded in front of one's eyes. Especially, one without tangible, corporal evidence of a corpse as proof. It haunted you every night with its miasmal uncertainty.

He could smell her in the air of this city, her fragrance wrapping him like a warm cloak. This was her city, she haunted it. If he stood still and shut his eyes, he could breathe her in, from the first day he pulled her to him, she in that red dress that transformed her into the woman of the world she never was, doused in a musky fragrance which would reel him in hypnotically, every time he got within a foot's distance of her. It was only years later, when he had dissolved himself in her over and over, would he find out she used a perfume her mother had custom made. The perfumers in the old market made it for her. They supplied custom blends to some of the best parfumeries abroad, never mind their dilapidated exteriors and humble workshops. It was a special blend of sandalwood, jasmine, musk and roses, and more, that he didn't know nor care to know. The perfume was very expensive. A small vial would permeate the house for months, if it broke. He should know. He had flung one to the ground and shattered it in one of his rages. She had stopped wearing perfume after that. It was shortly after Aryan's birth, when the trouble between the two of them began rearing its ugly head. That was when she began retreating further into her own mind. He didn't realise it then. He'd reacted with his impulsive hot-headedness every time she did something that grated on his nerves. It just pushed her further away from him into a world he could not draw her out from.

The next day, she stopped perfuming herself. It was also the day the relationship between them stopped being sexual. The ritual of her daubing the perfume behind her ears and on the insides of her wrists, every time she emerged from a bath, ended. Her skin, alabaster with the blue veins travelling under the paleness, uneven tributaries of a river on a map that would not be traced by anything but human longing. Her hair damp, and dripping rivulets down her shoulders. Her body, still soft and giving, from the hot water that had pummelled it a few minutes ago. And when she was lactating, this fragrance would overlap with the smell of milk that would gush from her breasts when Maya sucked on them, a combination he found oddly arousing.

But that was then. The night she reached out for him, when Aryan was a month old, he shrank away seeing her belly bared, floppy and loose, the folds wobbling on their own accord. It descended into a hell of accusations and a standoff, where sex was the first bastion to fall in the war that would eventually decimate the relationship between them. The perfume vial was one among the things he threw in an uncontrollable moment of anger. She stopped perfuming herself. They never had sex again after that argument and she rapidly spiralled into a private hell that made her accessible only when she had the requisite calibrated dosages of medication flowing through her veins.

'Aisha,' he called out into the unresponsive air, imagining it wrap itself around him, the fragrance caressing him. 'Stop being a dramatic fool,' he told himself, blinking his eyes, feeling the unaccustomed moistness within dissipate into dry practicality. She was gone, and he was left with the task of resolving the mess he'd put his children's inheritance into.

He dialled the only person he could count on to be of any help, his sister. She answered on the third ring, her voice worried, as he knew it would be. His relationship with his sister was tenuous but affectionate. Like any well-meaning sister, she had violently opposed his getting married to Aisha.

'She's a bit strange,' she'd said without mincing her words, the first time he had introduced her to Aisha, and declared their intention of getting married. 'You know I have no issues with the different religion, but something is not quite all there with her.'

Of course he didn't pay heed to her warnings. Love is a country where you leave the passports of rationality at the customs when you enter, to be collected when you exit.

'Ritudi,' he said, without greeting, without preamble, 'I'm in trouble, and you have to help me.' He hadn't spoken with her for months. He had never felt the need to.

She was a widow, of comfortable means, a huge house, and a hectic social calendar, the do-gooder in her tony neighbourhood. Their worlds never collided. There was always that surety that she would take care of the kids, if he asked her to—she was family after all, and blood ran thick and dark, forming slender, unseen ropes that lashed them all together, too taut to be broken. She was terribly fond of the kids. She had just kept away after Aisha descended into delusions that she, and everyone around her, were trying to kidnap the children, and child-traffic them into a life of stone-breaking, in remote quarries in the distant Southern states, from where she would never be able to track them down.

'Where are you? There's no one answering the phone at home.'

There was a brief, uncertain pause. He stayed silent, wondering what could be said. She continued.

'Why did you put the children into boarding school? What is going on, Prithvi? Don't you think I deserve to know what's happening with you and the children? You are the only family I have now that Ma-Baba have both passed away.'

'I don't have the time to get into everything right now, but I want you to go to school and take the children away with you. Can you do that? Just keep them with you till I come and get them. You have already been named next of kin, in case of emergency. I will email the school and ask them to hand over the kids to you for the winter break. I will come to collect them in a few days.'

'I will do that of course. Nothing would make me happier than to have the children home. It has been years since I've spent time with them.' She paused for breath. She had a lot to say and it all came rushing out as she spoke. 'Who was the lady who kept answering the phone, every time I called on the landline? She refused to tell me and never passed on my messages, did she? And you would never take my calls.'

'She was Aisha's half sister, she was staying with us when Aisha went away and… it is too complicated to get into details right now, but the fact is that she has disappeared too, and she's taken the kothi papers with her, actually all of Aisha's papers. When I went to register a missing person's complaint, the police accused me of conspiring to kill Aisha, in order to sell the mansion. I had no option but to flee. They're chasing me. I'm a fugitive now. I don't know if they've got a warrant out for me yet or not. I need a lawyer, Ritudi.'

He ran out of words, these were more words than he had spoken in a stretch, for a long while now. It was unfamiliar, this rush of speech from him. Outside the window, a pigeon fluttered undecidedly and settled on the window sill, looking in, expectantly wary at the human within.

'Where are you now?'

'I can't tell you, but I'm safe. I just need to lie low for a few days and hopefully things will die down. I have registered a missing person's complaint for Heer, that's Aisha's half sister. And I don't know how to tell you this, Di, but Aryan thinks his mother is alive, and a waiter who used to serve us at a restaurant we frequented often on Mall Road claims to have seen her too. I asked around, and the locals claim she is living in a house beyond the ridge.'

'Did you try to find out more, or were you happy that someone had taken her off your hands?'

'I did go there,' he replied, 'But I couldn't find out anything, the place is guarded with dogs and an electrified fence. I thought I heard her voice screaming but the other chap with me couldn't hear it. I could have been imagining it…'

'I hope you realise you are not making any sense. But then, when did you ever? Anyway, let me speak to a friend, whose husband is a lawyer, and figure out what you should be doing. Have you told the children?'

'I'd told them I'd be going away for a few days, so they're not going to be too worried. I'm sending an email to the school, you need to reach there on Saturday. They will be releasing the children by around 10 am.'

'Don't worry, I'll be there, and they will be safe here with me till you come to collect them. Poor things.'

The conversation paused. There was a long silence on the other end of the line

Then, Ritudi asked the inevitable, 'Tell me about this girl Heer. Why was she living in the house with you, when Aisha was dead, and the children were in boarding school? What's the real story, Prithvi, why did Aisha commit suicide?'

Prithvi kept quiet. 'I…'

'You were sleeping with her obviously, and that's okay. You're an adult and no longer my kid brother that I need to haul you up from time to time.'

'Ritudi, you haven't been listening. I don't think Aisha's dead at all. I think she's alive, or at least someone who looks like her and sounds like her.'

'Then what was all that about her jumping off a bridge?'

'I don't know... I don't know anything right now, Ritudi.'

'Do you need money?' Trust Ritudi to come up with the most practical of all questions, and remain unfazed by the accusations that he could have committed murder.

'Not for now. I have enough to last me a few days. I'm just trying to sort out a few things, and get the property papers back into place before Heer sells it off.'

'How could she do anything? And how can you sell the property if Aisha's still alive?'

'All the documents are missing, Ritudi, and I have no idea who has taken them.'

At that moment, the disparate pieces of the jigsaw puzzle that had been fluttering around discordantly in his mind, snapped themselves into place. From the dim recesses of his brain, he figured out something he should have over the past couple of months. Heer had come to their home with an agenda, and Aisha's disappearance had given it all on a platter to her. In the spaces between Aisha's suicide and Heer's walking away, was a conspiracy that he had been too foolish, too preoccupied with a grief he would not acknowledge to notice. And this, he knew, with a sudden sinking sensation that plunged his intestines into ice, would prove to be his undoing.

7

The next morning dawned, cold and foggy. The grime had coagulated into oily streaks of residue on the window that trickled down in lines within the vapour, as he breathed on it. From a vacant distance, he heard the muezzin's call to prayer, a shepherding of the faithful towards their religious obligations. Prithvi called for tea. A boy arrived, clad in a pair of trousers he had long outgrown, and an oversized sweater which was inexpertly patched together with mismatched bits of wool. He had pulled it down over the wrists, revealing only the fingers, which were strangely knobbled at the knuckles, and overgrown for the rest of him.

'*Aur kuch, saab*?' he asked, looking him up and down, in a manner displayed by those who are often called upon by the authorities to recant all they remember about some inhabitant of the lodge.

'*Kuch nahin*,' Prithvi replied, dismissing him without looking at him, handing him the tip he had been waiting for. Making eye contact formed a connection, and making a connection was dangerous. He wanted to slip through the town unnoticed, uncommented upon, unremarkable.

He pulled on a jacket, the same one he had worn on his run

from the mountains to the plains. Here, the air was loaded with not just the cold tendrils of the fog but the grime of the city and the sediment of industrial residue floating in the air. He was not very familiar with the city, and like all cities, this one too sprouted new landmarks and demolished the old every few years, caught as it was in the orgiastic throes of redevelopment. He was at the mercy of the auto rickshaw driver to take him through the unrelenting warren of lanes and by-lanes that would eventually open up into wider roads, and then the huge imposing, rusting gates of the kothi.

He bathed awkwardly with the sliver of soap that the hotel provided, and dressed himself with the unease of someone uncertain of how the day would progress. He checked out of the lodge, mentioning that he might be back if he did not manage to complete the work he had come for.

The fog had lifted a bit, and the chill of the morning had been dissipated by the warm, intrusive rays of a feeble early winter sun. His clothes, the paltry few he had bought, made for a light parcel in the duffel bag he carried. His face was now covered by a two-day growth of beard. If they were searching for a clean-shaven male, around six feet tall, they might just pass him by.

The auto rickshaw driver he hired to take him to the house looked at him warily, before acquiescing, after stating a ridiculous amount to be paid as the pre-decided rate for the route. Prithvi looked and sounded like an outsider, even though he had grown up in a town not much different from this, and not too far away. There are distances one traverses in the course of one's life that go beyond the measurable. He sat warily in the green and yellow auto, feeling his head bump against the roof of the rickety vehicle, every time they hit a speed breaker or a bump in the road.

There was a sudden sense of foreboding when the gates to the kothi loomed up in front. As he stepped out, he felt diminished and wary, and realised that the kothi looked much the same.

The gates to the house were locked shut, and the side gate, the one kept open always for the staff and the suppliers to enter, was locked too. The pathway to the main house, that was once swept clean every day by a dedicated sweeper, was now littered with the detritus from other lives outside the crumbling walls, lives that had begun their insidious invasion into the house. The house itself was showing signs of decay. The stench of neglect had seeped into the walls, and the moss and exposed brick told him the story of a death, and the resulting disdain for maintenance. The buzzer at the gate wasn't working, so he rattled the chains that held the gates together, to announce his arrival. He should have called before coming. He had the caretaker's mobile number. The landline had long been disconnected.

It was an imposing house, a kothi, as they called it, built in the eighteenth century in the Baroque style. It had came down to Aisha via the intricate links of family and descendants to Aisha's paternal family. The mantle of the inheritance fell upon Aisha's father, who fought valiant court cases for its ownership, and outlived other branches of the dying family tree to stake his claim on it. He then forsook it to live out his life in another town, with another woman, who was not his wife.

The kothi had stayed with the family, through mutinies, through independence, through generations, and now it was time for it to be sold. The family tree itself had dried up, the sprawling line of descendants had all scattered and fallen to age, barren marriages and untimely deaths. It was impossible to maintain on a salaried income. The term 'kothi', perhaps, was a misnomer; it was a complex of buildings, a main house, flanked by many outhouses, a courtyard. Within the main two-storeyed squat house, were an intricate reticule of the public spaces where visitors could be received, and the private spaces, where the women of the zenana could be kept secluded from the gaze of insolence from strangers. Between the public and the private, there was a courtyard; so one could be observed by anyone from a window looking onto the courtyard. The second floor was the zenana, where Aisha grew up, where her daadi died, and her mother went mad. There wasn't any zenana anymore, just the echoes of ghost laughter and tinkling anklets that one could hear, if one listened carefully. Especially on foggy winter nights, when the moon was a nimbus of light behind the clouds.

The children barely appreciated the stately, ruined magnificence of it and were always keen to end their visits to the kothi, because it depressed them. They would rather stay in a hotel with hot and cold running water, twenty-four hour room service, and heaters in the room if they were visiting in winter. They did not care that the kothi was on the banks of a river that swirled lazily at a slight distance, away from their bedroom windows, the rushing of the water when it was in spate creating white noise for the tumult that the lives within the homes struggled to cope with.

The kothi was a white elephant, and Prithvi had said so often enough to Aisha. 'Convince your mother to sell it off, and she can move in here with us. The money you get will be enough to live out the rest of our lives in luxury.'

She had shaken her head, determined and pensive. 'That is my childhood. Where I come from. If I sell it off, I will have no roots. Nowhere to run away to.'

'Why would you want somewhere to run away to?' he had asked, puzzled. This was before things went bad between them, when they lay entwined in each other, after passion was spent, but words still filled the spaces between them.

'You never know. Every woman needs a place to run away to. A place where she will never need to return from, if she doesn't want to.'

'But I will find you if you run away here,' he had laughed. 'I will know where you are.'

She had propped herself up on the elbow and stared at him,

her face shadowy and serious in the straggly autumn moonlight filtering in through the window panes.

'When I do decide to run away, you will never find me. Remember that. Not only will you never find me, but you will lose yourself trying to find me.'

He had laughed and pulled her to him and forgotten her words, because at that moment they had meant nothing. Now they did.

The memory came to him with a start. He couldn't find her. And she had run away. That he was now certain about. She wasn't dead, as he'd imagined her to be. She had run away. Never to be found again. And he was slowly losing himself trying to find her or find the truth about what had happened to her.

The gates were rusting from their hinges, he was sure a swift hard push from him would push them down, but he waited, knowing the gates would be opened. The iron chain with the heavy padlock was looped over the top of the gates, and he could discern that it would take no key to open it. It just had to be lifted up and disentangled from the other. The grounds, he could see through the iron gates, were overgrown with weeds.

The caretaker, a wisened man in trousers held up with a disintegrating rope belt, ambled up to the gate, a muffler wrapped around his head, a woollen hand-knitted waistcoat keeping the chill out of his hollowed, caved-in chest.

His footsteps quickened as he recognised who was at the gate. 'Am coming,' he called, 'I'm not as spry as I used to be, I'm sorry,' he called, as he hobbled up to the gate. Unlocking the chain, he welcomed Prithvi into the grounds. It was a huge expanse of trees, and a driveway that led first to an outhouse and then onwards to the main house, which was barely visible from the main gate. They walked companionably to the main portico, which was on the verge of collapsing. The vines were creeping all over it, their roots driving themselves deeper into the stone and mortar and splitting deep, violent gashes across the surface. It had barely been a couple of years since Aisha's mother had passed away. That was all it had taken to have the house crumble in on itself.

'What a surprise,' said Irfan chacha, who was known as 'Irfan chacha' to everyone. Even though he might have had a family name he would have been proud of, it had never trickled down to Prithvi's ears.

'It was a sudden decision,' replied Prithvi, guiltily, knowing that the premises were probably locked up and musty, and the kothi wouldn't be habitable. He had no intention of staying there, he just needed to see it and then visit the advocates who had been custodians of the property. Irfan chacha hobbled ahead, his gait altered by rheumatism and age, asking him when had he arrived, did he intend staying long, there were property taxes to be paid, the electricity had been disconnected, a few windows needed glass put in, because the pigeons were creating a mess.

'It is so strange that you are visiting a few days after Aisha bibi visited with that strange man.'

Prithvi stopped mid-step, hearing the crunch of the fallen leaves underfoot punctuate the sentence that had him catch his breath.

'What? When did Aisha visit? She's dead.'

'Dead?' Irfan chacha gave Prithvi an amused look. 'Of course she's not dead, she came here, four days ago, spoke with me, cried a little for her mother, and showed a man the property. She told me she had sold it to him. And that she would give enough to me to buy a small house back in my village, and live out the rest of my years in comfort. She's definitely not dead. Unless that was her ghost who came here.'

He paused, shook his head, and his face crinkled up in affectionate laughter. 'And that ghost, these days, chain-smokes.'

Prithvi grabbed at a pillar that held up the canopy over the porch to prevent his knees from buckling under him. Irfan chacha, who was a step or two ahead, didn't notice the impact of his words. Prithvi pulled himself back together and followed Irfan chacha to the main door, its grand façade and portico, reached by two rambling porches that spanned the breadth of the house. The tiling was now cracked and uneven, insects making their way into the gaps, creating homes they had no fear of being displaced from. Above the door, the emblem of a state long dissolved into the Indian republic, still stood guard over the vestiges of the crumbling nobility.

He gestured dramatically for Prithvi to precede him to where the faded, dusty formal guest room awaited him, through a smaller adjunct receiving room. Prithvi was still trying to assimilate what he had just heard. Aisha was not dead. She had visited, cried for her mother, and showed a man the property, she had smoked her cigarettes. And she had now sold the property. He had only cursorily glanced at the board nailed to the wall outside without really registering the words on it.

He ran back out to the gate, through the long driveway, feeling the earth resist the pounding of his feet, and read it again.

'This is the property of M/S Capital Hospitality. Trespassers will be prosecuted.'

He stormed back into the house.

'How can this have happened? Aisha committed suicide months ago.'

Irfan chacha looked at him, his head cocked to one side like a rooster, his expression concerned. He led him politely to the sitting room and gestured at the decrepit sofa that was worn and fraying, the dust covers barely managing to keep it from falling to pieces.

'I really don't know what you are talking about, janab, but she is very much alive. I might be old and these cataracts in my eye need to be removed, but I couldn't be that mistaken.'

There was a long silence while Prithvi tried to catch the flittering skeins of the changed situation, and weave them into a tangible explanation for what he had just learnt. Aisha was alive. Or someone else had taken her place.

'What did the man accompanying her look like?' he asked Irfan chacha.

'He was tall, he had light brown eyes and a deep scar on his wrist.' This man, he was everywhere. Him with the light brown eyes, and the scar on his wrist.

'And he probably drove an SUV with a Delhi registration number, didn't he?' he asked Irfan chacha.

'I don't understand cars, and I can't remember what he was driving. I didn't look outside to see which car they drove up in. Do you know who he is?' He looked at Prithvi with his head still cocked to one side, his expression measuring him up, finding him wanting. 'I found it strange that Aisha bibi would come home accompanied not by her husband but another man who behaved like her husband.'

A sudden racking cough attacked him and his words. He turned his body to a side to let it have its way with him. When he stopped, he wiped his mouth with the back of his dirty sleeve and looked at Prithvi carefully.

'You have lost weight from the last time I saw you. There are circles under your eyes. You say your wife is dead, but I have met her in the flesh. It is not my place to question what is happening, but is there something I should know?'

'My wife is dead,' Prithvi said, his voice catching on the wave of some distant emotion for Aisha. It now washed over him in thick, hard bursts, lashing him, so his voice choked and the eyes spilt over with tears, which dribbled down the side of his face. He wasn't crying for Aisha, he realised as the tears dripped into his mouth, making him taste their saltiness. He was crying for the life he should have led, the wife he could have had, the love that they would have shared, had it not been for the demons that had taken over her mind. Irfan chacha stared at him, at a loss to the appropriate behaviour here. Dare he assume a social equality and offer comfort, or should he stay ineffectual the way someone who isn't close enough to offer comfort would be?

'My wife is dead,' he repeated. 'This woman who came here must have been an imposter, a look-alike. Her sister, her half sister.'

'That can't be true,' the old man shook his head, and settled down on the floor, pulling out his roll of beedis and a battered matchbox, lighting one up and puffing on it deeply.

'Her half sister was over fifteen years younger than her. The woman who came yesterday was Aisha bibi's age. No one can fake looking so much older. And she knew me, she knew the house, she went to her mother's room on her own, sat there, and cried and cried, until I thought she would choke. When she finally stopped crying, she took the man she was with on a tour of the main house, and the outhouses. I wasn't accompanying them, so I didn't know what they discussed, if that's what you're going to ask me. She asked about my family, about my son and my wife back in the village, she knew their names, she knew about my grandchildren and that my daughter-in-law had completed her teacher's training and now teaches at the village school. She knew everything. It couldn't be a look-alike. A person who only looks like her wouldn't know about these things.'

Prithvi put his head into his hands and sighed deeply. The room around him was being split open by the straggly rays of light that were entering it from the shuttered windows. Dust motes danced vacantly in the beams. The room, once so impeccably maintained, was disintegrating from the disuse that sucks the life out of homes not habited by human beings. Houses without people to breathe life force into them crumble into brick and mortar, and then, slowly, fall apart. Nature reclaims them. Trees force their roots under their foundations, moss claims the walls, insects dig crevices into the skirting and the wind sneaks into gaps caused by the lack of attention, and scoops up the things it can, swirling them around, dancing the dance of the mindless.

He could see the cracks reaching out tentatively from the ceiling, crawling towards the ground, the patches of sunlight filtering in where the roof had fallen away, the plaster peeling off in ragged patches fighting a losing battle with the dampness. A few years more of neglect and the house would crumble in on itself, and vagrants would sneak in to save themselves from the chilly winters, defying an increasingly frail Irfan chacha and his inadequate lathi, which no longer held its command as the hand wielding it weakened its grip with rheumatism.

Irfan chacha rubbed his rheumy eyes with the back of one hand and pulled out another beedi from his stash stored in the waistband of his pyjamas, before lighting it up. He puffed on it with the deep, life-drawing breaths of someone who knows his lungs won't allow him the luxury of doing so for much longer.

'She was very thin, she's lost a lot of weight. In fact, I even asked her if she was keeping well. She looked like she had some serious illness, wasted away, shrivelled up.'

He paused and looked up at Prithvi with the intent look that some creatures have when they are trying to assess if you presented danger.

'I asked her about you and the kids. She told me that the kids were at boarding school now, and she saw them occasionally, and that the two of you had separated.'

Prithvi narrowed his eyes. Had they separated? That was not the story he was living out. He assumed that his wife had committed suicide and her body couldn't be found. He never tried to have it found either. He had slipped conveniently into the role of a widower.

'Did she say where she was putting up?'

'There is no electricity or running water here now. She had

come with the intention of staying I think, but then the man looked around and said they couldn't stay here, and they would go to a hotel.'

'Did they name a hotel?'

'No.' Irfan chacha cast an appraising gaze at Prithvi's depleted appearance. 'What happened to you?' he asked with the lack of tact that comes from the casting away of the reticence, when it becomes clear that the employee is no longer beholden to the employer.

'Nothing happened to me, I just happen to be trying to find out what happened to Aisha. And her sister, Heer.'

'Heer?' Irfan chacha scratched his head with one insistent knobbly finger. 'She did have a half sister, but her name was not Heer. It was something else, I remember telling Badeybibiji too that it was a strange name to burden a little girl with.' In small-town India, the name you were bestowed with could destroy you.

He looked blankly at the ceiling, trying to will himself into recalling the name he had forgotten. 'It will come to me shortly,' he said, and settled himself back on his haunches with a sigh. 'The name, it will come to me. As I grow older, my joints and my memory have gone. That girl, she died when she was eleven. I remember that clearly, Badeysaab had been called for the funeral. I found it strange that he took the news so calmly, as though it was the death of a distant acquaintance. She looked like Badeysaab, I'm told. I had never seen her, but that's what I was told, that she looked exactly like her father. Aisha bibi though, was different. Aisha bibi got the best of both her mother and her father. I could never understand what Huzoor saw in that woman, she was nothing like Badeybibiji. She was so ordinary to look at, so ordinary. And he was so very handsome, so tall and what a personality. After all, *thoda sa angrez khoon tha na.*'

Irfan chacha knew the secrets of the family and thought Prithvi did too—the mingling of the blood through some liaisons not mentioned in public, the inherited genes throwing in the unusualness of the tall, the fair, the light eyes, the hair that was a soft brown, but which glistened golden, when it was caught unawares by an errant ray of morning light.

'I'm very sure her name was Heer,' Prithvi insisted, 'She stayed at our home, for a few days, before Aisha passed away, and Aisha told me she was her half sister, and she did look at lot like Aisha. In fact, she looked exactly like Aisha, a younger version of course, but very much the same.'

Irfan chacha stood up, with slow jerky movements, and shuffled towards an inner room. He emerged a few minutes later, bearing an album, one of those with photographs printed out and pressed with their cold plastic sleeves, preserving for posterity, moments that would eventually get erased from memory. A photograph proved that moments and people existed, when memory proved false. He wetted the tip of his finger with his tongue and turned the sleeves packed with pictures from a part of Aisha's life he had never known nor had been made privy to.

'Here she is,' Irfan chacha finally said, stopping with his finger on one photograph on a page with more than a dozen photographs. 'This was the Badeysaab's album, one he kept in his room, under lock and key. Of course, when he died, the Badibegum had all the cupboards and drawers opened by the locksmith and found this. She threw it out telling me to burn it, but something made me keep it safe. Someday, I thought to myself, it would be needed. I was right.'

It was a studio portrait, with an awkwardly painted Mughal garden behind the subjects of the photograph. A tall, sharp-featured man stood with the erect, self-conscious stance of one who needed to be the focus of attention at all times, his hand resting lightly on the shoulder of a tiny woman, who stood coyly next to him, barely coming up to his shoulders. In front of them, a young girl stood, clutching onto a doll with half its hair off the scalp, and the ragged patchy scalp showing through. The girl was wearing a be-ribboned, velvet and lace dress, evidently dressed up for the photograph, her hair smoothened down fiercely with a combination of hair oil and stern maternal combing, but stray strands escaped and stood around her face, defiantly awkward. She was a pretty child in the manner that all young children are pretty, their eyes yet undimmed with unanswered questions. She was beautiful, but she was dead. If she had died young, who was the woman he had been sharing a bed with? Who was she, and how had she come into the house, and most importantly, how did she look almost exactly like Aisha? He clutched his head with his hands placed his elbows on his knees, willing his head to stop swarming around like a million bees on street crack.

He looked around at the kothi. There were gaps where antique furniture and artefacts had been. How many pieces had been sold by Aisha's mother to fund her ailing last days because Aisha had not been able to send her money or had Irfan chacha been selling them off on the sly? A sharp quill of self-reproach pierced him as he realised he had morphed into a pecuniary tyrant, grudging Aisha even the basic funds required to run a home, without cutting corners on everything. He had been doing it for her good, he'd told himself. After all, there had been those days, when Aisha had gone berserk shopping online, and ordering tons of things they didn't need, maxing out the credit card he'd given her, hundred rolls of toilet paper, fifty boxes of cereal, fifty kilos of rice. And the clothes, clothes she would never wear, clothes that didn't fit her, slinky, seductive, satin and lace exquisiteness, bodycon bandage dresses that she packed away in a trunk and shoved into the attic. Reams and reams of fabric that would never touch her body, ordered in a crazed spell of wanting to escape the image she'd created of herself—colourless, dull, regulation jeans and t-shirt-clad.

She had stopped wearing her jewellery, he realised. Had she

been selling off her jewellery, to fund her shopping sprees? The pieces that had adorned her ears had dropped off, into the abyss of no return, until her wrists no longer clanked with the two thin gold bangles that had once been permanently stationed there. He had noticed when she stopped wearing her solitaires in the ears. They had been her mother's. 'I've kept them in the locker,' she had told him when he'd asked, more out of concern that she had misplaced them in one of her fugue states.

He hadn't bothered to check. There were so many things he had never bothered to crosscheck. Like the fact that Heer was her half sister. Or her supposed half sister.

'Could you remember the name of that girl? The girl in the photograph you just showed me?' He gestured towards the album, now kept neglected on a side table.

'Arey nahin. It is age, my memory is not what it used to be.'

'Are you leaving now?' Irfan chacha asked, as Prithvi rose, involuntarily dusting the seat of his trousers to displace the residual dust which might have adhered to it.

'Yes, I need to go meet the lawyers and check about this sale of the property you're talking about, and about this board outside claiming that Capital Hospitality is now the owner of this house and the grounds. I need to stop it.'

Irfan chacha shook his head. 'How can you do that, when Aisha bibi herself sold it? After all, isn't she the owner?'

8

It was late in the afternoon by the time he found the lawyer's office. He had only visited them once and that too with Aisha, a few days after her mother had passed away, to sign on the documents transferring ownership to her and to read the will that left behind the crumbling house, and the adjoining plots of land.

He was greeted with surliness from a paan-chewing peon, who led him from the reception area to the dark, musty inner chambers.

'What a pleasant surprise to see you, Mr Thakur. Are you here about the sale of the kothi?' The man behind the wide, polished wooden desk, his shirt sleeves rolled up and his woollen sleeveless vest frayed with years and use, did not rise to meet him, nor did his expression indicate any pleasantness in the surprise he mentioned.

'Yes,' Prithvi forced himself to smile tautly, 'I'm here to check about the sale.' It was the truth. RS Chaturvedi, of Chaturvedi, Dubey and Sons, looked at him with discernible suspicion, taking off his reading glasses in order to look Prithvi over closely. His nostrils flared and subsided with what seemed to be a sniff of disapproval.

'Please sit down, can I get you some tea? Coffee? How are

the kids? They are in a boarding school now, aren't they?' The pleasantries were essential to being dispensed with, before the business at hand could be got down to. That was just the way it was in these places, unlike the rough and tumble of busy cities where pleasantries were the first to be dispensed with.

A thin finger of ice crawled up Prithvi's spine. The kids had been put into boarding school after Aisha died. How had this man gotten to know about that? Had someone been in touch with him?

'The kids are fine,' he brushed off the topic and the unease it brought, a searing guilt that corroded his intestines in a way no acid could.

The senior Mr Chaturvedi was ramrod straight with the posture that came from the cane and boarding school rigour of yore. His face was slowly folding into itself with the wrinkles that the years brush painstakingly onto skin. He had been known to have a bit of a crush on Aisha's mother. Prithvi remembered Aisha speaking about it with a slight laugh when she'd first taken him to the lawyer's office. 'He'll be in mourning for Ammi, be warned. He'll probably be more heartbroken than Abbu would have been. He didn't see the ugly side of her after all, it is easy to love the pretty face. It is tough living with the mind gone ugly.'

Those were prophetic words. Had she been referring to her mother, or had it been prescient, about their own relationship? He would never know.

Aisha's mother had been a tremendously handsome woman, with the kind of withering gaze that had suitors take blades to their wrists when scorned. It was her fabled beauty that had drawn Aisha's father to her. It was the very same beauty, made rancid by proximity and awareness, that pushed him away into the arms of the very plain woman, who would eventually become his second wife.

'I've been meaning to get in touch with you actually. Aisha is dead. She died in the aftermath of the cloudbursts and landslides that hit the mountains up ahead in August. She jumped off a bridge, a shepherd saw her jumping but we never ever found the body. The police assumed it had gone downstream and would eventually surface somewhere but it never did, or if it did, we didn't get to know… ' He let his voice trail off, and the faint hint of sadness swarm over his face.

The old advocate's face crumpled into disbelief, his forehead questioning.

'Are you serious?'

'Yes, I am.' He gave an involuntary shudder, and continued swiftly. 'That is very strange indeed,' said the senior gentleman, steepling his fingers and resting his face on them, his forehead creased into a crisis of contemplation.

'Anyway, I wanted to ask you about this board I just saw on the walls of the kothi when I went there. How can Capital Hospitality now own the property when I haven't sold it? I hold the power of attorney on the property, as you know.'

'Well, I'm sorry to inform you that Aisha has indeed sold the kothi to Capital Hospitality a month ago and was here just a few days ago to sign on the final papers to transfer ownership.'

Prithvi felt his intestines liquefy at the words. A buzzing began in his head, the sound of a million bees angrily circling the impossibility of what the lawyer said had happened.

'How can that be possible? She's dead I tell you, she's dead. I have the suicide note. And I have the power of attorney for all the property.'

'A suicide note won't do, I need the death certificate, I need proof that she is truly dead and that you have not institutionalised her, as you've always been threatening her you would do. And I wouldn't need that too, because I have seen her in person, and know she isn't dead. As for the power of attorney, she had that revoked months ago. You don't really keep up with your correspondence, do you?'

Prithvi let out a small, involuntary groan of despair.

The lawyer continued grimly, 'Yes, I know about that threat to have her institutionalised, and I know that you got her to sign the power of attorney over to you one fine day after beating her to pulp. You never checked your mail coming in and going out of the letter box ever. She didn't trust you, I'm sorry to say. Not one bit. Who would blame her? You were an abusive husband, and she wanted to escape.'

'You know that isn't true. I did my best to keep her on an even keel, but she refused to take her medication, go for her therapy sessions. It was difficult. I even moved out of Delhi, and to the mountains because she was so paranoid about the neighbours in the city, I thought if she was alone, she would be better.'

'No. You isolated her so you could drive her completely mad, and grab her property and then do away with her. Do you think she didn't know that? She knew it all and she was in constant touch with me. I helped her.'

There was a sharp intake of breath, and he saw the white-haired attorney looking at him, from across the desk, something in his stance and expression reminding him of a king cobra. Hood unfurled, ready to strike in a split second, movement too quick for the eye to register, and the fang puncturing skin, dripping in its venom, sending its victim into a state of paralysis, and then in a few agonising minutes, death.

Prithvi recoiled and leaned back in the chair as far as he could go. A slow smile spread across the old lawyer's face, a smile full of intent and guile.

'You did not choose to send me the notification of her death. Now you show up, telling me she is dead, and without any proof of the same. Why should I believe you? And why would she commit suicide? She was coming into town that day to meet me, the day she got stuck. I couldn't make it there. I called her when I was midway, and told her to turn around, but it was too late. She was already there. She had with her all the documents that day, the papers to your home, her home, her jewellery that she had taken out from the locker a couple of days ago. She was planning to run away, and take the children with her eventually once she had the paperwork completed. But something delayed her. Anyway, to cut a long story short, she's out of it now and has sold the property. So, young man, I think you had better leave. There is absolutely nothing you can do about this.'

Prithvi felt his heart race crazily, and the room began to spin around him.

'You must understand, Aisha had issues. Mental issues. She was on medication. She was suspicious of everything, everyone, even me. She thought I was trying to get at her property, and trying to institutionalise her, but that wasn't true. If that were true, why would I have lived so many years with her, struggling to keep the family going through all her episodes? I could have got her institutionalised a long time back, if I cared. But I loved her. I wanted her back, I wanted my Aisha back.'

He could feel his eyes begin to blur with the beginnings of tears, he blinked them back furious with himself at this momentary lapse of composure. Men didn't cry. Hadn't his father always told him so, refusing the relief of tears even when the cancer made pain a constant presence in his last days.

The lawyer stared at his own hands for a long moment. By default Prithvi looked at his hands too. The liver-spotted backs of the palms, with their angry veins standing up, blue and mottled, the knuckles gnarled and rheumatoid, from both the cold and cracking. For a dizzying moment, he could feel the hands around his neck, amazingly strong despite their apparent fragility and squeezing the breath out of his body.

'The police think I killed her and am responsible for her step sister's disappearance, please, try to understand, you have to help me. You know she is not dead, you can help me, you have to get this sale stopped, reversed, whatever it is, please help me...'

He hated the whining tone that had crept into his voice. But it was completely his fault. He should have got the paperwork done a long while ago, he should have started the process of selling the place off. Surely, the man was lying.

'Show me your papers.'

'That's just the problem, I don't have the papers, which is why I need your help. They've all gone missing from the locker.'

The old man laughed.

'You don't have the papers because your wife herself handed them over to me.'

'But I have the power of attorney to deal on her behalf.'

Could she have truly revoked the clause making him guardian of the property with complete power of attorney upon her death or mental incapability?

'You *had* the power of attorney. Now you don't anymore. As I said before, it has been revoked.' His voice was very gentle, like he was trying to explain something to a tantrumming child.

Prithvi put his head in his hands.

'How can that be possible? She is dead, I tell you.'

'Well then, it was probably her ghost that came across for a visit, and did all the signing required. The money has already been transferred into her account,' the advocate said, his voice dry as crackling leaves and as ominous. The room was hushed, still. The creaking fan overhead the only movement. Behind the advocate's head, the glass-paned bookcases reflected the back of his balding head, and Prithvi's perplexed countenance, playing out their own reversed conversation.

'What account? Aisha only had one joint account with me,' Prithvi replied.

'That's what you thought, but there was a lot that she had,

which you did not know about. That she kept hidden from you,' the lawyer replied, clearly enjoying his role as harbinger of bad news and dispenser of justice. He continued, without waiting for a response.

'I must tell you, it was quite a shock for me to hear that your marriage had broken down, to the extent that she would need to keep her legal matters private from you. I think she was planning to leave you and was trying to find a place she could go away to.'

Inside his head, loudspeakers began blaring questions that he had no answers to.

'Would you know anything at all about her half sister, Heer?'

'I'm sorry I don't. That part of her father's life was far away from us, the Badibegum wouldn't allow any mention of it but of course, there were whispers. You could go to the town she used to lived in and find out more about her if you are keen of course, but her name wasn't Heer, that I am sure of. She went by her mother's surname and her name was very strange, and of course, she's been dead now for many, many years… ' He paused, furrowing his brow in deep thought, making his forehead collapse into a maze of vertical and horizontal lines. His hair, or what remained of it, was combed carefully across his head, like a giant egg with a spider crouching over it.

He named a town—it sounded familiar, it was not too far away. And he said he had an address for the woman who was Aisha's father's second wife. 'She passed away last month, almost exactly a year to the day Begumsahiba passed away. It was rather strange, how both these women passed away in the same month, barely a year apart. Her daughter died when she was eleven, from a brain fever. That I know for sure.'

'She couldn't have passed away. She was living with me for months,' Prithvi said, beginning to pull apart the skeins of the differing narratives he knew and had heard, and trying to make some sense coalescence from all the threads that were right now tangled into hopelessness.

The lawyer sat back in the leather wing-backed chair, now worn from use and in urgent need of re-upholstering. 'Well, whoever was living with you was not your wife's half sister, that I can say for certain. One can never know what goes on in a marriage. Why would this handsome, socially respected man desert his wife and daughter, two of the most beauteous women I have ever seen, to set up a humble home in a small town far away? What did he lack in his first marriage that he sought in his second? The Badibegum was beautiful. I was, in fact, quite smitten by her myself, but she would have none of it, not even when her husband abandoned her. He didn't deserve her. Of course, she went downhill soon after that. Perhaps she had already begun losing her mind before her husband moved out.'

The room was hushed. The late afternoon sunlight dappled in hesitantly through an open window. Soft gusts of a breeze rustled the trees outside. Birds chirped, readying to leave for their nests. It was chilly, even though it was the late afternoon. Winter would set in soon, here in these unforgiving northern plains of India. Chilly winds would seep through every crack, every gap and slice into one's body through exposed skin, through clothes and inner wear, reaching straight to the bone and numbing it.

'And of course, she went completely crazy after it happened. Though the rumours are she was halfway there before it did, that she was unbearable to live with. That she wouldn't bathe for months on end and that Aisha did all she could to keep her presentable and lucid, until her father had her sent away to boarding school and then to a hostel. I heard that she once chased her husband around the house with a knife and almost sank it into his shoulder, before she was overpowered by the household staff. She went bad quickly after that, you were only allowed to meet her when she was kept calm by medication. Aisha was careful about that, she refused to have her institutionalised. By the end, she was just a shell from all the medication. She was there, but not there, if you know what I mean. But you should have seen her back in her youth!' His eyes misted over with a memory from a time before the cobwebs closed in on them. 'She was so beautiful, so regal.'

That's where Aisha got it from, Prithvi thought, the realisation striking him so sudden and so hard that his head reeled. From her mother. As well as her fine-boned beauty, with her alabaster skin, and arched imperiousness. He had fallen in love with the woman he saw, and hadn't known about the woman lurking within, ready to crawl out and take over, making her a stranger wearing the mask of the woman he had loved. How was he supposed to know about the demons lurking within her neural circuits, when she had hidden it so adeptly with the trappings of beauty and sensuousness, and the slight edgy unpredictability that had been deliciously tantalising? He hadn't handled her changing into a stranger well, he had let her drift off into another dimension untethered, fencing himself up by stony-walled rejection, afraid to admit to himself that it scared him, the madness he saw in the split seconds before the medication took over.

'Did Aisha leave a phone number or an address? I really need to get in touch with her,' he pleaded. 'I have to meet her. I have to talk to her. I can't believe this.'

'She doesn't want to meet you, I believe. I have been instructed not to give out any details of where she is.'

The old lawyer looked at him with an expression that was a mix of wariness, concern and a fair bit of pity. Prithvi looked down at himself. He was depleted, a ruin of his former self, his shoulders sagging with defeat, the haunting questions that ran through his head every waking hour. *Where is Aisha, where is Heer, who is Heer, is Aisha alive, is Heer her sister, who jumped off the bridge, why was the body never found, was that a fake story about her jumping off the bridge, planted to mislead him, who, what, where?* The questions swirled around in his brain in a never-ending circuit that looped endlessly,

'I do have a number but I am not authorised to give it to you,' the lawyer repeated, his voice now coated in steel. 'But I can tell you that the holding company she has sold the property to, plans to convert it into a heritage getaway, on the lines of a very exclusive boutique hotel. This holding company is based in Delhi.'

'Can you hear me out, my side of the story?'

Prithvi could hear the pleading in his own voice and he detested himself for it. He could, if he wished, stand up, tower over the shrivelled man and knock him to the floor in a single punch, no matter that he was older and out of practice now. Perhaps he could just tell him the truth, the story as he knew it, and let him decide whether he wanted to share the details with him or not. After all, wasn't that what being human was all about, letting the other person take their own decisions and making one's peace with it, no matter what the decision was?

The older man gestured graciously for him to continue.

'You must know that I loved Aisha. Truly loved her. She had changed because of her illness. She didn't trust me. She imagined I wanted to kill her, she was sometimes dangerous, even to the children, I had been trying to get the children into boarding school to keep them away from the craziness at home, but she threatened to kill herself if I did.'

And so he sighed and continued. 'I never, ever raised my hand on her, only restrained her sometimes, when she grew violent. But this is the truth of what happened. You can choose to believe me or not. But I had to be stern with her, regarding her medication, with her out-of-control spending. She thought I was controlling her, restricting her.' It took him the better part of the hour, where he explained what had happened between him and Aisha from the last time they had met the lawyer, shortly after the demise of his wife's mother, for the transfer of ownership of the kothi to Aisha. He spoke about how difficult it had become to watch Aisha morph into a stranger, an unpredictable one, who roamed the house like the resident ghost, refused all physical contact with him, and spent her time cleaning the house obsessively. Not to mention her fugue states, where she would suddenly be gone, only to return a few days later, with no recollection of where she had been or what she had done. 'It had been getting progressively worse. She was seeing a doctor, but she didn't take her medication regularly, of that I am sure. She had actually become dangerous to be around.'

He told him about the landslides, the returning home to find her half sister in residence, Aisha's disappearance, and how things unfolded after that, gently prodded along by fate and the needs of the body. By the time he finished his narration, the table before them had the rings of evidence of the many cups of the sickly sweet tea they had been calling for. The man was sitting back in his chair, lacing his fingers together, rocking himself slowly back and forth, as if trying to lull himself into a stupor.

'You think she really jumped, she ended her life?'

Prithvi nodded.

'My dear boy, when did you plan to inform me about her suicide? You did know, didn't you that there was huge property at stake here.'

'I'm sorry,' Prithvi replied, 'I meant to do it, but somehow never got round to it.'

'I must confess, I find this all rather hard to believe because I was just visited by your wife and I do recognise her. I've known her since she was a child. I've seen her grow up in front of my eyes into the beautiful woman she became. Of course, we were rather surprised when she decided to marry you, because honestly, you came from a very different back ground. She is very much alive. And well rid of you. I don't believe your story.'

Prithvi flinched. He stared back at the dapper man, his face carefully arranged in a concerned question mark, the disapproval seeping through his pores like a miasmal stench.

He continued, 'I wasn't very surprised when she told me that she was separating from you the other day, I always thought that the two of you were not very suited for each other. Oh yes, when you are young, there is hormonal desire and lust, and all those things...' He suddenly stopped, realising that he had said more than he was supposed to. His last line hung in the air between them like a half-formed moon, uncertain, undefined, yet lighting up the dimness around, with an incandescence that revealed all that needed to hide.

'I wish you all the luck, Mr Thakur, but I really cannot help you with any more information.'

With that he stood up and stretched out his hand for a firm handshake. His skin was dry and soft, with the slight crumpled feel one might feel if one crumpled up rose petals in one's palm, beautiful yet damaged.

Prithvi scribbled down his phone number on a piece of paper and handed it across to him. 'Just in the event there is something you think I should know, or if you decide you can tell me any details, do feel free to call me on this number.'

Capital Hospitality seared through his brain in blazing neon. That was the name of the company. Capital Hospitality. The board outside the gate of the kothi. The skeins of thoughts circling his mind like a preying eagle, suddenly spotted prey, felt the loose ends begin to come together. How had Capital Hospitality acquired the property, unless they had access to the documents and to Aisha as well?

'Can you tell me the name of the person at Capital Hospitality who was representing the company during the dealings? Could you describe him?'

'A gentleman called Aniket Sharma, he was dealing with me. The papers were actually signed in Delhi and sent back to me, so I never actually dealt with the owners. How do I describe this man? He was perfectly ordinary, medium height, wheatish, black moustache, nothing that distinguished him.'

Aniket Sharma was not the man Prithvi had met. He had met another man, smooth, compelling, his gaze strangely hypnotic. If only he could remember his name. He resolved to check out his wallet and empty it of all the flotsam and jetsam of visiting cards he had shoved carelessly into it. The man had handed him a card and the dignified blue and grey of Capital Hospitality on it was all that he had retained. It had been a long time ago, a couple of years at the very least, and Aisha had turned down the offer. He hadn't contacted the man after that. He would google it up, the moment he exited this office.

He needed to find himself another lawyer first.

'Thank you for all your help, sir,' Prithvi rose heavily, keenly aware that the increasing chill and the number of cups of tea had made his bladder clamour noisily for release. He would go back to the room in the lodge, and figure out what his next move should be.

'Excuse me, could you please direct me to your washroom?' he asked the peon, impassive and unhearing from all the years of being stationed outside a room, where confidential things were discussed. The peon raised a bony hand and pointed down the corridor in a sepulchral manner, where the lack of light made it end in an indistinct blackness.

Prithvi went down the corridor, which seemed to have no doors opening anywhere, to finally come up suddenly upon a door that opened crankily, as he turned the handle. It creaked as he swung it inwards to reveal a dark room, which was dimly lit by two flickering bulbs. It was a huge space for a bathroom, with wooden benches and wood-framed mirrors, and cubicles with wooden shutters. He went into one of the cubicles and felt the piss pour out of him in gushes of pale yellow relief. As he washed his hands in the old yellowing porcelain basin with the fine cracks showing where age had assaulted it, he saw a blurry shadow behind him in the reflection ahead. He turned around. There was nothing there. He turned back to the mirror only to see the dim outline of something or someone rushing at him, and then there was a hand around his throat and another holding a cloth with something on it at his nose, until the dimness of the men's room blurred into grey, a sudden popping of the light bulb that lit up the inside of his head, plunging him into a searing, terrifying blackness.

9

When he opened his eyes, he was in a tiny room. The world outside the dust-caked windows was dark. A grimy bulb hung from a wire in the centre of the room, flickering disinterestedly. In the extreme corner of the room, he could make out a pile of what seemed to be discarded and broken furniture, heaped in a random manner. The windows, the little he could make out in the gloom, had iron bars set into the frame, behind which there were wooden slats. And the main door was shut.

Sometime between his passing out and coming to, night had taken over this part of the earth and brought with it the chill that cut to the bone, if one wasn't clad warmly enough. Which he wasn't. He had stepped out that morning with just a regular shirt, with a thin jacket over it. It had worked during the day, but the night was a different animal. The chill settled into your veins, turning the blood within into ice, wrapping its glacial fingers around the intestines and the heart, so that all you could feel with every breath, with every movement, were shards of ice piercing soft tissue.

He sat up gingerly and winced. The sudden movement brought the pounding back to his head with redoubled vigour, and the bile rushed to his throat. As he tried to move, he realised that his right leg was manacled to the iron leg of the bed he had been laid out on. The floor beneath wasn't too clean to begin with. The dust on the floor was evidence of an eerie, ghoulish march of flurried footsteps, which seemed to have dragged something broad and heavy inside. That would be him. He had been dragged in, with as much dignity as a sack of potatoes, and tossed onto this bed. Kept here, until he regained consciousness, with no medical attention, for quite a few hours. His clothes were dusty and muddied with being tossed around on unclean floors. The stench of decay did not add pleasantly to the rich pulchritude of aromas of neglect that swarmed round the chilly night air.

The windows, though shut, had slats which would have let in a chink of light had it been day blazing outside. The lone bulb hanging from the wire in the middle of the room had been switched on, in careful consideration of the possibility that he would wake and need some light. It cast a flickering, uncertain light throwing more shadows into forbidding existence, than reassuring brightness. The bed he was on was a hospital bed, probably a remnant of a bedridden patient, who had been confined to this spot. The mattress had sunk in with the weight of the body that stayed on it, day in day out, the lumpiness making the skin blister and turn to oozing bedsores that caretakers ignored, and which the patient was too far gone to realise. The thick odour of a fragrance mingled with the smell of congealed urine and sweat, wafted from the bedding. A fragrance that was familiar, the ittar Aisha used and her mother before her. Ittar her mother had got custom-made until the point she began losing her mind. The thin mattress made him feel every millimetre of the hard, unyielding iron rods below it.

Had he died and gone to hell, or was he still in the corporeal world, a world of flesh and appetites and lust and emotions? His head throbbed, his body winced at the sudden spikes of chilly breeze that snaked in its tentacles through window slats from broken panes to caress bare skin.

He was in one of the outhouses of the kothi. It was an outhouse that was so accustomed to being overlooked that it had learnt to make itself disappear beneath the shade of the sprawling mango tree that unfurled itself a few yards away from the door. It was the mango tree that was filtering the dappling speckles of stray moonlight that made its way into the room through the gaps in the slats, only to be wiped out into neutrality by the flickering light of the bulb.

He sat up gently. His throat felt raw and bruised. The back of his head felt painful. He touched it with tentative fingers. It felt like a raised lump from an impact. He pulled his fingers away and sniffed the dark, sticky stain on them. He could smell the metallic rustiness of dried blood. Bile rose to his throat, he threw up, wiped his mouth on the sleeve of his shirt. His sweater was rancid with the smell of stale sweat.

How long had he been lying here, his leg manacled to this bed? The watch on his hand had been removed, as had his shoes. He had no blanket, no covering. The room was in a ferment of disuse. He could smell the dust and the desolation in the air. The ceiling was hanging low, ominous and threatening, a loose window shutter somewhere was flapping in the indolent night breeze. He patted around in his pockets for his phone, which he already knew, wouldn't be on his person. On cue, it rang. The soft ring shattered the aching silence that hung over the room. It was kept, in almost ceremonious precision, on a small trestle table next to the bed, within reach. The ring startled him. He reached out and looked at the number flashing on the screen. Private number said the message flashing on the screen.

'Hello,' he said, his voice cautious. There was nothing but the silence of the wary for a few seconds breathing heavily down the line.

'Hello, are you completely conscious now?' asked a deep, male voice. Unfamiliar, yet familiar, in the strangest way. He had heard this voice before. The language was English, the accent boarding school clipped, the words measured to the barest essential. The air of growing up in a cocoon of entitlement seeped through the static into the receiver. 'I'm sorry about needing to knock you out, but you were getting a little inconvenient.'

'Who are you?'

'Does it matter?'

This was a voice he should know, Prithvi thought, given the familiarity with which it spoke to him, although he couldn't quite place it. A figure rose to his mind, the figure of a tall man, with piercing eagle-brown eyes, and hair falling thick to below his ears, streaked with the burnished gold of one who spent much of his time in the outdoors. Capital Hospitality. The man he'd met for a drink on a trip to Delhi, the man who had plied him with too much alcohol and probing questions, before getting him dropped back to his hotel, and never contacting him again. It all came back to him.

'I remember you now. Why have you done this?' Prithvi waved an impotent hand at the leg manacled firmly to the bed, the chain long enough for him to go to the bathroom right next to the bed, but not far enough to the door which was a long way off, perhaps over twenty feet away.

'Why did I knock you out and put you in confinement in this room, where you're sitting looking at the windows and doors, wondering if you can make an escape?'

Prithvi froze, he was being watched.

'Where are you?'

There was a brief laugh. 'No, I can't see you, of course, but that would be what you would be doing wouldn't you, if you found yourself imprisoned in a strange room? Why did I do this to you? It is rather complicated. It began as a plan to get your wife's property by side-stepping you, but then I realised your wife wanted to get rid of her life with you too. So I just helped her a bit. It took some convincing, but finally both of us got what we wanted.'

'We? Us?' he asked. The iron of the chain holding his foot to bed scraped against his skin, making the spot raw, he had probably turned and tossed, when he was out of consciousness.

'What are you talking about?'

There was a short burst of laughter at the other end of the line. 'Here,' the voice said. 'Speak to your wife.'

Prithvi felt his blood freeze in his veins in the second of silence between one voice falling quiet on the line and the other taking it up.

'Hello, Prithvi.'

It was Aisha. Her voice. She was alive. All that grieving, all that gut-wrenching pain he went through thinking she was dead, and that perhaps he had been part of why she'd jumped off the bridge, slammed into his chest like a headbutt from a dwarf. Damn and blast that shepherd who had assured him on all the gods in the pantheon that he had seen her jump off the bridge.

His head throbbed and it wasn't from the bump at the back of his head from where he had fallen on the hard floor. His tongue was like a block of wood in his mouth, which was, in turn, acrid, with unrinsed vomit still sticking to the back of his teeth, to the palate, to the throat.

'Hello, Aisha,' he said. Strangely, over the waves of sound trickling into his ears, he could smell her perfume flooding into the room, musky, mysterious, specially created for her mother, by the famous perfumers of the city who then began sending her stock by parcel to where she was. Aisha would never begin her day without daubing herself with the perfume at all her pulse points. Her cupboard, her clothes, her body, all exuded that musky fragrance like a cloak. It comforted her. The smell of her mother embracing her, had kept her sane, but only just so. Until the point she had completely tipped herself over the edge. The scent was her, it wrapped him right now, the warmth of her, her cunt dripping with its moistness, clamping onto his penis in quick waves as she came. The scent of her perfume was entering his nostrils, confusing him.

'How are you, Prithvi?' Her voice was tender, concerned.

'How do you think I am? And how are you still alive, I thought you were dead, or did you intend me to think you were dead?'

'You wanted me dead, Prithvi. Let's cut the pretending. I bet you were celebrating the day they told you I had jumped off the bridge, that your plan had been successful. How sad I've messed up all your fine plans yet again, haven't I?'

She laughed, a deep, rolling, belly laugh, the laugh that had made him seek her out across a room the first time he had heard it, a laugh he had all but forgotten, a laugh that was unfettered, and free. He felt his penis getting turgid, a primeval, visceral reaction that her laugh never failed to elicit. He couldn't remember when he had last heard her laughing.

The absurdity of his situation did not escape him. Manacled by his ankle to a bed of iron, in a room that was dark, dank with dampness and moss, and the stench of rat's urine and faeces, the only thing keeping him company, and getting aroused, in response to a laugh, a laugh that had reeled him into a relationship, and then a marriage. He hadn't heard her laugh that way for a long, long while. It made him ache in a core he had thought was dead, or buried beneath layers of accumulated misery and dissonant lives.

'Why did you do this, Aisha, don't you know I love you, how it affected me, the children? Why all this? Why did you do this?'

'More questions? You always were like this, Prithvi, you haven't changed a bit despite all that has happened in the past year. Poor you.' She laughed again.

Her voice was like silk, smooth and deep, comforting, the

way it used to be. He wrapped his head in it, in the unexpected comfort of hearing her as she used to be, not as it was when she descended into her hell of manic screaming fits. Or the opposite phase, the lying in bed for days while the dirt collected in layers on her body, and the tearing of the sheets into bandages to cover the places, where she had peeled off her skin, exposing the raw dermal layers beneath, the sores and scabs peppering her body like war medals. She had fought her battles with invisible demons those days.

He could smell the rancidity on himself. He felt vaguely drunk, disoriented. If someone saw him now, he thought, they would dismiss him as an alcoholic, a filthy one, a low life. They would be disgusted by him. He would be disgusted by him.

'What is this game, Aisha? Where are you?'

'Not anywhere you can find me, Prithvi. You don't need to know anything.'

His brain began fogging over. The pieces of the puzzle kept floating elusively in his head and refused to fit together, to make sense.

'Heer, your half sister, who was she? Everyone I met says your half sister is dead. Who was that woman?'

There was a faint laugh from the receiver, a voice not at the mouthpiece, but listening in. The voice changed as it spoke, it was Heer now on the line. 'Just let's say she was no one related to your wife. Or rather I was no one related to your wife, but poor thing, she was so desperate to have some family to clutch onto, she believed all I told her.'

Heer. On the phone. Aisha was gone, as suddenly as she had arrived. Or had she never arrived in the first place?

'What is going on?' he asked again, 'Where's Aisha, who are you, Heer?'

'Did you like my Aisha voice?' The voice on the phone asked, speaking exactly in Aisha's measured, precise cadences, before slipping back into a rougher texture of grittiness that only survival can inflect into a tone.

The disparate pieces of the puzzle slowly fell into place, sinking in slow motion into their pre-destined slots. Some pieces were yet to find their slots. They floated in the space-time continuum within his consciousness, aimlessly, out of his grasp, like most missing pieces do, tempting, yet unreachable. This was Heer, or the woman who called herself Heer, who had done it all. Sold the kothi, visited the lawyer's, transferred funds into an account he knew nothing about.

He punched the thin mattress, feeling the pressure against his knuckles, unsatisfying, too thin to be giving.

'Where is Aisha? What have you done with her? What have you done with the kids? How did you manage to sell the property?'

'Everything is easy if one knows the right people, Prithvi, you of all people know that. Poor Aisha, she was so desperate to escape from you, she swallowed the bait we gave her hook, line, and sinker. And then it was easy, getting her to do whatever we asked her to, open another bank account, get the power of attorney revoked…'

The voice trailed off. He kept silent.

'Where's Aisha now? Where are the kids now?' he finally asked.

'The kids are at school where you had left them, of course, and Aisha is at peace.'

'I'm going to get you arrested for impersonation. You cheats, how dare you do this? I want to see Aisha, and I am going to go to court and get all the sales reversed.'

'How can you do that, when Aisha herself sold it? You can't do a thing, Prithvi, we've done this watertight. Everything has been checked and triple-checked.'

Her voice was soft, even-pitched. She was calm. It was a calm not brought on by the palliative of prescription medication, but the calm of an even-keeled mind as she spoke.

She laughed again, but it was another laugh, brittle, high-pitched, it scratched on the ear drum with its forced hilarity. He felt his stomach clench up, getting ready to dislodge the remainder of the contents within.

'What sort of a crazy game is this, Heer? You deliberately created this trap for me to walk into, did you?'

'I didn't create it, Prithvi. Aisha did. Unfortunately, it kind of backfired on her. I was just hired help. But then all's well that ends well.'

'What do you mean, she created it?' Things were still not fitting into place, jagged edges that didn't make sense floated around, bereft of anchoring into reasoning.

'She wanted to sell the property, rid herself of the power of attorney she had given you to deal on her behalf, to do it without your knowledge and get away from you. She reached out to old negotiations she'd left unfinished. We finished them for her. She's happier now though, I'm sure.'

'I will sue you.' His voice was flat, defeated.

'On what grounds will you do that? You don't even know my name, I will disappear into the nowhere I came from, and you will never be able to track me down again. I've already changed my appearance, I look nothing like the Heer you know or remember.'

The silence hung undecidedly on the tenuous connection between the two of them, wary, circling, awaiting the next word, the next statement that would take this further from where it was.

'I'm going to go to the police. Inspector Pant…' He began.

'Oh, he was to keep you inside for some time, till we sorted out all the paperwork, but unfortunately you foiled that bit of the plan. We managed though.'

The crackle of sudden static blazed through the quiet night air.

'Goodbye, Prithvi. It was nice knowing you.'

The line went dead. He dialled back, but the call went into a blank darkness where there were more questions than answers. Aisha. Heer. Whom had he spoken with right now? He didn't know. He needed to find out. He would get out of there and find out. He would track the call down, go back to the house in the hills, with the imposing gates, with the hounds guarding the grounds, where he had last heard Aisha's voice. He would enter the grounds and find her, if she was still there.

The manacle on his leg clicked open as he pulled weakly at it. It had never been locked. He had assumed himself shackled to the bed, just as he had assumed himself shackled into a marriage that had slowly become a cage. The door, he realised, was open, just that slight bit, an apologetic kind of half way through ajar. It had been open through it all. He threw the chain away and sat up, feeling the world spin around him briefly, until the mewling strength of his exhausted body beat down the dizziness. His stomach growled with the realisation that he hadn't eaten for hours.

'I will track her down and find her, and we will be a family again, and I will make sure she knows how much I love her,' he thought to himself, carefully putting on his socks and shoes. The nerves of his feet, manacled for so long, had the blood rush back into them, painfully dissolving the pins and needles. As he stepped onto the floor, his feet finally clad, he realised that he didn't know where to go anymore, or where to begin and sat right back on the creaking bed, waiting to be found. When he finally looked up, Aisha was standing right there, at the open door, an expression of indescribable tenderness on her face. He looked at her, and smiled, he was home. Was he awake, or was he hallucinating? Everything felt thick and heightened like a memory which is unreal, yet real as it happens. The strange thing he realised, in a distant recess of his concussion-fogged mind, was that he could see right through her, into the darkness lit by the pale light of full moon that shone behind her, and beyond her, the dark outline of the mango tree she'd always wanted to be buried under. And he got to his feet, realising that she was pointing, with a long, transparent arm, at the mound of earth freshly packed under that mango tree, almost like something, someone, had been buried there in a hurry.

Acknowledgements

To all the brave women out there, who battle their monsters every day. Real. Or imaginary. For telling me your stories, for letting me into your heads and trusting me with your pain. I owe you so much.

To my mother, for teaching me early in life that all one needs is the conviction in oneself and the determination to go on.

To Madhulika Mathur, for putting me on the path to writing this. It began as a novella way back in 2013, and grew and grew, until it became a story completely different from what it set out to be originally.

To Rashmi Menon at Amaryllis for being the editor every author needs, to handhold one through the dark, dank paths of despair and self-doubt. And Megha Parmar, Vikas Rakheja, and Manoj Kulkarni at Amaryllis for being the bulwarks of support they are.

To Archana Pai Kulkarni for polishing this up and spotting where I've 'segued' a bit too often.

To Mishta Roy for all the kickass covers she's made for me, from my very first book *The Reluctant Detective*, to *Once Upon A Crush*, *The Face at the Window* and now for *Missing, Presumed Dead*.

And finally, to Krish, for realising that when Mamma is writing, she is writing, and the world, including the child can wait. And being gracious enough to give me that space.